THE LITTLE GIANT BOOK® OF DINOSAURS

Thomas R. Holtz, Jr.

Illustrated by Terry Riley

STERLING PUBLISHING CO., INC.
NEW YORK

Library of Congress Cataloging-in-Publication Data

Holtz, Thomas R., 1965–
 Little giant book of dinosaurs / Thomas R. Holtz; illustrated by Terry Riley.
   p. cm.
  Includes index.
  ISBN 0-8069-7391-9
  1. Dinosaurs—Juvenile literature. [I. Dinosaurs.]
  I. Riley, Terry, ill. II. Title.
QE861.5.H65 2001
567.9—dc21   00-067082

10 9 8 7 6 5 4 3 2

Published by Sterling Publishing Company, Inc.
387 Park Avenue South, New York, N.Y. 10016
Text ©2001 by Thomas R. Holtz
Illustrations ©2001 by Terry Riley
Distributed in Canada by Sterling Publishing
℅ Canadian Manda Group, One Atlantic Avenue, Suite 105
Toronto, Ontario, Canada M6K 3E7
Distributed in Great Britain and Europe by Chris Lloyd
463 Ashley Road, Parkstone, Poole, Dorset, BH14 0AX, England
Distributed in Australia by Capricorn Link (Australia) Pty Ltd.
P.O. Box 6651, Baulkham Hills, Business Centre, NSW 2153, Australia
Manufactured in Canada
All rights reserved

Sterling ISBN 0-8069-7391-9

For Alex, Drew, and Abigail

CONTENTS

1. **DINOSAURS ARE DISCOVERED**   10
2. **HOW DO WE KNOW ABOUT DINOSAURS?**   13
3. **WHERE DID THE DINOSAURS COME FROM?**   17
4. **WHAT ARE DINOSAURS?**   20
5. **THYREOPHORANS, THE ARMORED DINOSAURS**   25
   Scutellosaurus   *28*
   Scelidosaurus   *32*
   Huayangosaurus   *36*
   Stegosaurus   *40*
   Gastonia   *44*
   Edmontonia   *48*
   Ankylosaurus   *52*

6. MARGINOCEPHALIANS, THE RIDGE HEADS   56

Homalocephale   58
Stegoceras   62
Pachycephalosaurus   66
Psittacosaurus   70
Archaeoceratops   74
Protoceratops   78
Zuniceratops   82
Einiosaurus   86
Triceratops   92

7. ORNITHOPODS, THE BEAKED DINOSAURS   96

Heterodontosaurus   99
Hypsilophodon   104
Tenontosaurus   108
Muttaburrasaurus   112
Camptosaurus   116
Iguanodon   120
Altirhinus   124
Ouranosaurus   128
Protohadros   132

	Anatotitan	*136*
	Hypacrosaurus	*140*
8.	**SAUROPODOMORPHS, THE LONG-NECKED PLANT EATERS**	**145**
	Saturnalia	*148*
	Plateosaurus	*152*
	Shunosaurus	*156*
	Mamenchisaurus	*160*
	Jobaria	*164*
	Diplodocus	*168*
	Apatosaurus	*172*
	Amargasaurus	*176*
	Camarasaurus	*180*
	Brachiosaurus	*184*
	Argentinosaurus	*188*
	Saltasaurus	*192*
9.	**THEROPODS, THE BIRDLIKE MEAT EATERS**	**197**
	Eoraptor	*202*
	Herrerasaurus	*206*
	Coelophysis	*210*
	Dilophosaurus	*214*

Ceratosaurus	218
Majungatholus	222
Torvosaurus	228
Suchomimus	232
Allosaurus	236
Giganotosaurus	240
Sinosauropteryx	244
Pelecanimimus	250
Ornithomimus	254
Tyrannosaurus	258
Troodon	264
Caudipteryx	268
Oviraptor	272
Beipiaosaurus	276
Deinonychus	280
Velociraptor	286
Archaeopteryx	290
Rahonavis	294
Shuvuuia	298
Confuciusornis	302
Hesperornis	306

10. MODERN BIRDS	**310**
11. THE WORLDS OF THE DINOSAURS	**313**
Triassic Period	318
Jurassic Period	322
Cretaceous Period	328
12. WHERE DID THE DINOSAURS GO?	**333**
Extinction	333
Survival	337
Glossary	**340**
Dinosaurs by Epoch	**342**
Dinosaurs by Location	**344**
About the Author	**351**
Index	**352**

• 1 •
DINOSAURS ARE DISCOVERED

There was a time when nobody knew about dinosaurs. The bones and teeth and footprints of dinosaurs were found all over the world, but people thought they were the bones and teeth and footprints of giants or elephants or huge birds. In the late 1700s, though, scientists began to realize that these **fossils** were the remains of prehistoric animals.

Most of the fossils that scientists found were from shellfish like clams and snails; others were from plants. Some were from flying reptiles that the scientists named **pterodactyls** (pronounced terra-dak-tls), which means "wing fingers."

Other fossils were sea reptiles, like the **ichthyosaurs** ("fish lizards"), the long-necked **plesiosaurs**

11

("near lizards"), and **mosasaurs** ("Meuse River lizards").

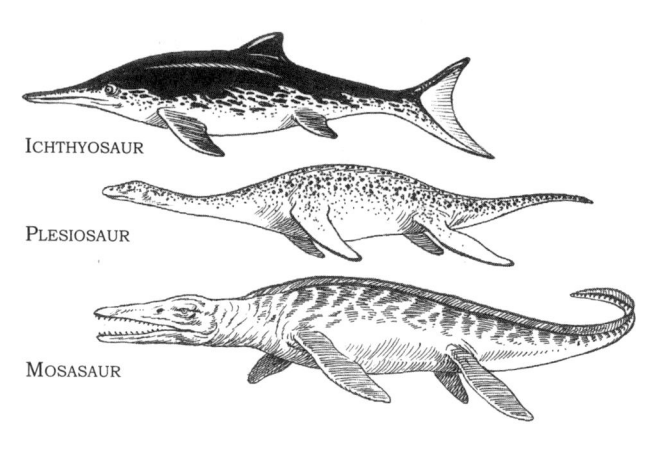

ICHTHYOSAUR

PLESIOSAUR

MOSASAUR

In the early 1800s **paleontologists** (scientists who study fossils) recognized that some of these fossils were from giant land reptiles. Although no one had ever found a complete skeleton of these reptiles, scientists could tell that they were a very special kind of animal. In 1842, paleontologist Sir Richard Owen named these land reptiles **Dinosauria,** which means "fearfully great lizards." Dinosaurs had finally been discovered.

• 2 •
HOW DO WE KNOW ABOUT DINOSAURS?

All we know about dinosaurs we know from their **fossils.** A fossil is any part of an animal or plant, or traces of their activity, preserved in rock. Clams and snails leave shells and burrows as fossils. Plants leave wood and leaves and pollen. Dinosaurs leave bones and teeth, as well as footprints and other traces.

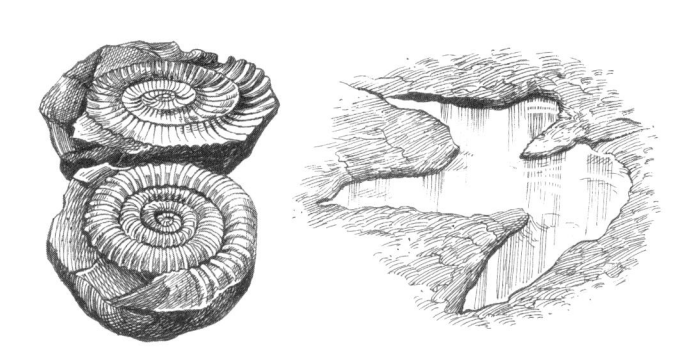

Before a dinosaur could become a fossil, it had to die. It could have died from being attacked, or from being sick, or from old age. If the body of the dead dinosaur were out in the open, other animals would eat up most of it. So, in order for the dead body to become a fossil, it had to be buried quickly, by mud or sand. If a dinosaur died near the banks of a river, or during a flood or a sandstorm, it is more likely that part of it would become a fossil.

When mud or sand is buried for a long time, it turns into rock. Water seeping through it is full of minerals that help glue the bits of sand or mud together. These minerals also fill in the spaces in the bones and teeth, so that they too become hard as a rock.

Footprints can also become fossils. If a dinosaur walked along the shore of a lake or sea, and water washed mud or sand into the footprints, these traces could be preserved. So could eggs and nests, or even dinosaur droppings! Very rarely the impression of the outside of a dinosaur, its skin and scales or feathers, will be preserved, but mostly what we find are bones and teeth. In fact,

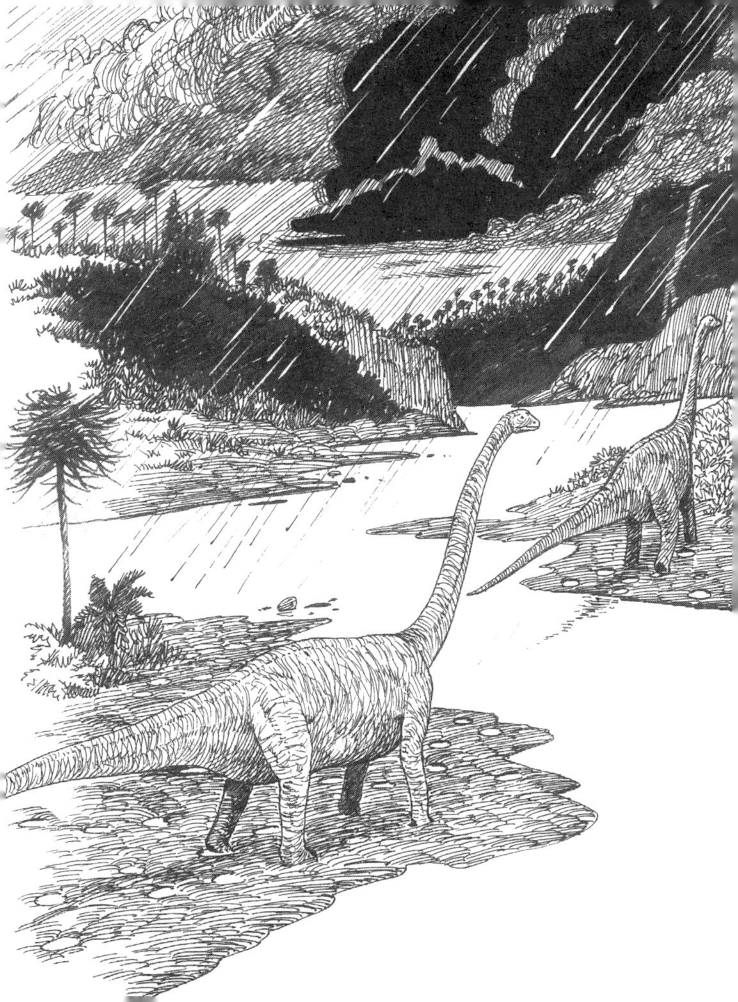

we know about some dinosaurs only from their skeleton. We don't know what the whole dinosaur looked like!

Over time mountains rise up in regions that were once low land, and rivers cut valleys into rock. When this happens, fossils can be **exposed.** If people are walking through those mountains or in the river valley and spot the fossil, they can dig it out of the rock. It is only from these chance findings that we know anything about dinosaurs.

· 3 ·
WHERE DID THE DINOSAURS COME FROM?

The first dinosaurs appeared on Earth 230 million years ago. Before that, other groups of animals ruled the land—relatives of crocodiles and ancestors of mammals. Where did the dinosaurs come from?

Like all animals and plants, dinosaurs were descended from earlier life forms. The offspring of every group of animals and plants look a little bit different from each other and a little different from their parents. These differences are called **variations.** In the wild more animals and plants are born than could possibly survive. There isn't enough food and water and space for all of them. If any of the offspring has a variation that gives it an edge, it has a better chance of living to become a parent. If it becomes a parent, it can pass on its own variation.

Over millions of years, these variations cause **descendants** to look different from their **ancestors.** This is called **evolution.**

The ancestors of the dinosaurs lived in the Triassic Period, 240 million years ago. (See page 318 for more about this period.) They were small reptiles, less than 1 foot (30cm) long, with long legs directly under their body. This helped them run very fast and escape the larger animals that ruled the land. They walked mostly on their hind

Little *Lagosuchus* from Argentina is a possible ancestor of the dinosaur.

legs, so their hands were free to grasp food.

The long legs underneath their bodies and their grasping hands were variations that helped the dinosaur ancestors to survive. These features and others, over millions of years, enabled many dinosaurs to grow to giant size while still being good runners. Other dinosaurs used their grasping hands to kill other creatures or to climb in trees. All these modifications came from the same ancestor.

• 4 •
WHAT ARE DINOSAURS?

Not all extinct creatures are dinosaurs. The fin-backed *Dimetrodon* lived long before the dinosaurs, and was in fact a "protomammal": an animal related to the ancestors of mammals. Woolly mammoths and sabretooth cats lived after the Age of Dinosaurs, and were true mammals (while dinosaurs were a type of reptile). Ichthyosaurs, plesiosaurs, mosasaurs, and pterodactyls lived at the same time as dinosaurs, but none of these marine or flying reptiles were dinosaurs.

When Owen first named "Dinosauria" in 1842, he only knew about three types of dinosaurs: the meat-eating *Megalosaurus*, plant-eating *Iguanodon*, and armored *Hylaeosaurus*. He recognized that these creatures were different from other fossil reptiles because their legs were underneath their body—not sprawling out to the side—and because they had extra backbones in

MEGALOSAURUS

their hips to support their weight. At that time Owen knew only about large dinosaurs; we now know that many dinosaurs were actually very small.

Scientists give names to groups of animals and plants based on their **common ancestry.** If an animal or plant is a descendant of a particular ancestor, it is considered part of that group; if not, it isn't. All dinosaurs, they say, are descendants of the most recent common ancestor of *Iguanodon* or *Megalosaurus*.

Iguanodon (see page 120) and its relatives are the **ornithischian** ("bird-hipped") dinosaurs. They have a special extra bone at the end of their lower jaw, and one of their hip bones points backwards. The armored thyreophorans, ridge-headed marginocephalians, and beaked ornithopods are all ornithischians.

Megalosaurus and its relatives are the **saurischian** ("lizard-hipped") dinosaurs. They have a large thumb claw, and in many of them the hip bone points forward. Long-necked sauropodomorphs and birdlike theropods are saurischians.

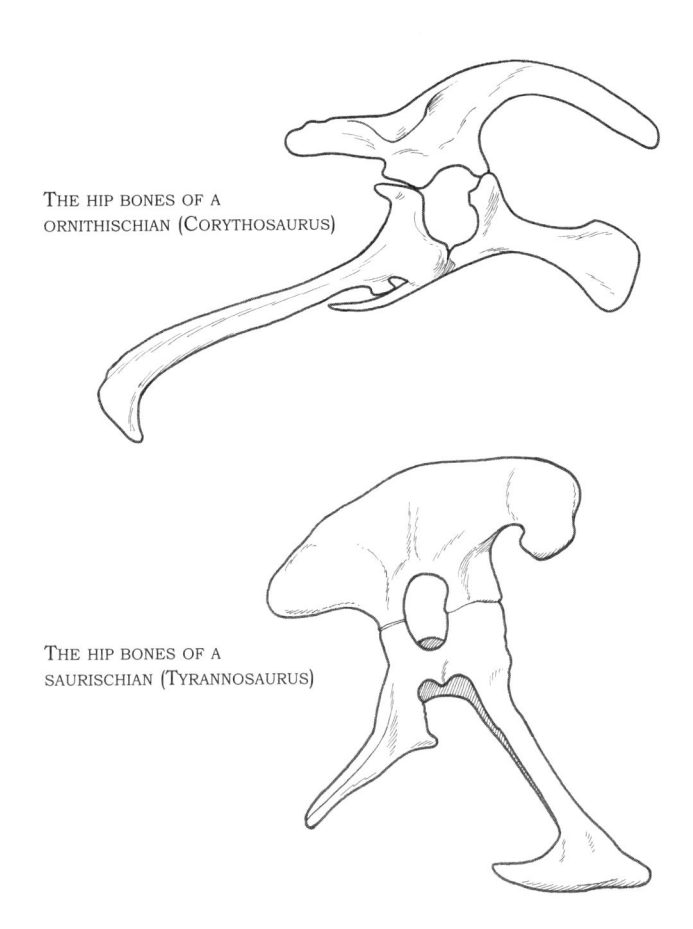

The hip bones of a ornithischian (Corythosaurus)

The hip bones of a saurischian (Tyrannosaurus)

FAMILY TREE OF DINOSAURS

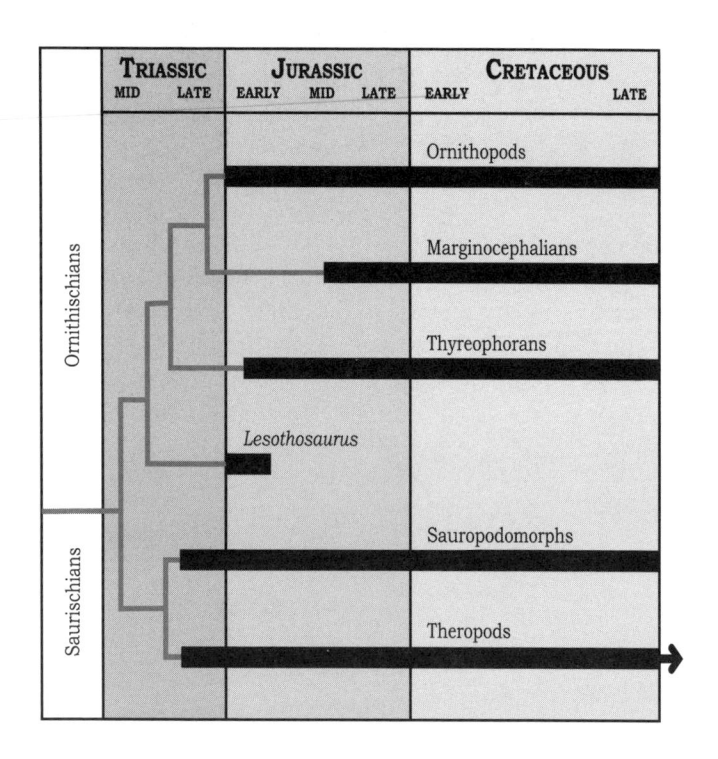

	Triassic MID LATE	**Jurassic** EARLY MID LATE	**Cretaceous** EARLY LATE
Ornithischians			Ornithopods
			Marginocephalians
			Thyreophorans
		Lesothosaurus	
Saurischians			Sauropodomorphs
			Theropods →

24

• 5 •
THYREOPHORANS, THE ARMORED DINOSAURS

The world of the dinosaurs was full of some pretty fearsome predators, so plant eaters needed protection. In some cases, the plant eaters became huge; in other cases, they became fast.

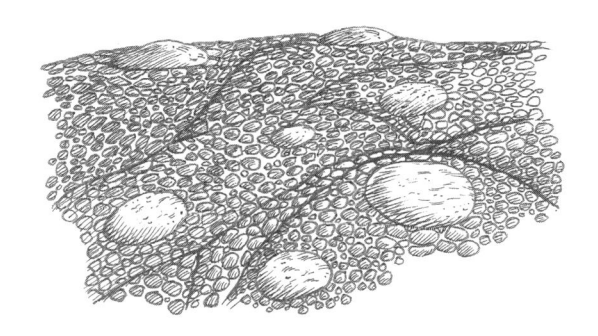

One group of ornithischian dinosaurs developed armor to protect themselves. These armored ornithischian dinosaurs are called **thyreophorans,** which means "armor bearers." They all had bony shields called **scutes** that were embedded in their skin.

These scutes had a scaly covering, like a turtle's bony shell or an alligator's bony back. They would protect the dinosaur from attack, because if a meat eater tried to bite through the scales, it would probably break a tooth.

There were many kinds of thyreophorans. Primitive ones lived early in the Jurassic Period, which started 205 million years ago. (See page 322 for more about this period.) **Stegosaurs,** a group of thyreophorans whose backs had tall plates and spikes, first appeared in the Jurassic Period, too, and died out early in the Cretaceous Period about 110 million years ago. (See page 328 for more about this period.) The most heavily armored of all were the **ankylosaurs.** Some of these even had armor over their eyelids, to protect their eyes when they were shut!

Some fossils of ankylosaurs come from the Jurassic Period, but they are far more common in the Cretaceous.

FAMILY TREE OF THYREOPHORANS

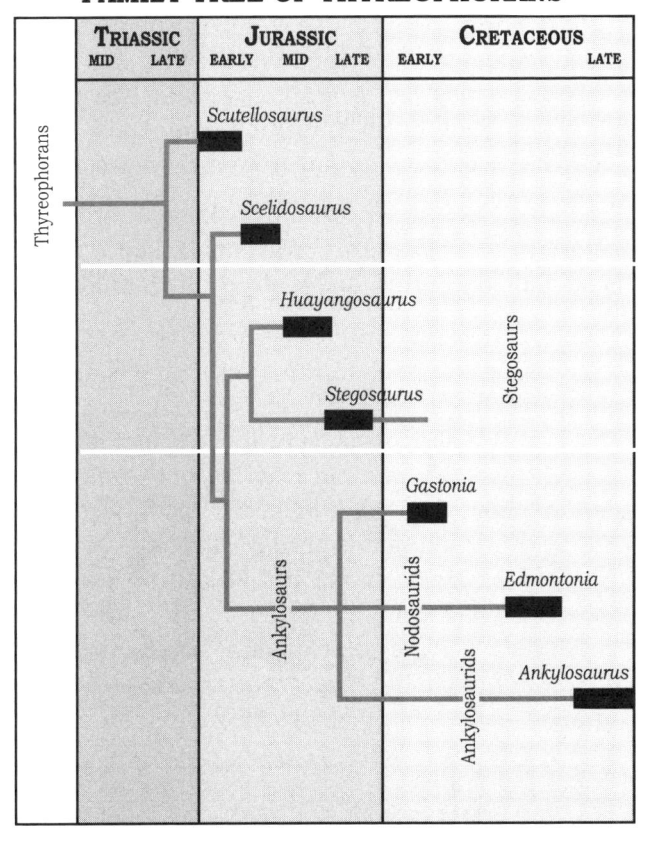

	TRIASSIC		**JURASSIC**			**CRETACEOUS**	
	MID	LATE	EARLY	MID	LATE	EARLY	LATE

Thyreophorans

- *Scutellosaurus*
- *Scelidosaurus*
- *Huayangosaurus*
- *Stegosaurus* — Stegosaurs
- *Gastonia*
- *Edmontonia* — Nodosaurids
- *Ankylosaurus* — Ankylosaurids

Ankylosaurs

Scutellosaurus
"Little armored reptile"

Length: about 4 feet (1.2m)
Diet: plants

The first and most primitive known armored dinosaur, *Scutellosaurus,* was small, had a small head and short arms, and walked on its hind legs.

EARLY JURASSIC

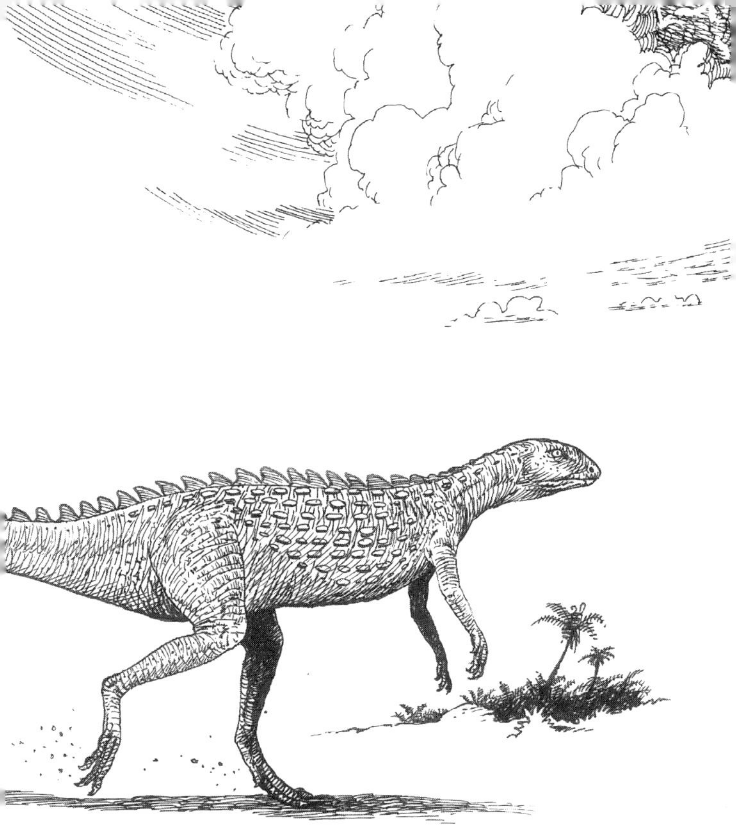

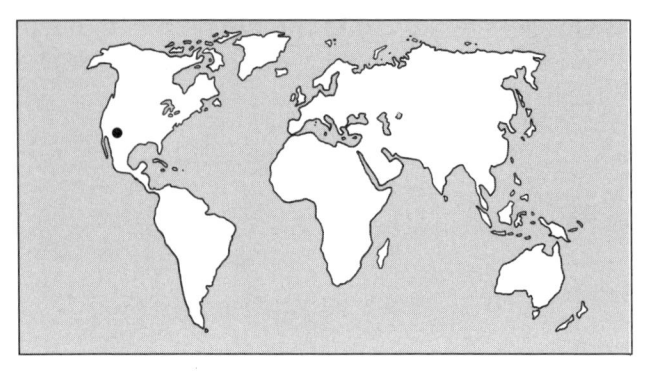

FOUND IN ARIZONA

It had hundreds of small armor plates or **scutes** covering its back and tail. If a small predator tried to attack it, the plant eater could curl up with its armored tail wrapped around its body. If the small predator tried to bite into its back or tail, it probably couldn't cut through the armor and might even break a tooth trying. All these small armor plates probably made *Scutellosaurus* slower than the other plant eaters that lived at the same time. The scutes would help against a small attacker, but if a bigger meat eater attacked, its much larger teeth and claws could probably get through. Something else would be needed to defend against these bigger predators.

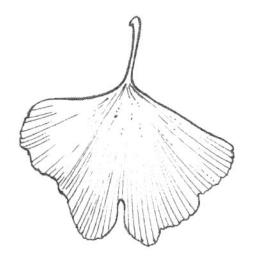

Scelidosaurus
"Knee reptile"

Length: about 13½ feet (4 m)
Diet: plants

Descended from *Scutellosaurus* or a similar dinosaur, *Scelidosaurus* represents the next stage in the history of the armored dinosaurs. Because

EARLY JURASSIC

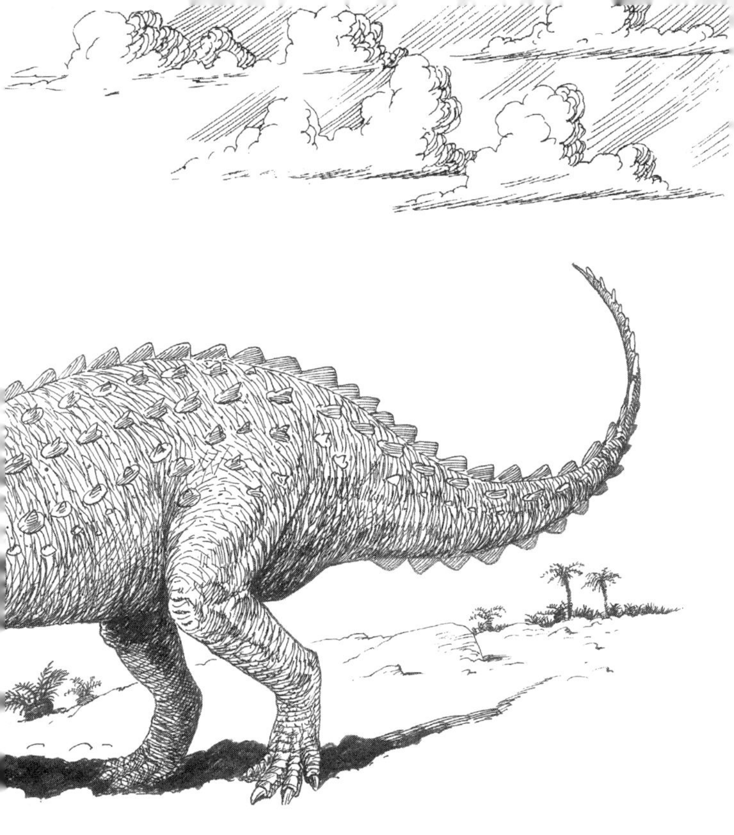

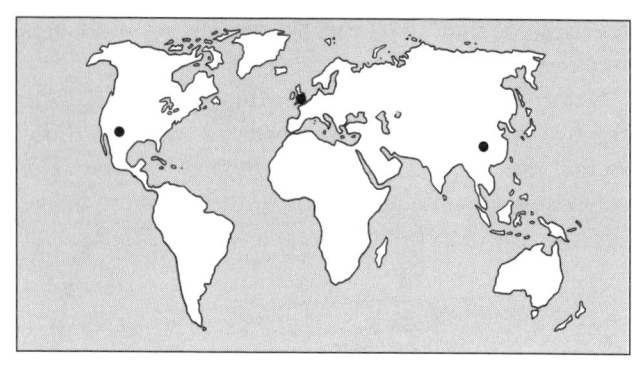

Found in England, Arizona, and possibly China

little armored dinosaurs could not defend against larger predators, they had two possible ways to go. Either they could become faster or they could become larger and more heavily armored. *Scelidosaurus* is much larger than *Scutellosaurus*, and has much larger armor plates. Very few predators of its time could have pierced its thick scutes. Such armor came at a cost, however. A big animal with lots of armor plates was too heavy to run very fast. In fact, *Scelidosaurus* had so much armor that it probably had to walk on all fours all the time, rather than run around on its hind legs like *Scutellosaurus*.

From *Scelidosaurus* or its close relations came the two main branches of advanced armored dinosaurs: the stegosaurs and the ankylosaurs. The stegosaurs became more mobile, with a more active defense; the ankylosaurs became walking tanks.

Huayangosaurus
"Huayang reptile"

Huayang was the ancient name for Sichuan, the province of China where this dinosaur was discovered.

Length: about 13½ feet (4m)
Diet: plants

Huayangosaurus was one of the earliest and most primitive stegosaurs known. Stegosaurs differ from other armored dinosaurs in a number of ways. Instead of many small scutes, they had a pair of rows of tall flat **plates** and sharp **spikes** down their back. Without the heavy armor of *Scelidosaurus*, stegosaurs were more flexible. Their tails had "war clubs" made of paired spikes that stuck

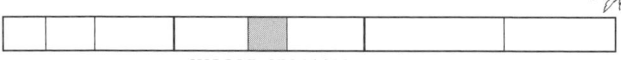

MIDDLE JURASSIC

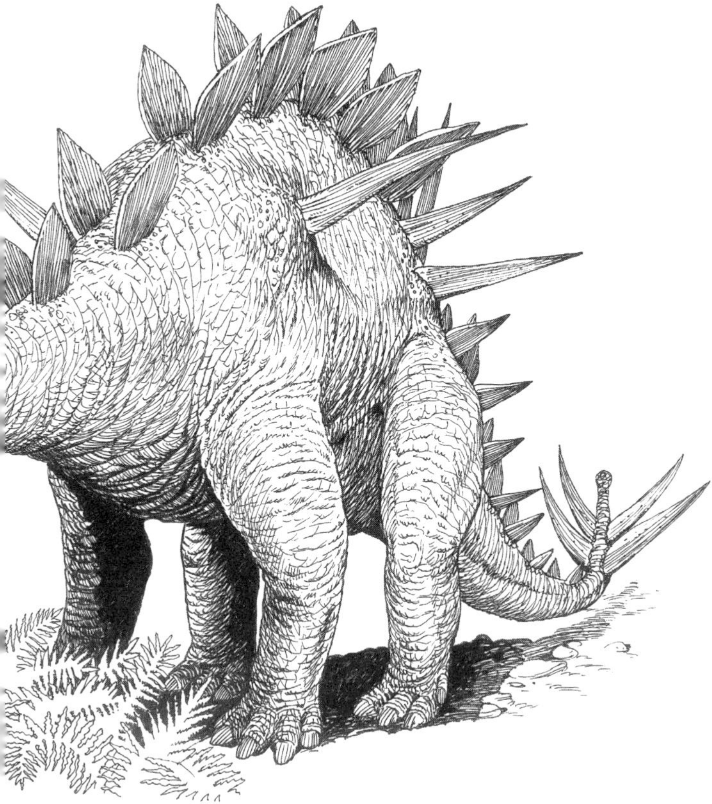

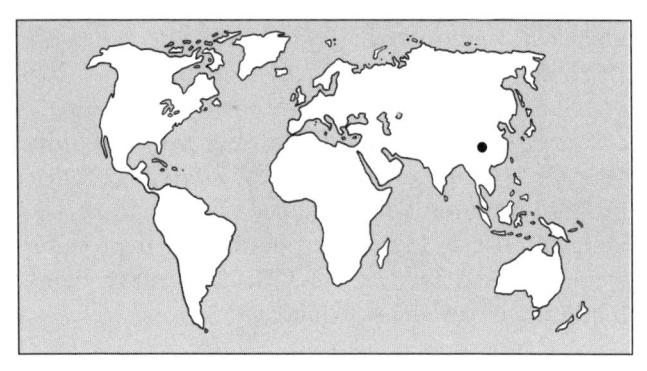

FOUND IN CHINA

out to the side. The stegosaur tail weapon, called a **thagomizer,** could swing out and smash into an attacking predator. This way stegosaurs evolved an active defense against meat eaters, using their specialized armor.

Huayangosaurus had a great big spike on each shoulder and some scutes over the side of its body as well.

Another Chinese Stegosaurus was *Tuojiangosaurus*. It had more spikes than plates on its back, and at nearly 20 feet (6m) long, was much bigger than *Huayangosaurus*. *Tuojiangosaurus* also differed from *Huayangosaurus* in that its front legs were much shorter than its hind legs. Some paleontologists think that it could rear up on its hind legs to feed higher in the trees. *Huayangosaurus* probably couldn't do that because its front legs were almost as long as its hind legs. It probably spent its time feeding on ferns and other plants that grew close to the ground.

Stegosaurus
"Roofed reptile"

Length: more than 20 feet (over 6m)
Diet: plants

Stegosaurus is probably the most famous armored dinosaur of all. Besides its thagomizer, it had very tall, very flat plates on its back. It differed from other stegosaurs in that its plates were staggered: instead of pairs of right and left plates, it had a

LATE JURASSIC

41

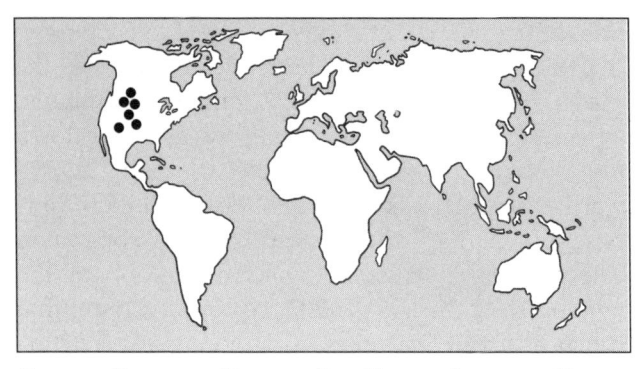

Found in Colorado, Montana, New Mexico, Oklahoma, Utah, and Wyoming, U.S.

plate on the right, then a plate on the left, then a plate on the right, and so on.

Paleontologists have wondered why *Stegosaurus* had such huge plates. They didn't make sense as armor, because they were filled with blood vessels. So if a meat eater bit into one, *Stegosaurus* would have bled. Maybe the plates made *Stegosaurus* look bigger. If it suddenly turned to show its side to an attacker, it would look much larger than face-on. Or maybe the plates were used to display to other

Stegosaurus to attract a mate or signal to each other that it would defend its territory. Or maybe the plates helped keep its body temperature stable. When facing into the wind they would cool down the dinosaur; when facing the sun they would warm it up. Perhaps the plates served all these purposes, or perhaps their actual use was something else altogether. Paleontologists once thought the tail spikes of *Stegosaurus* faced upwards, and that it had to use its tail like a scorpion, curling it forward. However, we now know that the spikes faced outwards and backwards, so the stegosaur could swing its tail from side to side to defend itself. We also know that *Stegosaurus* had dozens of small armored knobs in the skin of its neck, so its throat could still move from side to side, but was protected if an attacker tried to bite it.

Gastonia
Discovered by Gaston

Length: almost 20 feet (about 6m)
Diet: plants

Named after Robert Gaston, who discovered the dinosaur, *Gastonia* is one of the best known of the early ankylosaurs, the most heavily armored of all the dinosaurs.

EARLY CRETACEOUS

45

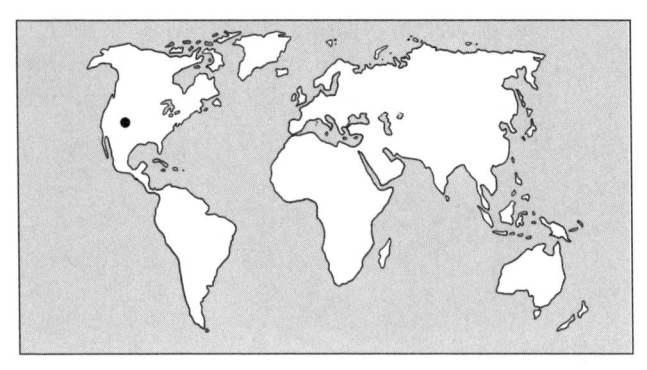

FOUND IN UTAH

Ankylosaur scutes often became fused into rings around their body. Armor plates became fused onto the bones of their skull. Over their hips the armor fused into big shields. Even the eyelids of some ankylosaurs had armor!

Gastonia had very large flat plates sticking out of the sides of its body and down its tail. These would have kept predators from getting too close. Even if they did get close, few meat eaters would have been able to break through *Gastonia*'s armor. The weight of the armor, however, would have made the ankylosaur very slow. *Gastonia* and its relatives probably spent most of their time with their faces close to the ground, cropping away at the low plants.

Edmontonia
Edmonton Formation

Length: 23 feet (about 7m)
Diet: plants

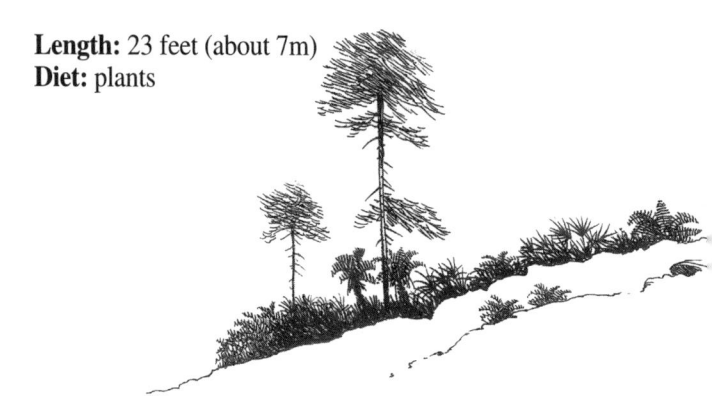

Named after the Edmonton Formation, the rocks in Canada where the dinosaur was found. The advanced ankylosaurs are divided into two groups, the **nodosaurids** (lump reptiles) and the **ankylosaurids** (fused reptiles). *Edmontonia* is

LATE CRETACEOUS

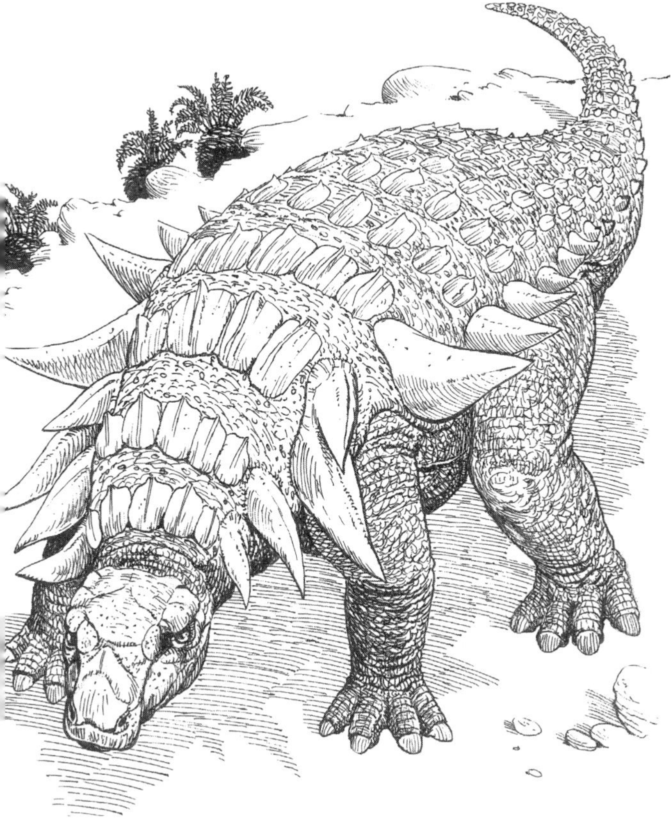

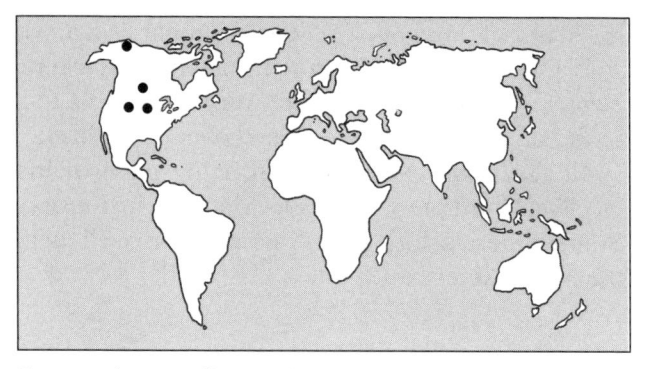

Found in Alberta, Canada; Alaska, Montana, and South Dakota, U.S.

one of the last, largest, and best known of the nodosaurids.

Edmontonia and its relatives had skulls that were long and sloping with thick armor plates on top to protect it. The spikes coming from its shoulder region were very large and had edges along them. They might have been used in combat between different *Edmontonia*, or perhaps to smash into the legs or bellies of attacking tyrannosaurs. If that didn't work, the strong armor on the back of *Edmontonia* would probably keep it safe from all but the most determined attackers. *Edmontonia* would have been very vulnerable to a meat eater only if it were turned over on its back.

Nodosaurids were found in many parts of the world in the Late Cretaceous Epoch—in Europe, South America, and even Antarctica, as well as in the North American West.

Ankylosaurus
"Fused reptile"

Length: around 25 feet (over 7.5m)
Diet: plants

Ankylosaurus was the last and largest of the armored dinosaurs. Its name is used for the whole group of advanced armored dinosaurs (the ankylosaurs) and for its special subgroup, the ankylosaurids.

LATE CRETACEOUS

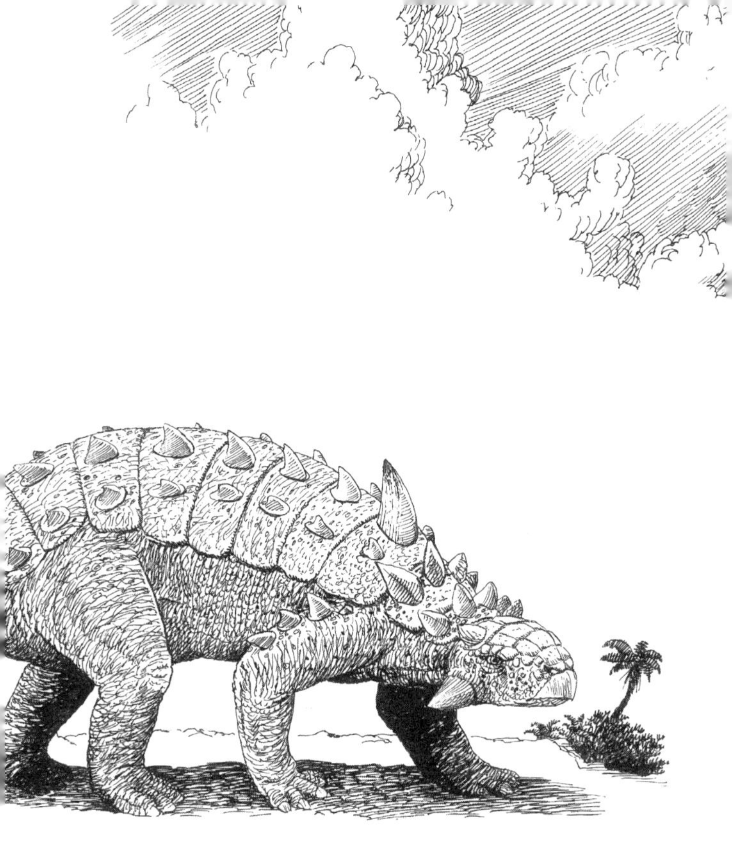

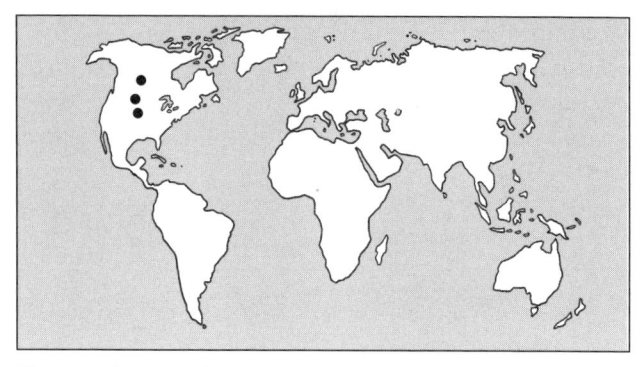

Found in Alberta, Canada; Montana and Wyoming, U.S.

Ankylosaurids all had short triangular skulls with small horns on the back. They were different from other ankylosaurs in that they didn't have big shoulder spikes or other spines along the sides of their body. Instead, they had tails that were very stiff for the last half of their length and ended in huge clubs. Like the thagomizer of the stegosaur, the ankylosaurid tail club was probably used to smash into attackers. Since *Ankylosaurus* lived in the same time and place as *Tyrannosaurus*, a powerful tail club would have been a useful weapon to have!

Ankylosaurids lived only in Asia and western North America.

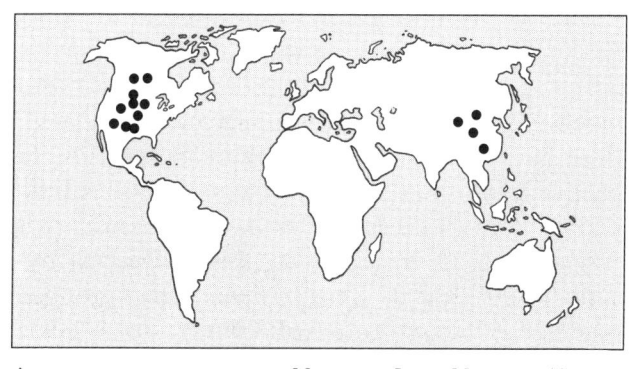

Ankylosaurids were found in Mongolia, Inner Mongolia (China just south of Mongolia); Saskatchewan, Alberta, Canada; Montana, Wyoming, South Dakota, Colorado, Utah, Arizona, New Mexico, and West Texas, U.S.

• 6 •
MARGINOCEPHALIANS, THE RIDGE HEADS

Two unusual groups of dinosaurs are the dome-headed **pachycephalosaurs** (thick-skulled reptiles) and the frilled horned **ceratopsians** (horned-faced ones). At first these two groups do not look very much alike, but they are actually closely related. Both have a ridge on the back of their heads. In pachycephalosaurs this ridge sometimes has little knobby bumps on it, but in most ceratopsians it forms a frill. Because of this ridge, pachycephalosaurs and ceratopsians are grouped together as the **marginocephalians** (ridge heads).

Like all ornithischians, marginocephalians were plant eaters. They defended themselves in different ways. Small ones could try to hide. Bigger pachycephalosaurs might have used their domed heads to ram into attacking meat eaters. Huge ceratopsians with long horns could probably fight even a tyrannosaur.

FAMILY TREE OF MARGINOCEPHALIANS

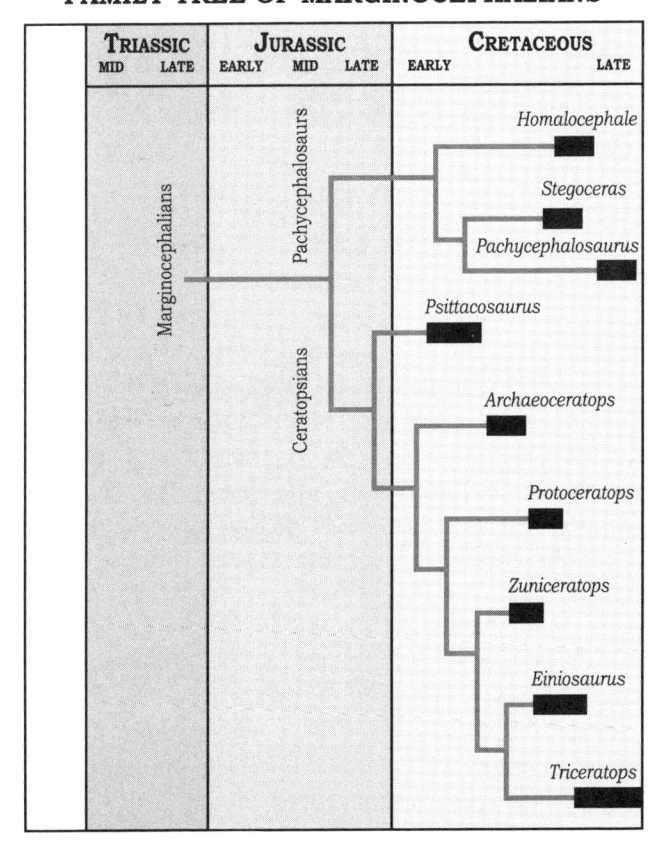

	Triassic	Jurassic	Cretaceous

Marginocephalians

Pachycephalosaurs
- *Homalocephale*
- *Stegoceras*
- *Pachycephalosaurus*

Ceratopsians
- *Psittacosaurus*
- *Archaeoceratops*
- *Protoceratops*
- *Zuniceratops*
- *Einiosaurus*
- *Triceratops*

Homalocephale
"Even head"

Length: almost 6 feet (about 1.75m)
Diet: plants

Homalocephale is one of the best known of the primitive pachycephalosaurs. Like all the other

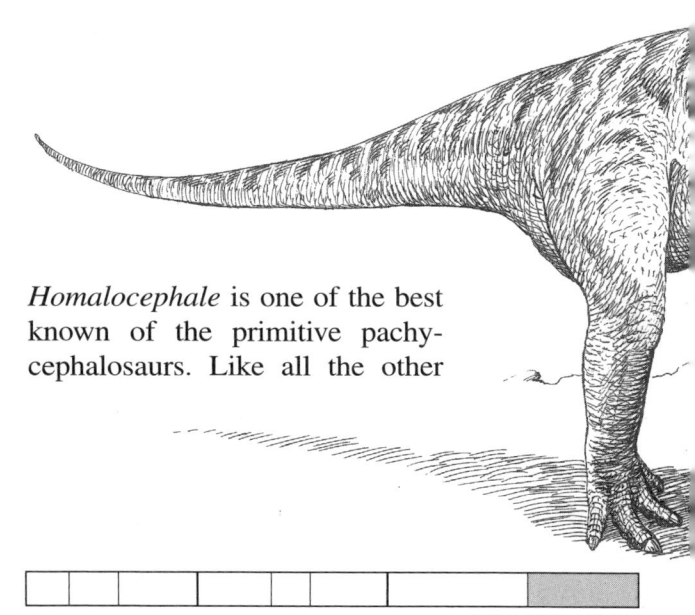

LATE CRETACEOUS

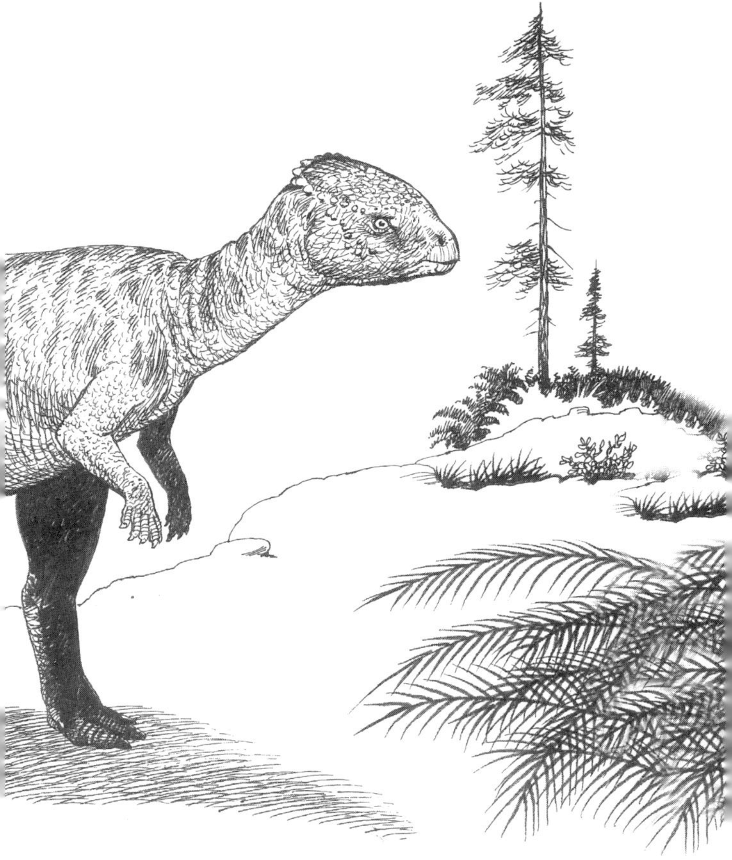

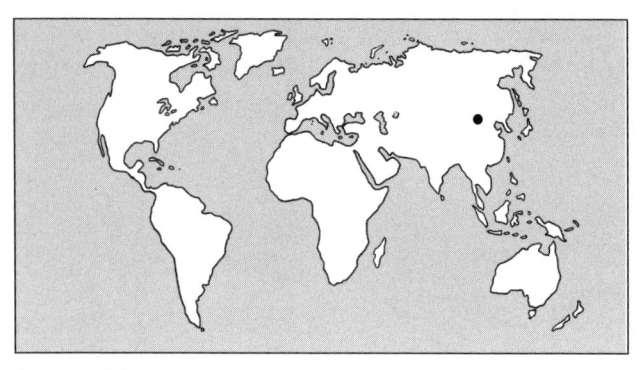

FOUND IN MONGOLIA

pachycephalosaurs, the bones on the top of its skull were thicker than in other types of dinosaurs. Unlike its relatives, its thickened skull didn't form a big dome.

Why should these dinosaurs have thicker bones on their skull? It wouldn't help them run any faster, or help them get food. What purpose could these thick heads serve?

It may be that *Homalocephale* and its relatives rammed their heads together when they got into an argument over territory, the way rams do, until eventually one of them was proven stronger.

There were many other pachycephalosaurs from Asia—dome-headed *Prenocephale* was one of the most famous—and some were found in the North American West, too.

Stegoceras
"Roofed horn"

Length: almost 6½ feet (about 2m)
Diet: plants

Looking at the head of *Stegoceras,* you'd think this little dinosaur might have been very "brainy." In fact, that dome is solid bone covering a small brain. *Stegoceras* can be said to have been a real "bone head"!

LATE CRETACEOUS

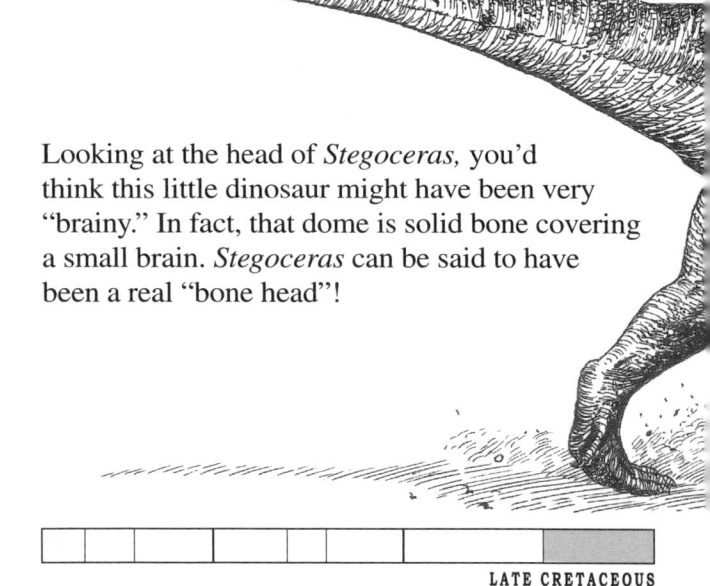

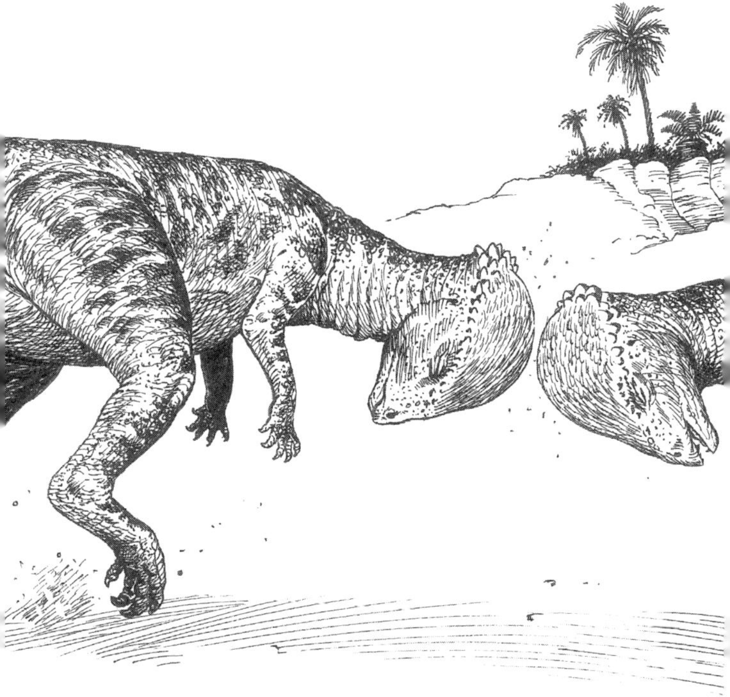

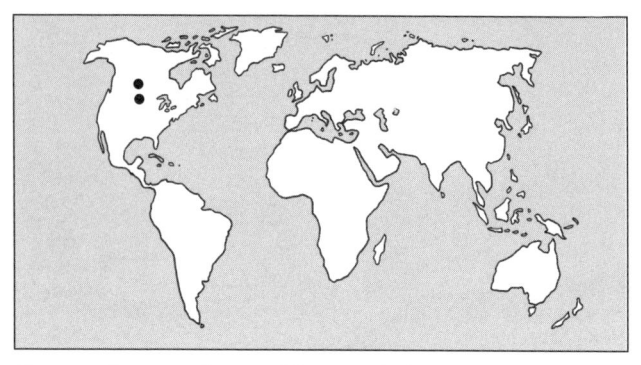

FOUND IN ALBERTA, CANADA; MONTANA, U.S.

There are two different types of skulls among the *Stegoceras* fossils: some with a slightly lower dome, and others with a slightly larger one. In modern animals males often have "showier" body covers, horns, or other structures than females. That may explain the differences we see in *Stegoceras* skulls.

The backbones of *Stegoceras* had a special shape that would help absorb the forces of impact—more evidence that these dinosaurs used their thick skulls to push and shove each other.

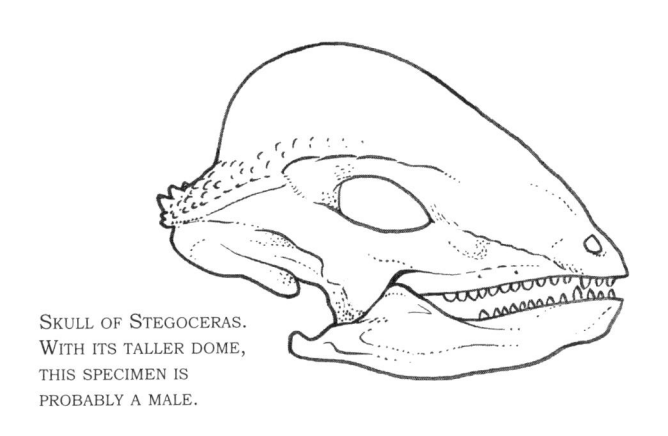

SKULL OF STEGOCERAS. WITH ITS TALLER DOME, THIS SPECIMEN IS PROBABLY A MALE.

One of the best-known North American dome-headed dinosaurs, *Stegoceras* was a plant eater. Its simple leaf-shaped teeth were probably good for chopping up leaves and ferns, but not as good as those of horned dinosaurs for slicing up tough vegetation or grinding up big masses of plants.

Pachycephalosaurus
"Thick-headed reptile"

Length: 12 feet or more (over 3.5m)
Diet: plants

Pachycephalosaurus was the last and the largest of all the dome-headed dinosaurs—the only known member of this group that was bigger than

LATE CRETACEOUS

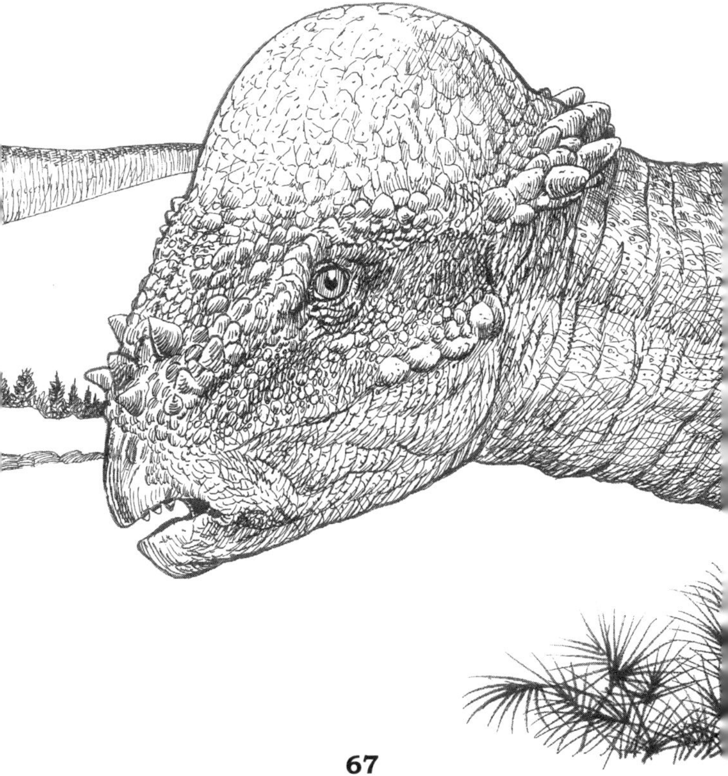

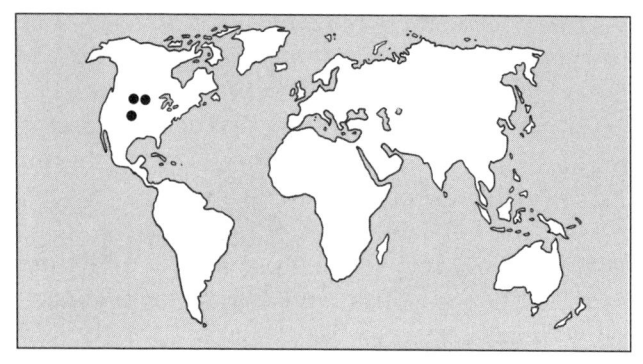

FOUND IN WYOMING, SOUTH DAKOTA, AND MONTANA, U.S.

an adult human. It also had the thickest dome (up to 9 inches or 23cm thick!) and larger knobs on the back of its head than any of its relatives.

Its world contained many of the last and largest dinosaurs: *Triceratops* and *Torosaurus*, greatest of the horned dinosaurs; *Anatotitan* and *Edmontosaurus*, two of the largest and most advanced duckbills; *Ankylosaurus*, the largest of the armored dinosaurs; and stalking the others, *Tyrannosaurus*, one of the largest land-living predators of all time.

How could *Pachycephalosaurus* survive in a world with the mighty *Tyrannosaurus*—one of the fastest of the big meat eaters? *Pachycephalosaurus* could run, but not that fast, and it was too big to hide in small spaces. It might try to ram *Tyrannosaurus,* but if it didn't hurt him enough, *Pachycephalosaurus* would be in trouble.

We have to remember, though, that dinosaurs were just a kind of animal—they weren't monsters from science fiction movies. Like the big meat eaters of the modern world, such as lions or tigers or crocodiles, *Tyrannosaurus* wasn't always looking for food. Most of the time it was probably resting or just walking around. *Pachycephalosaurus* too would have spent most of its time browsing and walking around. Dinosaur fights might have been very dramatic, but they were probably rare.

Psittacosaurus
"Parrot reptile"

Length: almost 4 feet (up to 1.2m)
Diet: plants

Although it doesn't look it, *Psittacosaurus* is one of the oldest known and most primitive ceratopsians (horned dinosaurs). It didn't actually have

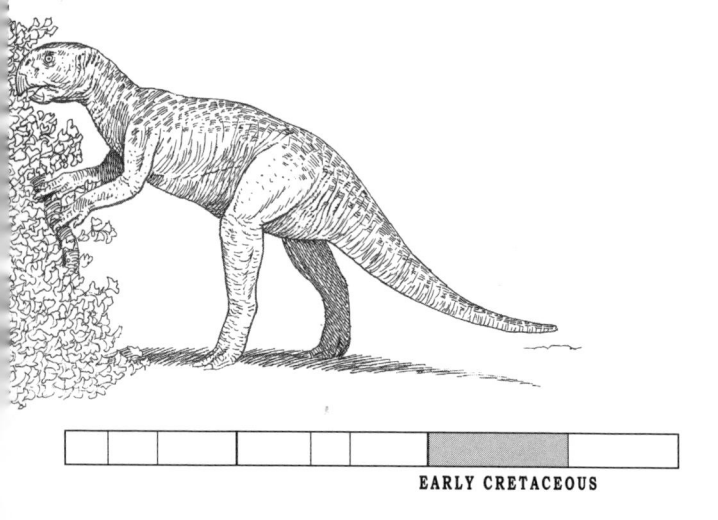

EARLY CRETACEOUS

71

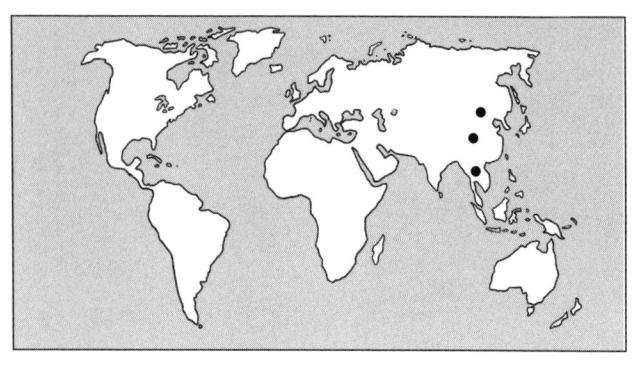

FOUND IN: MONGOLIA, CHINA, THAILAND

any horns, and (unlike all other ceratopsians) it didn't even have a frill. However, like all other ceratopsians it had a special extra bone at the end of its upper jaw.

Of all the dinosaurs (and other animals) known to paleontologists, only ceratopsians had this special extra jawbone. This shows that *Psittacosaurus* was a very early "horned" dinosaur, but that horns didn't evolve in ceratopsians until after this parrot-beaked dinosaur.

Like all ornithischians, *Psittacosaurus* was a

plant eater. Its jaws were deep and strong, and it was able to chop up and eat lots of tough vegetation. If its jaws and teeth were not enough, *Psittacosaurus* had a gizzard full of stones to grind up its food, too.

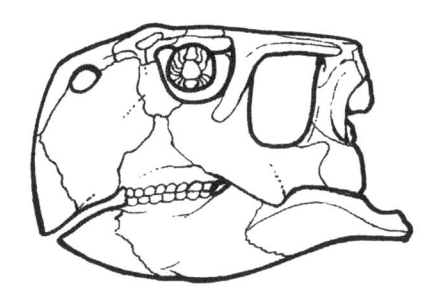

SKULL OF PSITTACOSAURUS

Psittacosaurus was a bit stocky, but it could still stretch up on its hind legs when looking out for a meat eater or when trying to eat leaves or twigs or fruit from low-hanging branches of trees. It might walk on all four legs, though, if it was feeding on plants growing low to the ground.

Archaeoceratops
"Ancient horned face"

Length: 3⅓ feet or more (up to 1m)
Diet: plants

At first glance, *Archaeoceratops* looks like a skinnier version of its close relative *Psittacosaurus*. It too was a plant eater, and probably fed on tough

LATE CRETACEOUS

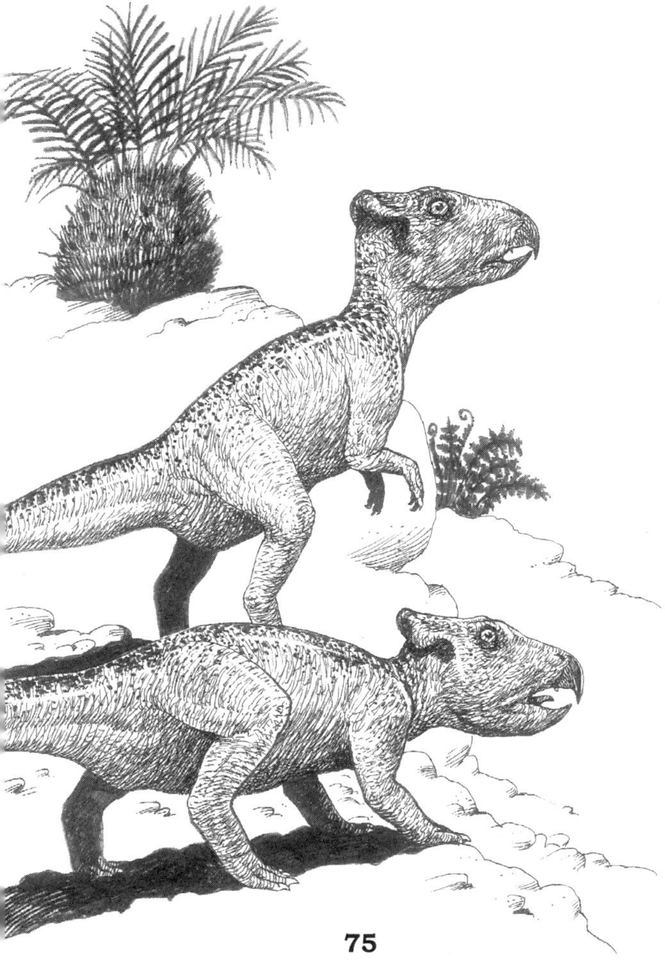

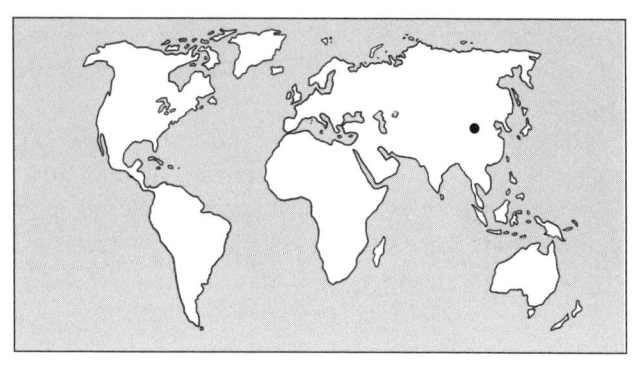

FOUND IN CHINA

vegetation, But there was a difference: *Archaeoceratops* had a small frill coming off the back of its skull.

While its powerful jaw muscles helped it cut through tough plants, those muscles need a bony surface to attach to. In *Archaeoceratops* when the back of the skull had grown outwards to form the frill, it made a much bigger space for the muscles that helped the jaws to close.

Because its skull was fairly small, *Archaeoceratops* could still walk on its hind legs. In fact, it was probably a pretty fast little dinosaur. Most of its descendants had skulls so big they could only walk on all fours.

Recently sites have been found in China where many *Archaeoceratops* were buried at one time. This suggests that it lived in groups. Some later ceratopsians (like *Einiosaurus* and *Centrosaurus*) lived in huge herds.

Protoceratops
"First horned face"

Length: 6½ feet or more (about 2m)
Diet: plants

Protoceratops was bigger and heavier than earlier ceratopsians like *Psittacosaurus* and *Archaeoceratops*. But that isn't the only difference. For one thing, the top of its snout came to a bit of a

LATE CRETACEOUS

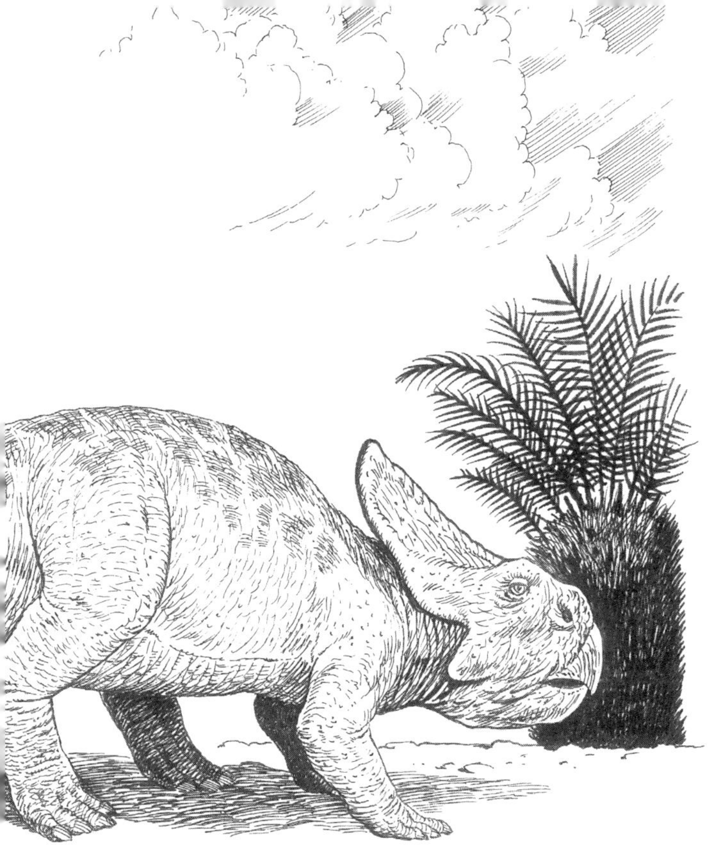

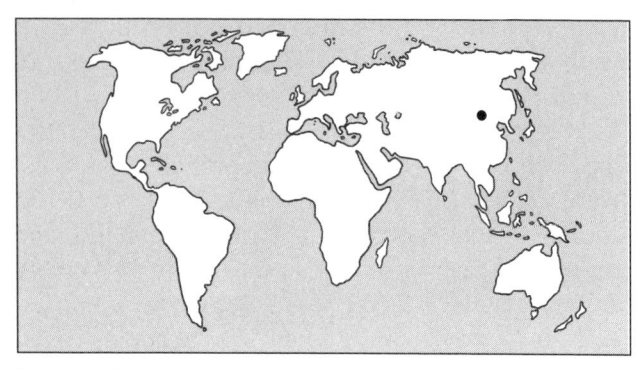

FOUND IN MONGOLIA

point—a foreshadowing of the true horn of later ceratopsians. More important, the head of *Protoceratops* and other advanced horned dinosaurs was very big—its skull made up a quarter or more of its total body size! The frill, which was small in *Archaeoceratops*, was much larger in *Protoceratops*. Because it had such a big head, *Protoceratops* would not have been able to walk around on just two legs. Like all the other advanced ceratopsians, it could walk only on all fours.

Why have such a huge head? The jaws of

Protoceratops were strong and powerful, and its teeth had a sharp edge. It probably ate lots of tough vegetation. At least some of the frill was used for the attachment of its jaw muscles. But the frill was so big that that probably isn't the whole story. In many animals today large broad surfaces—like the ears of African elephants and the tails of peacocks—are used to show off to other animals. It is very likely that *Protoceratops* used its frill to show off or scare off attacking meat eaters. It might have had color patterns (spots or stripes, maybe) on the front of the frill. Because the colors of dinosaur skin don't fossilize, we will probably never know for sure.

Protoceratops was a very common dinosaur in its time. Many dozens of skeletons have been found. It lived in a desert environment, where the blowing sands could cover the dinosaurs so quickly that skeletons have been found in the exact position in which they died—trying to dig themselves out of the sand. In one spectacular case, a *Protoceratops* and a *Velociraptor* were in the midst of a fight and were buried together, locked in the final position for 80 million years!

Zuniceratops
"Zuni horned face"

Named for the Native American people of New Mexico.

Length: 6½ feet (about 2 m)
Diet: plants

Recently discovered and known only from parts of different skeletons, *Zuniceratops* is the oldest known example so far of a true horned ceratopsian.

Although people sometimes refer to all ceratopsians as "horned dinosaurs," only the most advanced ceratopsians of the North American West actually

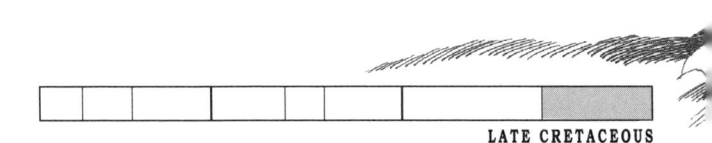

LATE CRETACEOUS

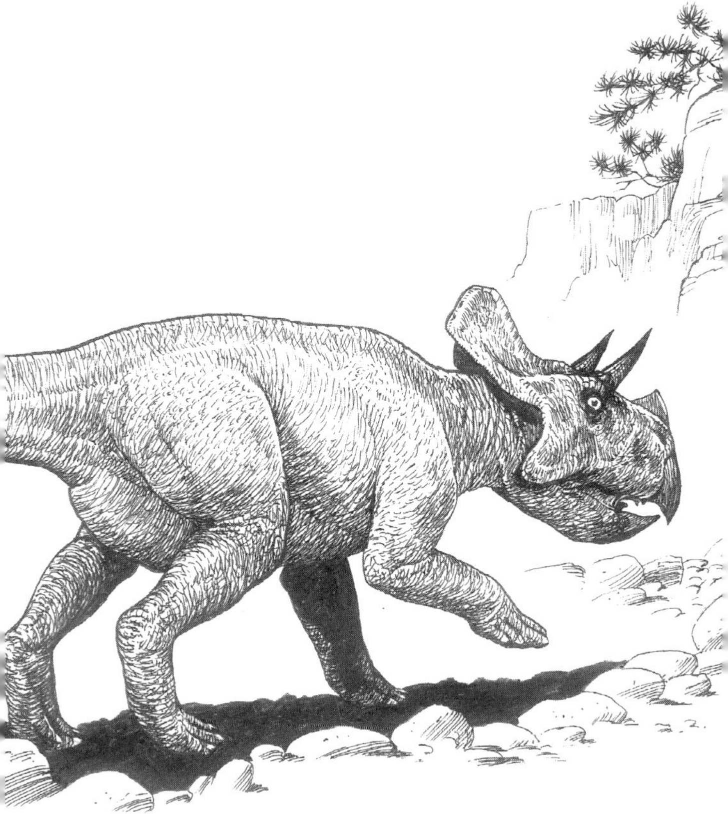

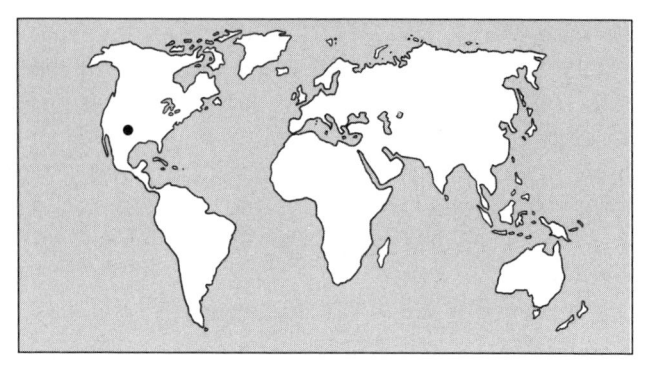

Found in New Mexico, U.S.

had horns. Asian ceratopsians either had no horns or, at most, a pointed top to their snout (like *Protoceratops*).

Zuniceratops shows the pattern we see in the later true horned dinosaurs: a horn on the nose and a horn over each eye. These horns were fairly short and stout in *Zuniceratops*, but they became longer in later forms.

Because all ceratopsians were plant eaters, *Zuniceratops* would not have used its horns to kill other animals. The horns over its eyes protected the base of the frill, where its jaw muscles were attached. The main use of these horns—and the horn on its nose—was probably in tests of strength with other *Zuniceratops*. If one of these dinosaurs placed its head against the other, the horns would lock together and the dinosaurs could have a shoving match, like antelopes or deer today.

Like deer and antelopes, though, the horns may have served yet another purpose—defense. *Zuniceratops*. may have used its horns to hold off meat eaters, hoping that the attackers would give up and seek a weaker victim.

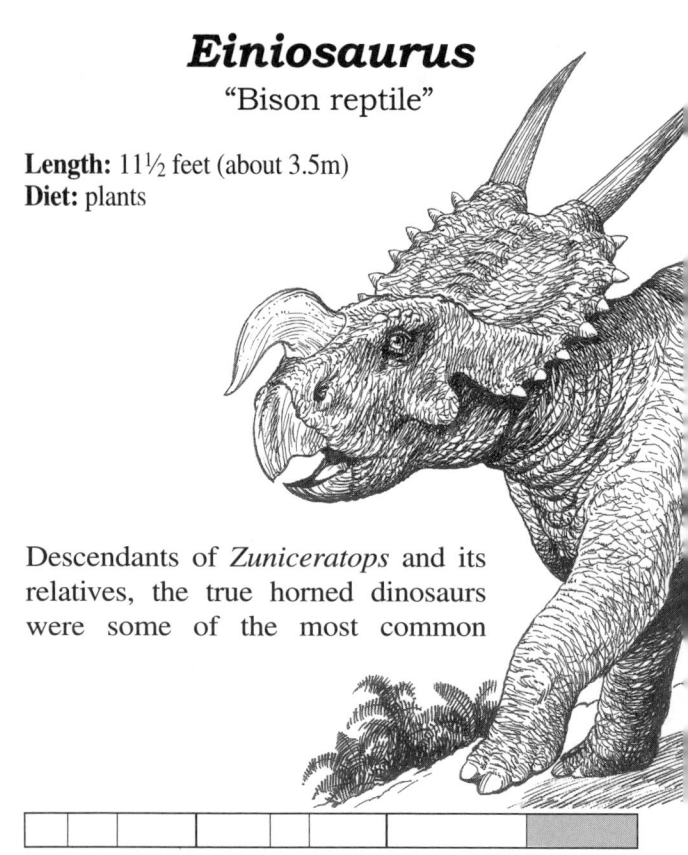

Einiosaurus
"Bison reptile"

Length: 11½ feet (about 3.5m)
Diet: plants

Descendants of *Zuniceratops* and its relatives, the true horned dinosaurs were some of the most common

LATE CRETACEOUS

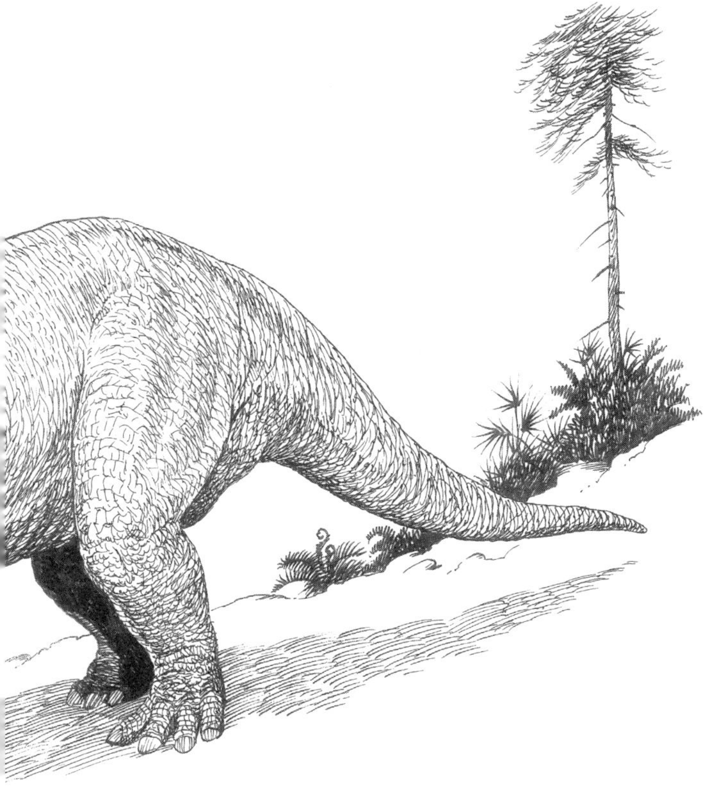

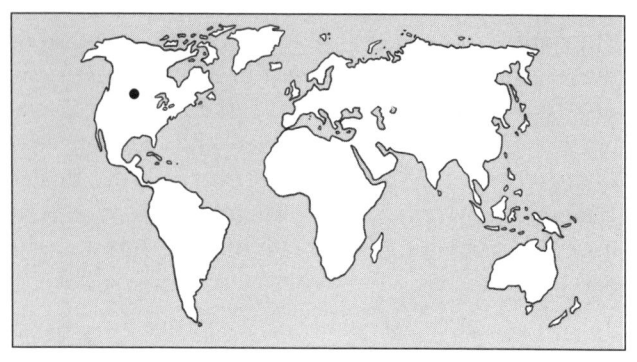

Found in Montana, U.S.

dinosaurs of the western part of North America during the last part of the Late Cretaceous Epoch. There were a great many species. In general, their bodies were very similar: they had huge skulls with powerful beaks, thick and powerful legs, and short tails. They had sharp rows of teeth to deal with the toughest vegetation. The main differences between the species of horned dinosaurs were in the pattern of the horns on the head and spikes on the frill.

There are two main groups of true horned

dinosaurs. *Einiosaurus* is representative of one of these groups. In *Einiosaurus* and its relatives the nose horn was much longer than the eyebrow horns. The snout was shorter and deeper, and there were often large spikes on the frill. In the case of *Einiosaurus* itself the nose horn was bent forward, something like a can opener, and the frill had only one pair of backwards-pointing spikes.

EINIOSAURUS NOSE HORN

In its relative *Centrosaurus* the nose horn had a slender upwards curve and the pair of frill-spikes pointed forward.

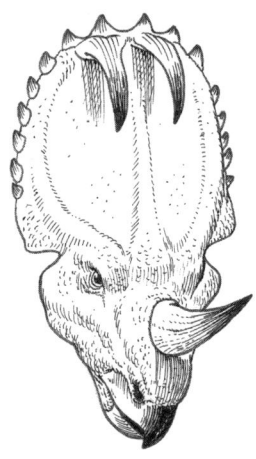

CENTROSAURUS NOSE HORN

In *Styracosaurus* the nose horn was straight and there were six large backwards-facing frill spikes.

In *Achelousaurus* and *Pachyrhinosaurus* the nose horn turned into a huge knobby mass in adults, and there were a pair or more of backwards-facing spikes.

STYRACOSAURUS
NOSE HORN

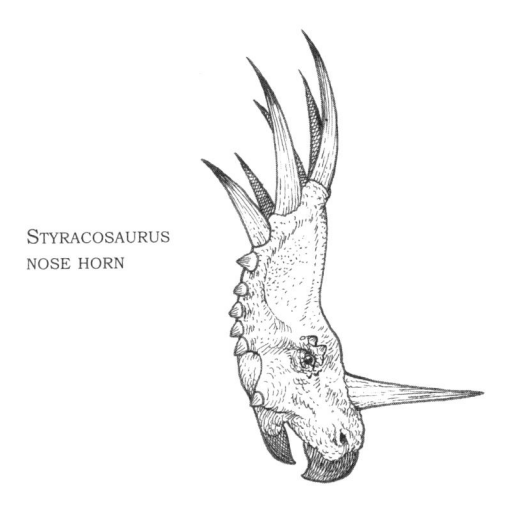

Einiosaurus and its relatives lived in herds. Sometimes paleontologists found the remains of babies, youngsters, and adults all jumbled together—probably members of a herd killed by a powerful flood or storm. From finds like these scientists can figure out how dinosaurs changed as they grew older. They discovered that a young *Einiosaurus* looked similar to a young *Centrosaurus, Styracosaurus, Achelousaurus,* and *Pachyrhinosaurus.* The features that distinguished these dinosaurs appeared only when they grew up.

Triceratops
"Three-horned face"

Length: 23 feet (about 7m)
Diet: plants

While *Einiosaurus* and its relatives form one major branch of the true horned dinosaurs, *Triceratops*, one of the last and largest of all—and its relatives—form the other.

In these dinosaurs the brow horns were almost always much longer than the nose horn;

LATE CRETACEOUS

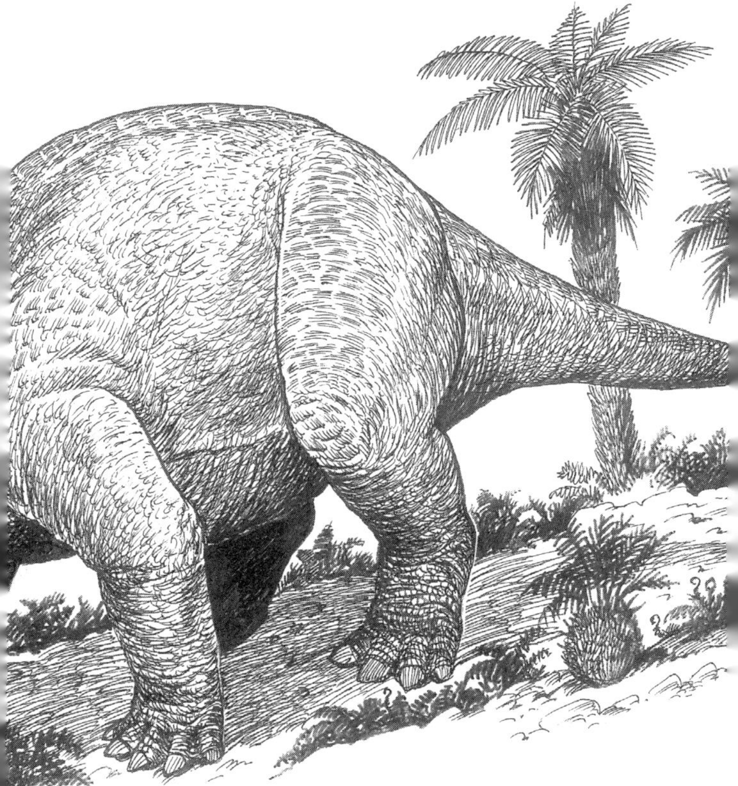

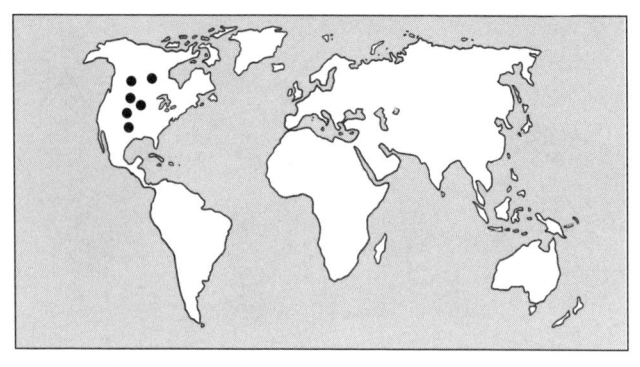

Found in Alberta and Saskatchewan, Canada; Montana, Wyoming, South Dakota, and Colorado, U.S.

the snout was long and not as deep; and the frill was generally very large. Instead of a few big spikes, the frills of these horned dinosaurs usually had many smaller triangular-shaped ridges along the edges.

Some *Triceratops* skulls are found with brow horns that were broken in life. The ends of the horns healed over so only a stump was left. From the position of the break in the horn, it seems likely that this happened when two *Triceratops* were locking horns in a shoving match.

THE THREE-HORNED
SKULL OF TRICERATOPS

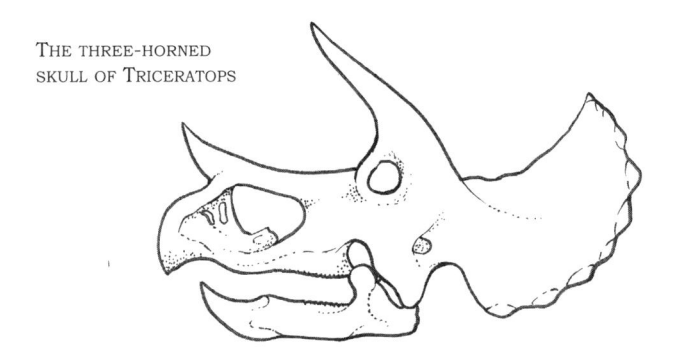

The horns of *Triceratops* would also have defended it against *Tyrannosaurus*, who lived at the same time and in the same place. *Triceratops* might have been one of the main foods of *Tyrannosaurus*. However, a healthy adult *Triceratops* would have been a powerful opponent of even *Tyrannosaurus*! Its large brow horns could inflict fatal wounds and its jaws (specialized for cutting through tough plants) could cause serious damage. So even though it was a plant eater, *Triceratops* was far from helpless. If *Tyrannosaurus* did hunt this giant horned dinosaur, it probably would have preferred to go after the young, the very old, or the sick.

• 7 •
ORNITHOPODS, THE BEAKED DINOSAURS

All of the ornithischian dinosaurs known to paleontology were plant eaters. In one group of ornithischians the jaws became very specialized for chopping and grinding up plant food. This group is the **ornithopods,** or "bird-footed" dinosaurs.

Like other ornithischian dinosaurs, the snouts of ornithopods ended in a beak. In ornithopods, however, the front end of the beak was lower than the rest of the upper jaw. Also, the joint between the upper and lower jaw was placed very low.

THE JAWS OF ORNITHOPODS WORKED LIKE NUTCRACKERS TO GIVE THEM STRONGER BITES THAN MORE PRIMITIVE PLANT EATERS.

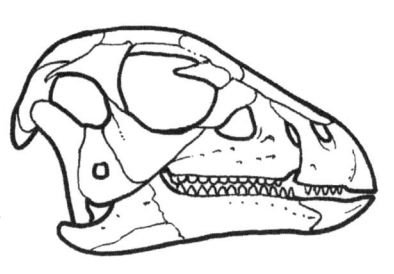

This combination of features gave ornithopods an extra special bite that helped crush up the plants they ate. Because of this, it might be more appropriate to call ornithopods the "beaked dinosaurs" than the "bird-footed dinosaurs."

Early ornithopods were all small two-legged animals, just like the early members of all the other groups of dinosaurs. Even the biggest beaked dinosaurs, like *Iguanodon* and the duckbills, walked and ran on just their back legs, but these giants also had hands, so they could walk on all fours.

Ornithopods didn't have armor (like thyreophorans) or horns and domes (like marginocephalians). The smaller beaked dinosaurs probably just ran and hid when meat eaters came around. Many types of big ornithopod lived in groups. By teaming up, one or two of the plant eaters might have been able to spot an approaching predator and alert the other members of the herd.

Ornithopods have been found on every continent, from the beginning of the Jurassic until the end of the Cretaceous Period.

FAMILY TREE OF ORNITHOPODS

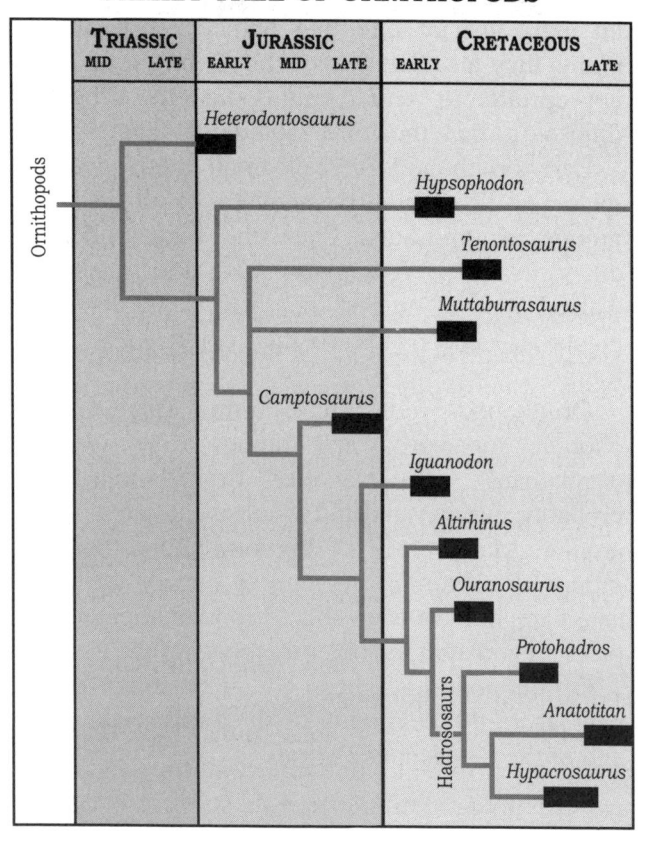

Heterodontosaurus
"Different-toothed reptile"

Length: 3⅓ feet (about 1m)
Diet: plants

Southern Africa in the Early Jurassic Epoch was home to many different types of dinosaurs. Compared to the giants of later times, these early dinosaurs were generally very small—most of them smaller than people. One of the most common was *Heterodontosaurus*, a primitive ornithopod.

Like most other early dinosaurs, *Heterodontosaurus* was a small two-legged runner. Like early saurischian dinosaurs, it had long hands with fingers built for grasping and holding. It was in its head that most of the differences between *Heterodontosaurus* and other early dinosaurs were found.

The teeth of most plant-eating dinosaurs were fairly simple, and looked something like leaves. But the jaws of *Heterodontosaurus* had three different types of teeth. In the front of the snout were small nipping teeth. Behind these were big fangs

Heterodontosaurus

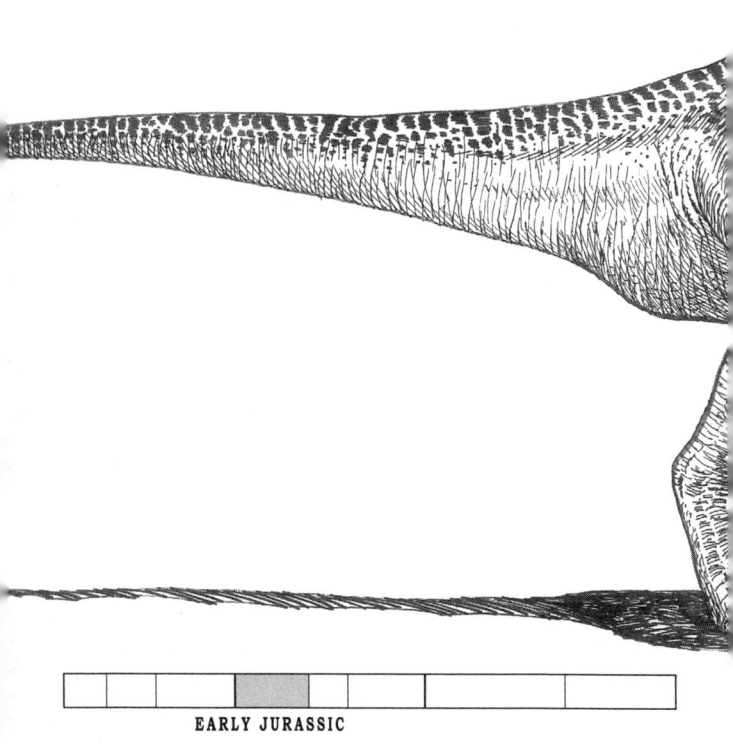

EARLY JURASSIC

101

like the canine teeth of mammals. Most of the teeth of *Heterodontosaurus* were shaped like little chisels.

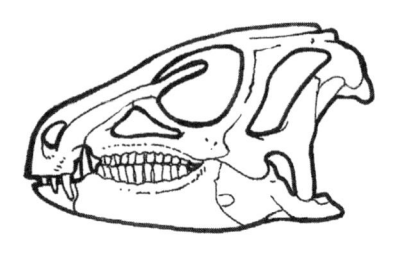

SKULL OF HETERODONTOSAURUS

The skull of this dinosaur was strongly built. By looking at its teeth and skull we can tell it was more specialized at eating tough plants than most other dinosaurs of its time. Its chisel teeth and strong skull show that it could bite down on hard plants and crush them up. But why should a plant eater have long fangs? It turns out that some small modern plant-eating mammals, like small antelopes and deer, sometimes have big fangs. They don't use them to bite and tear up meat, but

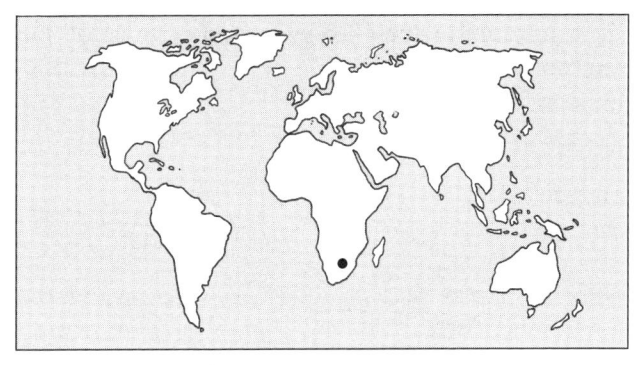

FOUND IN SOUTHERN AFRICA

to show off to each other when fighting. Perhaps *Heterodontosaurus* did the same.

Teeth like those of *Heterodontosaurus* were found in many parts of the world in the Late Triassic and Early Jurassic Epochs. After that, this primitive type of ornithopod became rare and more advanced types took over.

Hypsilophodon
"Hypsilophus tooth"

Named for a type of iguana lizard

Length: over 4 feet (about 1.25m)
Diet: plants

Hypsilophodon and its relatives were one of the most successful of all the groups of plant-eating dinosaurs. They first appeared in the Middle

EARLY CRETACEOUS

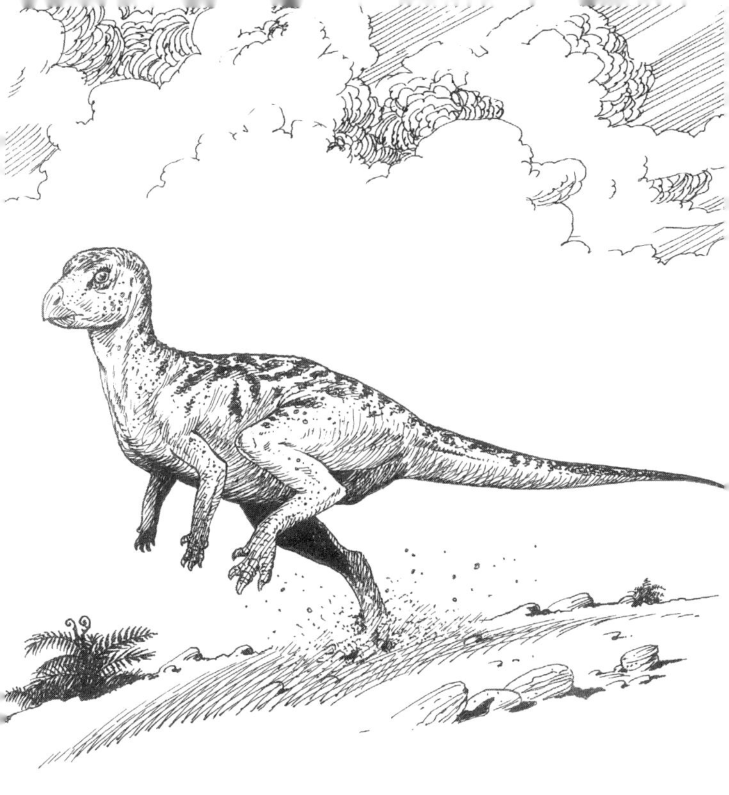

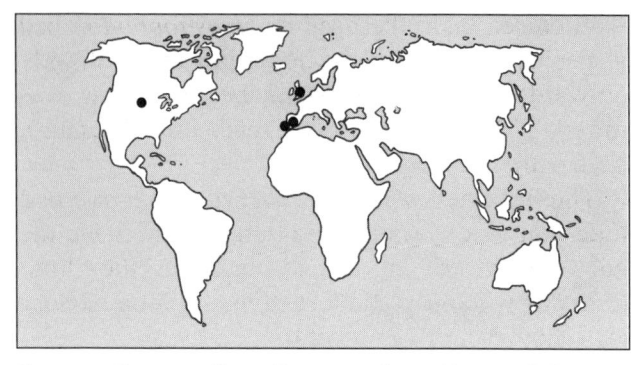

FOUND IN: ENGLAND, SPAIN, PORTUGAL, SOUTH DAKOTA, U.S.

Jurassic Epoch and survived until the great extinction at the end of the Cretaceous.

At first glance *Hypsilophodon* looks very similar to *Heterodontosaurus*. It was also small and two-legged. It didn't have fangs. Its hands were a bit shorter, and it was bigger over all compared to its Early Jurassic relative, but otherwise they seem alike.

Some of the main differences between *Hypsilophodon* and the earlier ornithopod are in the skull and in the tail. Instead of a rigid skull with chisel teeth, the head of *Hypsilophodon* had a special joint that let the upper jaw move slightly outwards and inwards when the lower jaw was raised. This gave the Early Cretaceous dinosaur a little extra chewing ability.

The back half of the tail of *Hypsilophodon* had long bony rods running through it. This made the tail stiffer, which helped balance the little dinosaur when it made fast turns. Its long slender legs show that it was a fast runner.

Hypsilophodon and its kin may not have been as interesting as stegosaurs or duckbills, ceratopsians or tyrannosaurs, but they lasted much longer and lived in many more places than those giants!

Tenontosaurus
"Sinew reptile"

Length: 20 feet (6m) long
Diet: plants

Over time the ornithopods became larger and larger. One of the most primitive of the large

EARLY CRETACEOUS

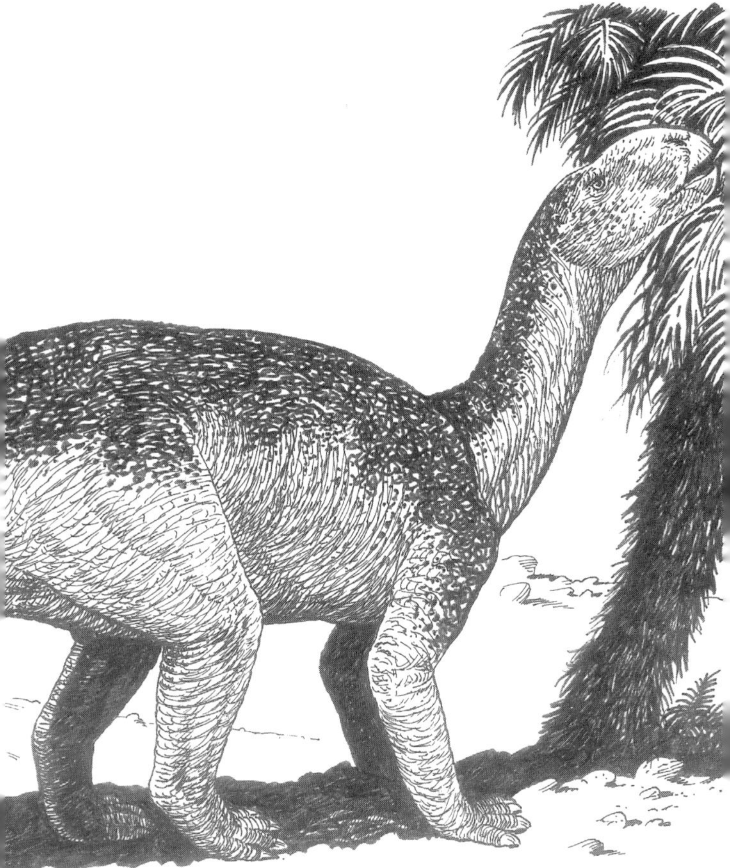

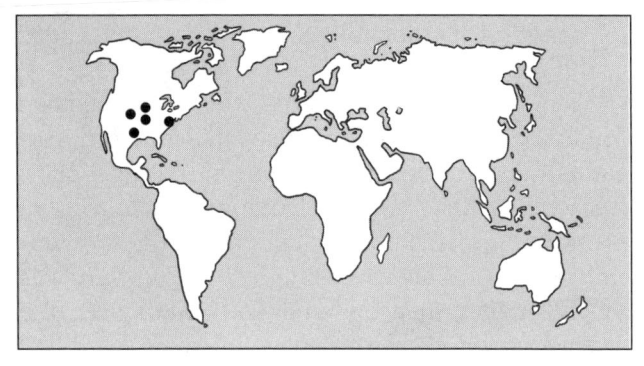

Found in Wyoming, Montana, Oklahoma, Utah, Texas, possibly Maryland, U.S.

ornithopods was *Tenontosaurus*. It was also one of the most common dinosaurs in North America during the Early Cretaceous Epoch.

In many ways *Tenontosaurus* was like a big heavy version of *Hypsilophodon*. Its skull was deeper from top to bottom and its arms and legs were thicker. Its tail was very long. There were some other differences, too. One of them, the lack of teeth along the front of its big beak, shows that *Tenontosaurus* was probably more closely related to *Iguanodon*, duckbills, and other advanced ornithopods.

Many skeletons of *Tenontosaurus* have been found together with the teeth of the smaller meat-eating raptor dinosaur *Deinonychus* (page 280). Because of this, some paleontologists think that *Deinonychus* was the main enemy of *Tenontosaurus*. But because any single *Deinonychus* was much smaller than an adult *Tenontosaurus*, the raptors would have had to gang up in packs to attack and kill one of the big plant eaters.

Like the smaller ornithopods, *Tenontosaurus* could walk and run on its hind legs. However, because it was so much bigger, it was a lot heavier than *Hypsilophodon* and its relatives. Although its long tail may have helped to balance its heavy front end, it seems likely that *Tenontosaurus* spent a lot of time walking on all fours. Because of this, the hands of this big plant eater are shorter and broader than those of *Heterodontosaurus* and *Hypsilophodon*.

Muttaburrasaurus
"Muttaburra reptile"

Muttaburra is a township in Australia.

Length: 23 feet (about 7m)
Diet: plants

Many types of big ornithopod had big noses. One of the most primitive of these was the Australian dinosaur *Muttaburrasaurus*.

EARLY CRETACEOUS

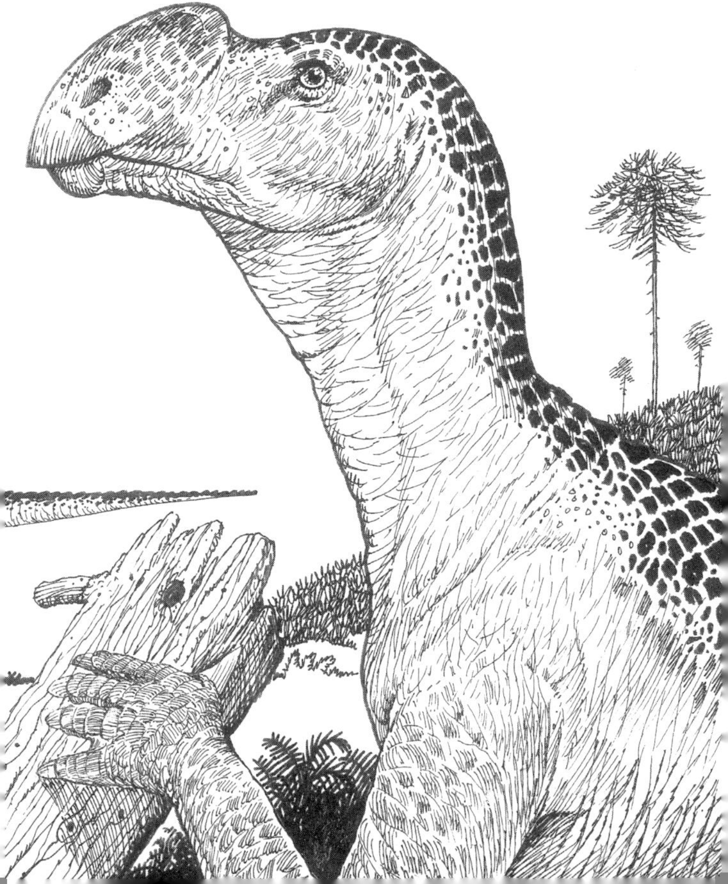

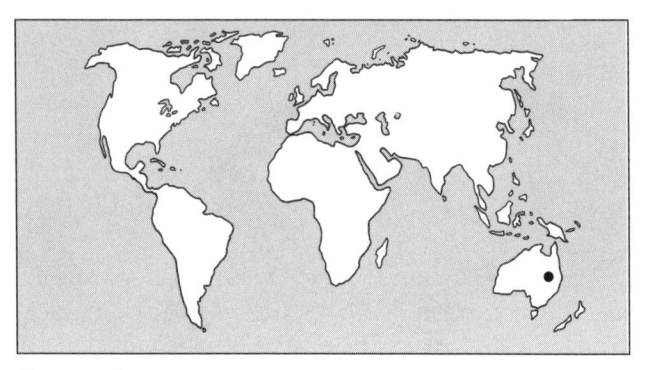

FOUND IN AUSTRALIA

Muttaburrasaurus looked something like *Tenontosaurus*, which lived at the same time far away in North America. Both were big and heavy compared to *Hypsilophodon*, and had thicker arms and legs. *Muttaburrasaurus* was unusual in the shape of its snout. The bones over its nostril flared upwards, so that it had a kind of crest on its nose. *Muttaburrasaurus* may have possibly used the shape of this crest to show off to others of its species.

Another possibility is that this crest supported a

fleshy nose sac. It's possible that the *Muttaburrasaurus* inflated the sac with air and made loud noises from its nose, the way frogs do with their throat sacs. However, until someone finds the skin impressions of the head of a *Muttaburrasaurus*, we may never be sure if they had a sac there or not.

When *Muttaburrasaurus* was alive, Australia was even further south than it is today. In fact, Australia and Antarctica were still connected to each other! Because of this it is possible that *Muttaburrasaurus* walked all the way to the South Pole. Though it was much warmer during the Age of Dinosaurs than today, the polar regions would still have been frozen during the winter. It's possible that these big-nosed plant eaters migrated into the more southerly regions during the warm season (when long hours of daylight made plants grow better), and then left those lands when winter frosts began.

Camptosaurus
"Bent reptile"

Length: up to 23 feet (7m)
Diet: plants

The rocks of the famous Morrison Formation of the American West contain the fossils of some of the best-known dinosaurs: *Stegosaurus*, *Diplodocus*, *Apatosaurus*, *Camarasaurus*, *Brachiosaurus*, *Ceratosaurus*, *Allosaurus*, and more. The most common ornithopod found in these Late Jurassic rocks was *Camptosaurus*.

LATE JURASSIC

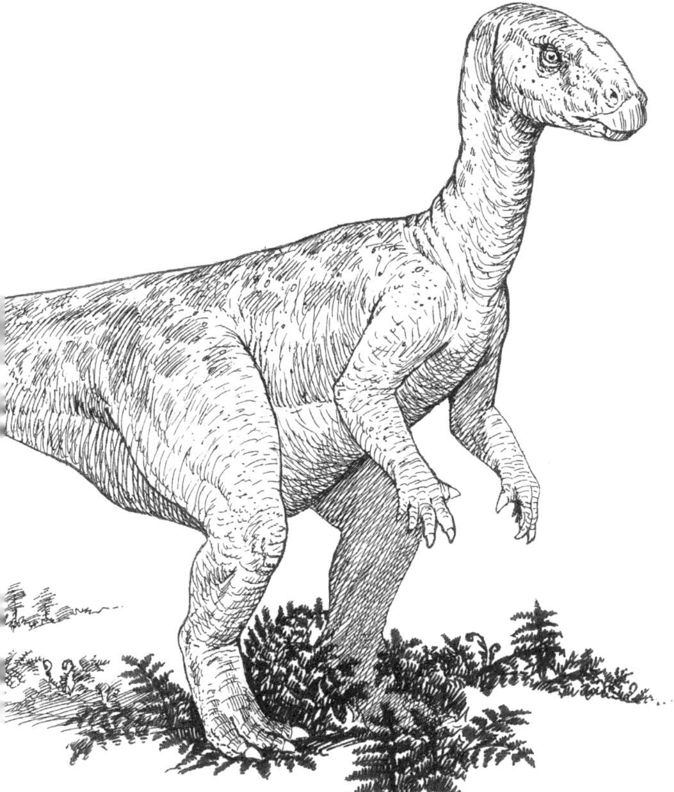

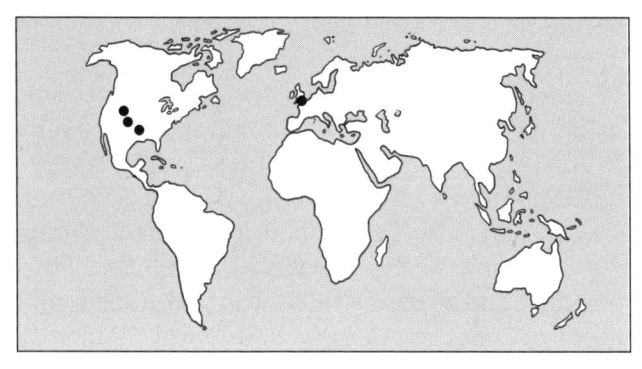

Found in Wyoming, Utah, Colorado, Oklahoma, U.S.; England

This dinosaur was more specialized than *Muttaburrasaurus* and *Tenontosaurus*. The end of its snout was more expanded. Its wrist bones began to be fused together, so its hands were even better for walking. Instead of having bony rods at the end of its tail, it had bony rods running along its backbone from the middle of the back to the front of the tail, making the middle part of its body very stiff. *Camptosaurus* had a big gut, and in order for its legs to fit around this belly, its thigh bone was more curved than in typical dinosaurs. That's why it was named the "bent reptile."

Camptosaurus probably spent a lot of time walking on all fours, but it could still rear up on its hind legs to feed higher in trees.

Best known from North America, *Camptosaurus* has also been found in England. During the Late Jurassic Epoch, the Atlantic Ocean was forming, and it seems there was still a land connection between Europe and North America. Other Morrison dinosaurs, such as the meat eater *Allosaurus*, were also found on both continents.

Iguanodon
"Iguana tooth"

Length: over 36 feet (about 11m)
Diet: plants

Iguanodon was one of the most common dinosaurs of the Early Cretaceous Epoch. It is also famous because it was one of the first dinosaurs known to science.

EARLY CRETACEOUS

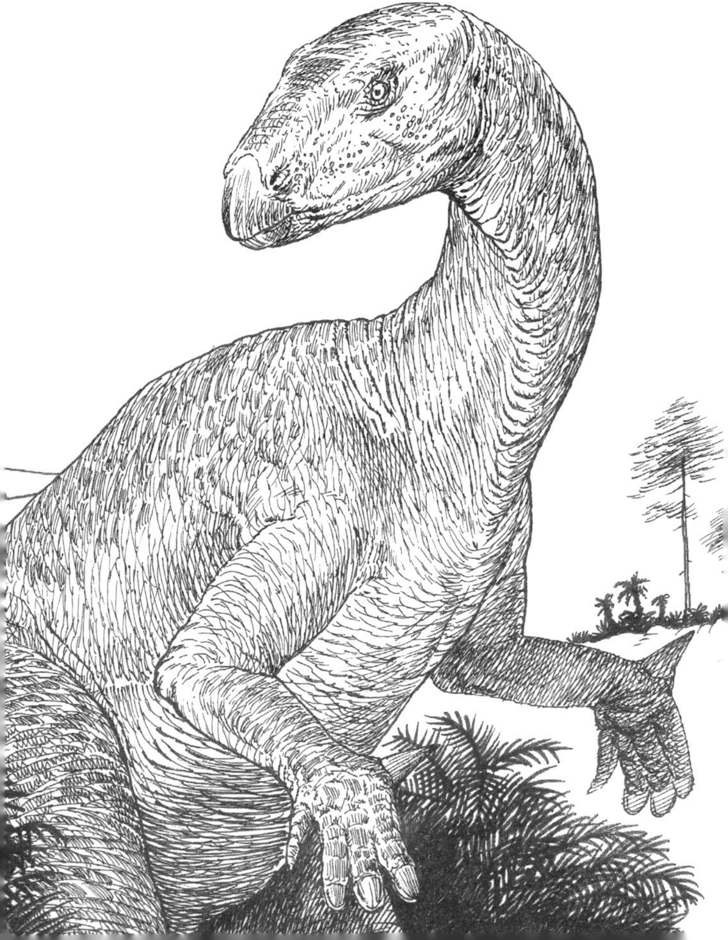

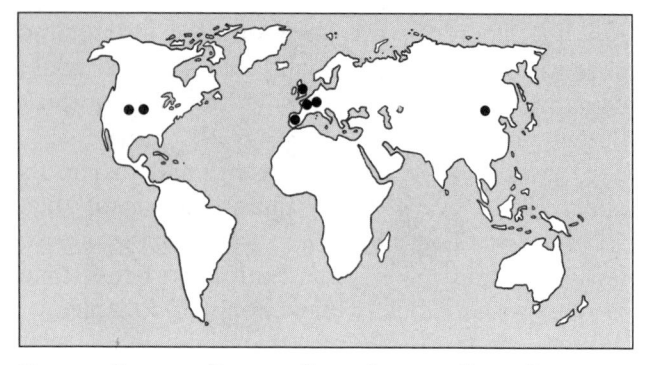

FOUND IN ENGLAND, BELGIUM, SPAIN, GERMANY, SOUTH DAKOTA, UTAH, U.S.; POSSIBLY MONGOLIA

Iguanodon was larger than *Tenontosaurus*, *Muttaburrasaurus*, and *Camptosaurus*. Like *Camptosaurus* it spent a lot of time walking on all fours. In fact, the middle three fingers of its hand had become more like toes: they were short and had hoof-like nails. Its thumb had become a heavy bony spike, which it may have used to pry open plants or to defend itself. (When it was first discovered, scientists didn't know that the spike was a thumb, and thought it was a nose horn!)

Iguanodon's pinky was very long and strong, and able to fold against the palm and wrist. It could use this pinky to hold on to branches or pick things up.

The skull of *Iguanodon* was big and strong. Its upper jaws were even more advanced than *Hypsilodon*, *Tenontosaurus*, and *Camptosaurus*. Its jaws could move in and out even better than those dinosaurs to help chew up the food it ate.

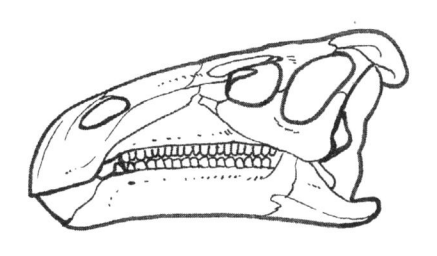

SKULL OF IGUANODON

Many skeletons of *Iguanodon* have been found, but the most complete fossils—24 of them—came from a quarry at Bernissart, Belgium.

Altirhinus
"Tall nose"

Length: 26½ feet (about 8m)
Diet: plants

Altirhinus was once thought to be a species of *Iguanodon* that lived in Mongolia. It had a gigantic nose.

Most of the skeleton of this new dinosaur was very similar to *Iguanodon*. Like that other

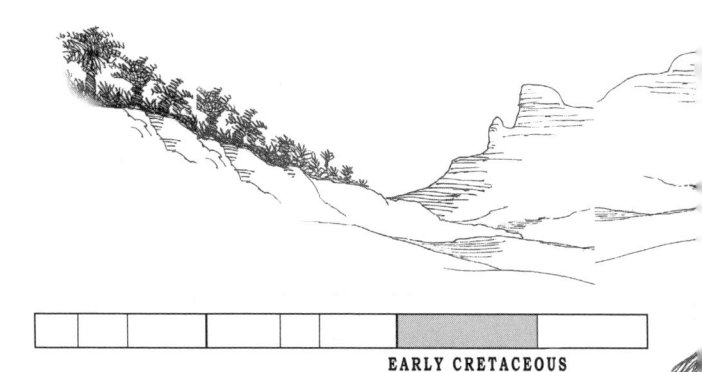

EARLY CRETACEOUS

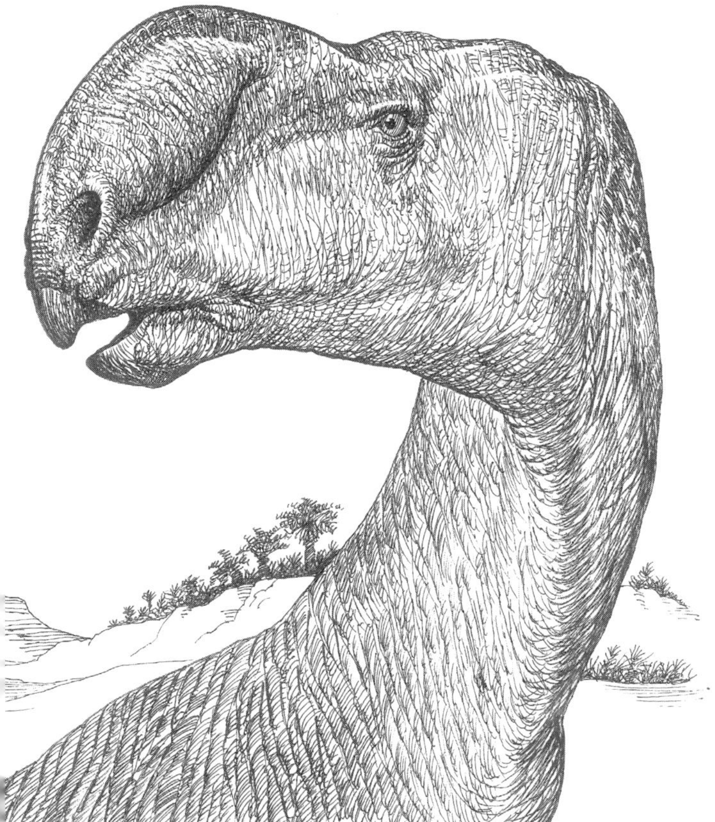

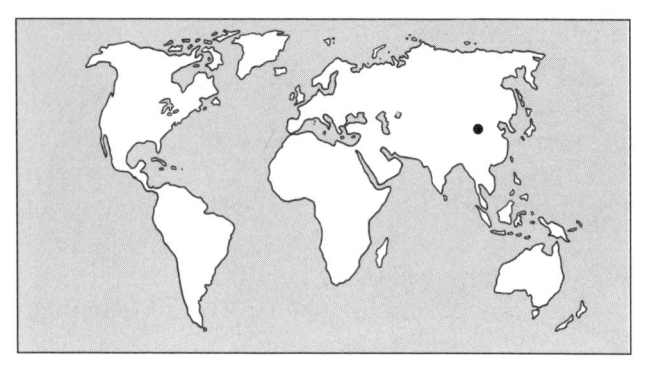

FOUND IN MONGOLIA

ornithopod, the Mongolian dinosaur had a spike thumb and grasping pinky. It was its skull that was very different. This new discovery had a very large front end of the snout, a little like *Muttaburrasaurus*. However, unlike the Australian dinosaur, this new discovery had enormous nostrils to go with the expanded snout. Because of its big nostrils, this dinosaur was named *Altirhinus*, "tall nose."

A fleshy sac probably covered the great big nostrils. This sac might have been used to signal to other *Altirhinus*, either by sight or by sound—or it might. have helped with breathing. Active animals living in dry areas need some way to trap the moisture in their breath so that their lungs don't get too dry. Since Mongolia may have been dry in the Early Cretaceous Epoch (although not as dry as it was later on), a way of trapping moisture would have been very helpful.

Other changes in the skull of this Mongolian ornithopod probably had to do with feeding. The front of the snout was even broader and lower than in *Iguanodon*, so that it could grab a lot of plants at once. In its jaws there were always two extra teeth already formed and ready to replace any tooth that was lost or worn down. So, as *Altirhinus* teeth got ground down during chewing, it always had plenty of new teeth to use.

Ouranosaurus
"Monitor lizard reptile"

Length: 23 feet (about 7m)
Diet: plants

Ouranosaurus was spectacular-looking—a big ornithopod with a fin on its back.

The Early Cretaceous world held many different types of big ornithopods. In the north African country of Niger lived

EARLY CRETACEOUS

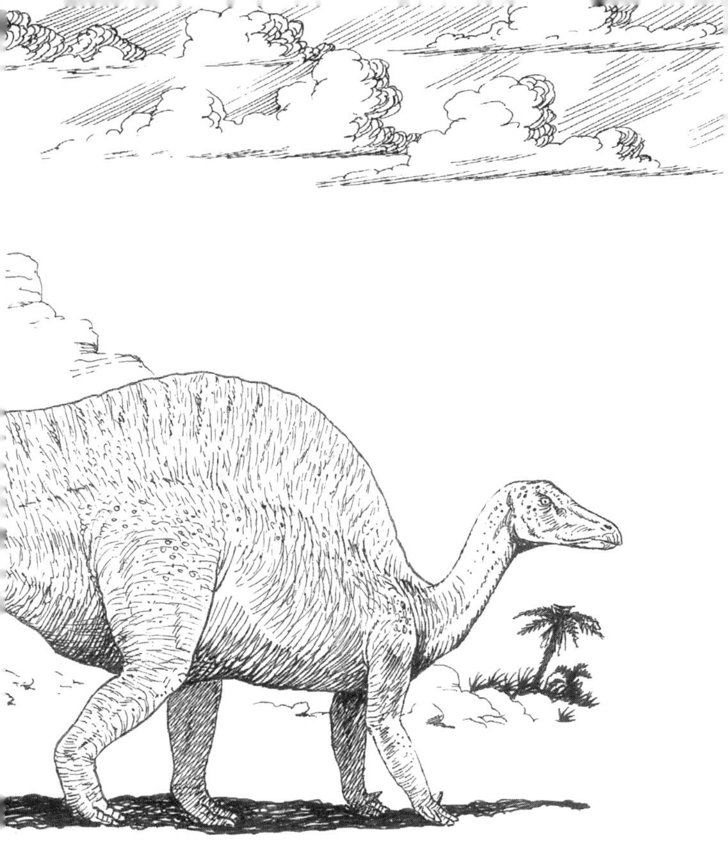

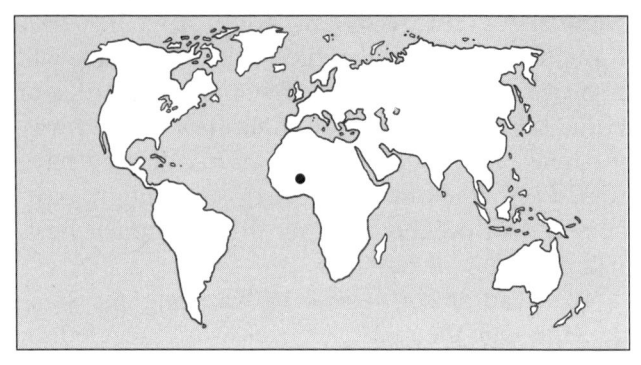

FOUND IN NIGER

Ouranosaurus. Although it is named after the "ourane," or monitor lizard (a modern meat-eating lizard), this ornithopod was a plant eater. Like *Iguanodon* and *Altirhinus* it had a spike thumb and a flexible pinky. Its arms and legs were more slender than those two relatives. The main differences between this African dinosaur and its relatives elsewhere were the spines on its back and its skull.

The backbones of *Ouranosaurus* had a series of tall spines coming off them. The largest of these were about 2 feet (63cm) long. Together they formed a thin sail down the back of the dinosaur. Like the tail of the peacock or the big frills of horned dinosaurs, the sail might have been a way to show off to other *Ouranosaurus*. It may have scared off attacking meat eaters. Or it might have helped cool off the dinosaur in the tropical heat. All these may be possible.

The head of *Ouranosaurus* was long and slender, although the end of its beak was expanded. In this way it looked like a true duckbilled dinosaur.

Protohadros
"First hadrosaur (duckbill)"

Length: 26½ feet (over 8m)
Diet: plants

The most advanced of all the ornithopods were a group called the **hadrosaurs** ("heavy reptiles"), also known as the "duckbills," because the very broad end of their snout looked something like the bill of a duck. During the Late Cretaceous Epoch duckbills were the most important group of plant eaters in North America. One of the earliest and most primitive of them was *Protohadros*.

Protohadros came from the very beginning of the Late Cretaceous Epoch. *Eolambia*, another advanced ornithopod from just about the same age in

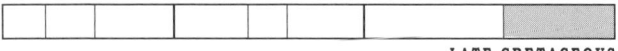

LATE CRETACEOUS

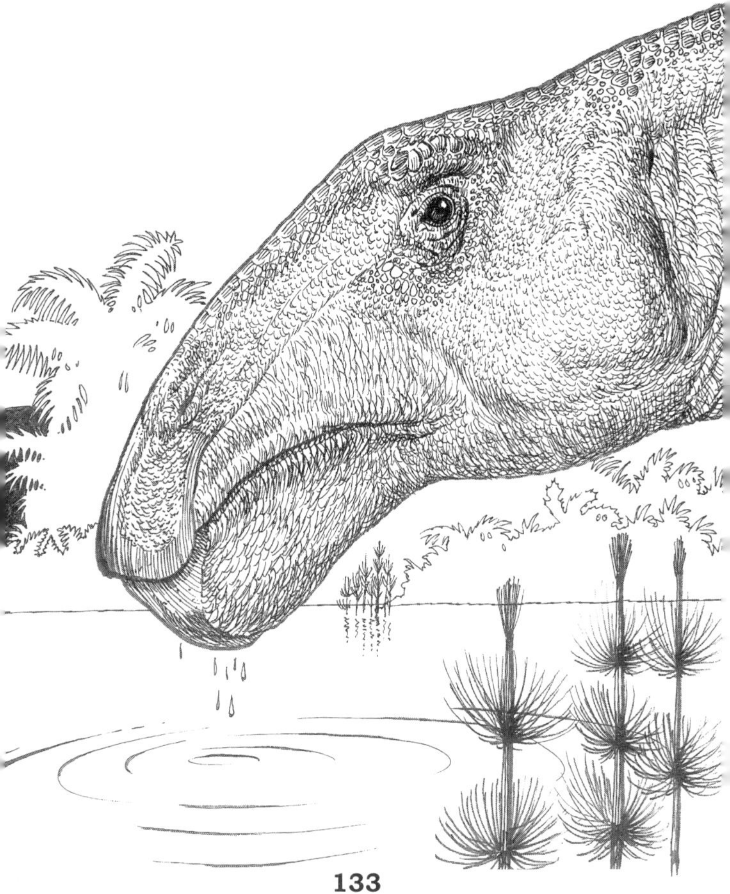

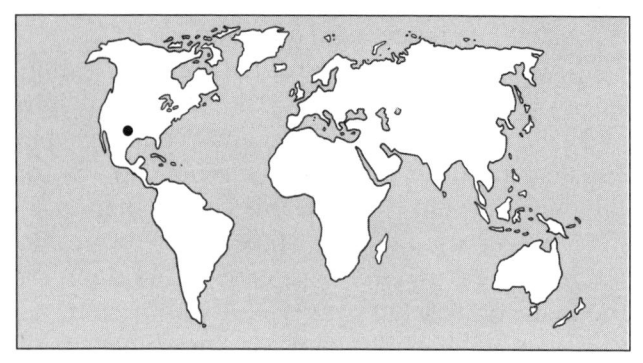

Found in Texas, U.S.

Utah, was almost a duckbill, but it still had a thumb spike. All true duckbills lost their thumb spike, and their hands became much longer and more slender. *Eolambia* and *Protohadros* are similar to *Altirhinus* in that they always had two extra teeth ready to replace any lost tooth.

In fact, *Eolambia* and *Protohadros* may have been descendants of *Altirhinus* or a close relative that migrated into North America from Asia. It seems likely that a land connection between Asia and North America opened up near the end of the Early Cretaceous Epoch, allowing Asian dinosaurs to migrate into North America.

Protohadros is famous for having a big "chin" on its lower jaw. This early duckbill lived in a swampy forest environment, so maybe its big chin and expanded snout helped it scoop up lots of low-lying swamp plants. But because other duckbills were also found where there were no swamps, there may be some other explanation for the shape of its snout.

Primitive duckbills were found in many parts of the world during the Cretaceous Period, including Mongolia, Argentina, and Transylvania (in Romania).

Anatotitan
"Titanic duck"

Length: 36 feet (about 11m)
Diet: plants

Anatotitan and its relatives form the broad-snouted branch of the duckbills. *Hypacrosaurus* and its relatives make up the hollow-crested branch of this group of ornithopods.

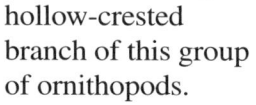

LATE CRETACEOUS

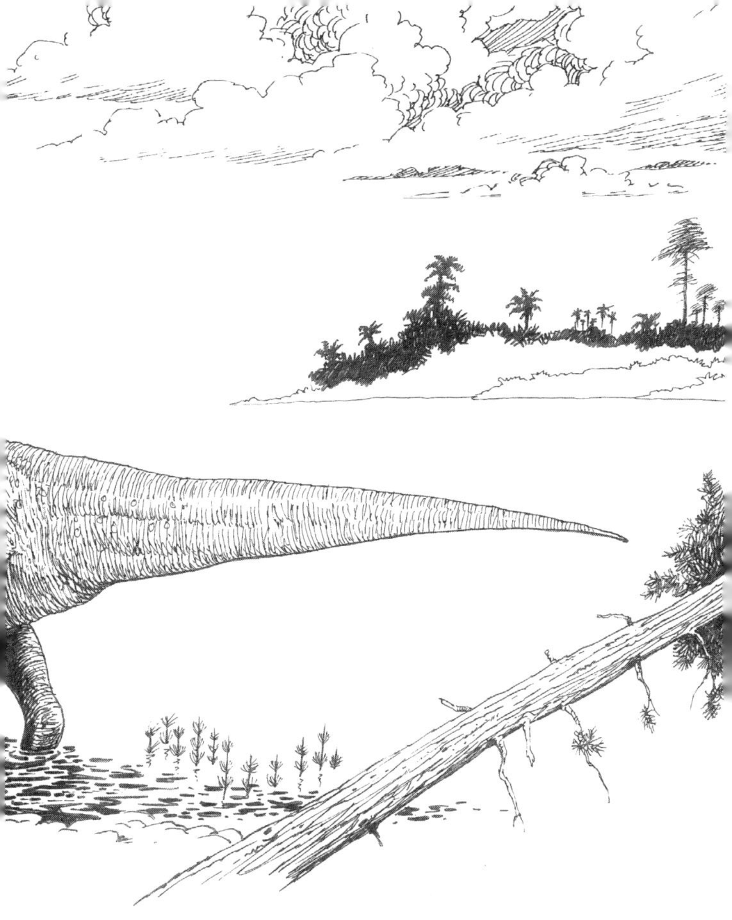

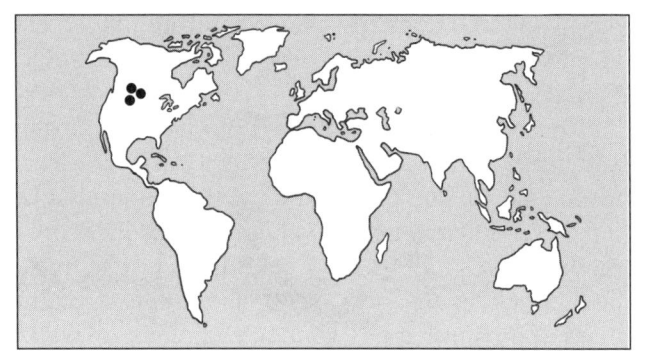

FOUND IN MONTANA, SOUTH DAKOTA, WYOMING, U.S.

The broad-snouted duckbills all had very wide ends to their beaks. They also had enormous nostrils, although these were almost certainly covered with a fleshy sac. Some broad-snouted duckbills had medium-sized snouts, while others had longer ones. The snout of *Anatotitan* was longest of all. It was the skull of this dinosaur that gave the hadrosaurs the nickname "duckbills." The broad-snouted hadrosaurs were very large. One of them, *Shantungosaurus,* grew over 51 feet (15m) long—bigger than any meat-eating dinosaur! The broad-snouted duckbills were therefore the largest known animals that were able to walk on just their hind legs.

Some species of duckbills, both hollow-crested and broad-snouted, lived in herds. Fossil discoveries in Canada and the U.S. show that parent duckbills would nest together in big colonies like some modern birds do. Baby duckbills seem to have been stuck in the nest, so their parents brought them food until they were old enough to walk. When they were old enough, the young joined the herds of duckbills.

In some ways, duckbills looked helpless. They didn't have armor or horns, and their legs were shorter and stockier than those of tyrant dinosaurs, the main predators of their time. By living together in herds, though, the duckbills had an advantage. Although any single duckbill was probably helpless against an attacking tyrant dinosaur, if one member of the herd saw, heard, or smelled the approaching predator, it could call out to the others—so they would be less open to surprise attack.

Hypacrosaurus
"Nearly the tallest reptile"

When it was discovered, it was the second tallest two-legged dinosaur, after Tyrannosaurus, of the Late Cretaceous Epoch of North America.

Length: 30 feet (about 9m)
Diet: plants

The descendants of *Protohadros* and other early duckbills were very common in the western parts of North America during the Late Cretaceous Epoch.

Complete skeletons of duckbills have been found, sometimes with the impression of their

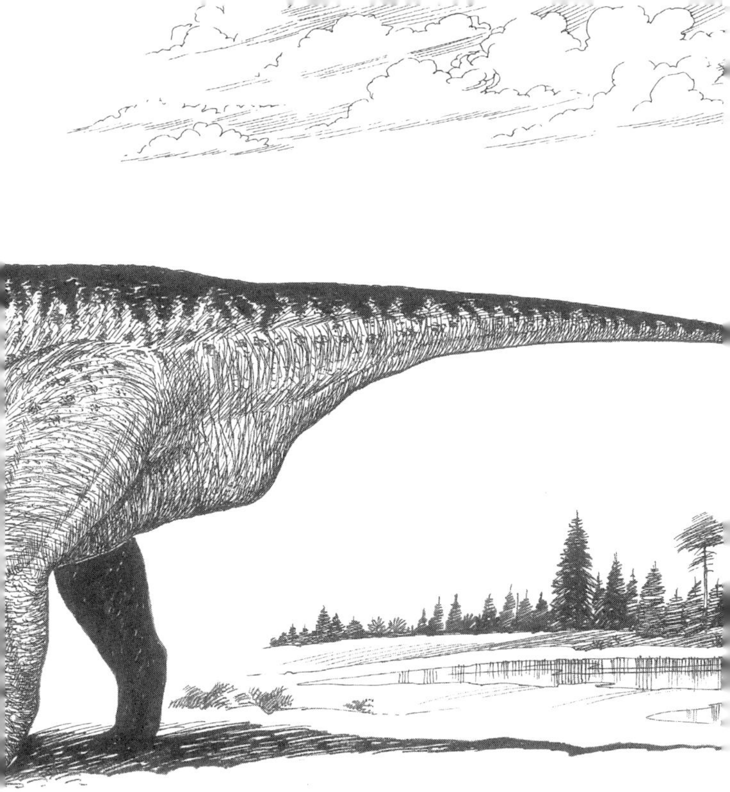

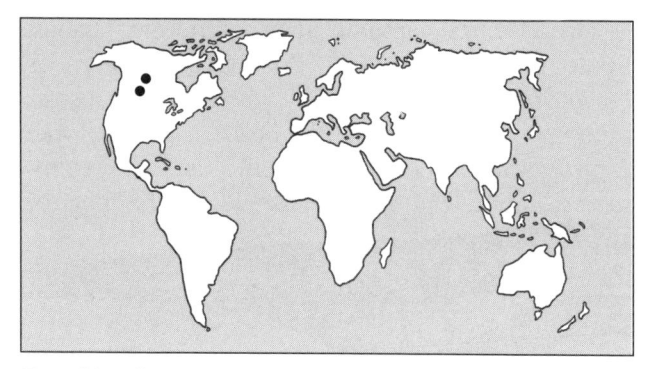

Found in Alberta, Canada; Montana, U.S.

skins. Although there were many different species, they were very similar. All had narrow hands without thumbs but with flexible pinkies. All could walk both on all fours and on just their hind legs.

There were two main groups of duckbills. *Hypacrosaurus* is a member of one of them—the hollow-crested duckbills. Here the nostrils were not much bigger than in *Ouranosaurus* or *Protohadros*, but inside the skull the air passage went way up into special crests before heading down into the lungs.

These crests came in many different shapes. Some hollow-crested duckbills, such as *Parasaurolophus*, had long tube-shaped crests running back from their heads. Others, like *Corythosaurus*, *Lambeosaurus*, and *Hypacrosaurus,* had tall narrow crests like the helmets of ancient warriors.

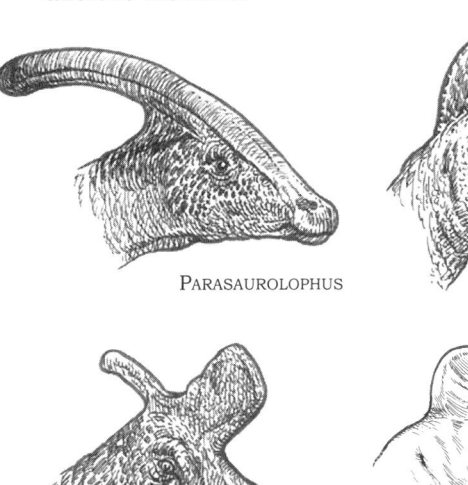

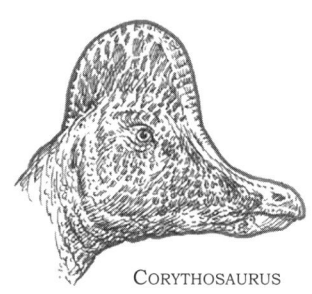

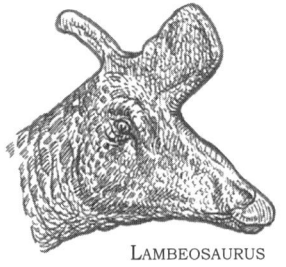

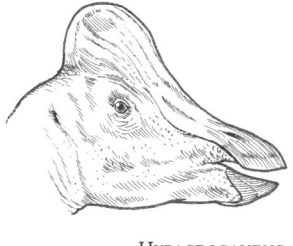

PARASAUROLOPHUS

CORYTHOSAURUS

LAMBEOSAURUS

HYPACROSAURUS

Why should these dinosaurs have such strange crests? One possibility was to trap moisture, as with the big nose of *Altirhinus*. Another was to make more room for extra smelling nerves, so that the duckbills could more easily smell approaching tyrant dinosaurs. Or these crests could have been used to make sounds. When air is blown through different-shaped tubes, it makes different noises. Because each species of hollow-crested duckbill had a slightly different shaped crest, they would make different sounds. The Late Cretaceous world probably sounded very strange with the loud hoots and calls of all the different types of hollow-crested duckbills.

· 8 ·
SAUROPODOMORPHS, THE LONG-NECKED PLANT EATERS

Ornithischians, like thyreophorans, marginocephalians, and ornithopods, are only one branch of dinosaur. The other branch is the **saurischians.** Within the saurischians are two main branches, the meat-eating **theropods** ("beast feet") and the long-necked **sauropodomorphs** (sauropod forms).

Some sauropodomorphs were the largest animals that ever lived on land, although the earliest ones were smaller than a human being. Their most distinctive features were their long necks and small heads.

All of them seem to have been plant eaters. They had leaf-shaped teeth instead of the steak-knife-like teeth of their relatives, the theropods.

The earliest sauropodomorphs were called the **prosauropods** (meaning "before the sauropods"). They were one of the most common groups of plant-eating animal during the Late Triassic and Early Jurassic Epochs. Their fossils have been found on every continent on Earth.

The descendants of the prosauropods were the **sauropods** ("lizard feet"). Sometimes called the "brontosaurs," or "thunder lizards," sauropods were *all* gigantic: even the smallest adult sauropod was bigger than a modern elephant! Sauropods too have been found on every continent. Some of them lived until the very end of the Age of Dinosaurs.

FAMILY TREE OF SAUROPODOMORPHS

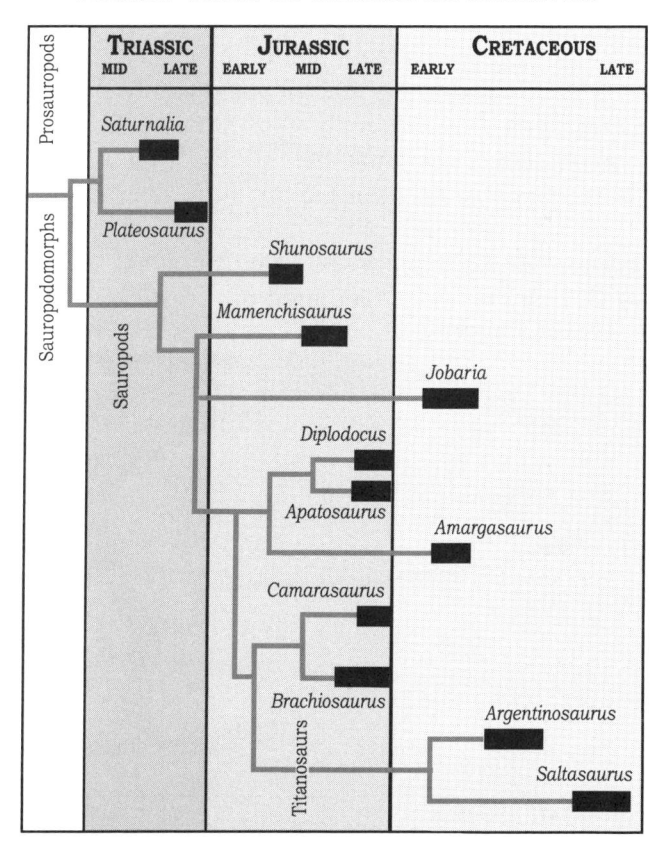

	TRIASSIC	JURASSIC	CRETACEOUS
	MID LATE	EARLY MID LATE	EARLY LATE

Prosauropods
- *Saturnalia*
- *Plateosaurus*

Sauropodomorphs / Sauropods
- *Shunosaurus*
- *Mamenchisaurus*
- *Jobaria*
- *Diplodocus*
- *Apatosaurus*
- *Amargasaurus*
- *Camarasaurus*
- *Brachiosaurus*

Titanosaurs
- *Argentinosaurus*
- *Saltasaurus*

Saturnalia
"Saturnalia"

Saturnalia is an ancient Roman festival.

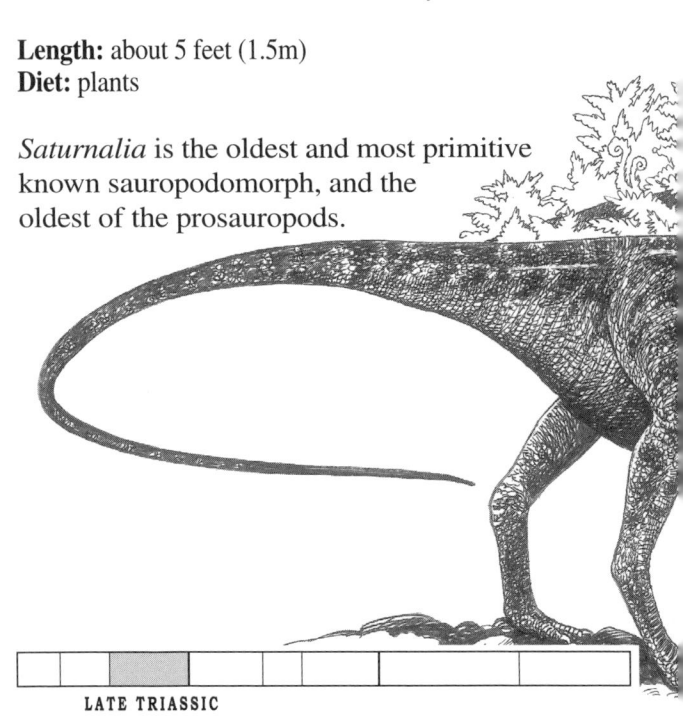

Length: about 5 feet (1.5m)
Diet: plants

Saturnalia is the oldest and most primitive known sauropodomorph, and the oldest of the prosauropods.

LATE TRIASSIC

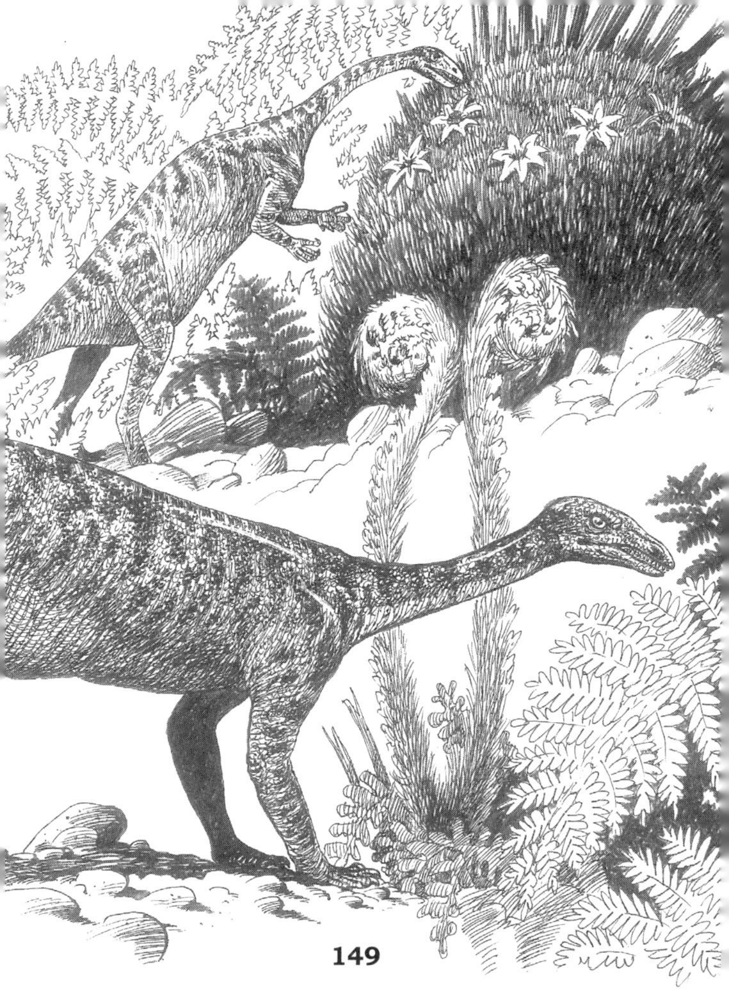

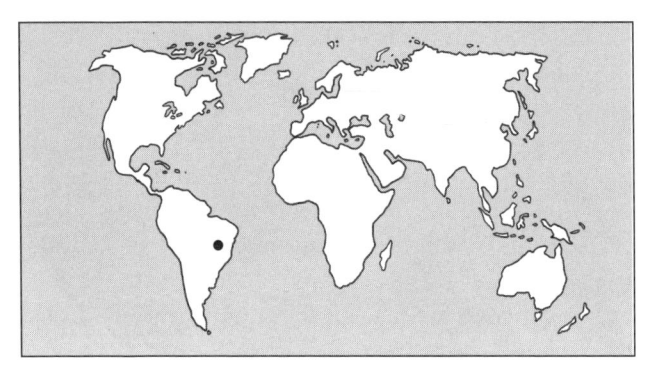

FOUND IN BRAZIL

Like all later sauropodomorphs, *Saturnalia* had a small head with small leaf-shaped teeth, a long neck, strong forearms, a fat body, strong hind legs, and a long slender tail. Like most early dinosaurs, it could walk or run on its hind legs. Its strong arms could help it walk on all fours if it wanted to.

What advantage did sauropodomorphs gain from their long necks and small heads? When *Saturnalia* and other sauropodomorphs first appeared, there were several other sorts of animals that were also eating plants. One of the things they all had in common was that they could only feed on plants growing low to the ground. Because the sauropodomorphs had long necks, they could reach up into the branches that were above the heads of any other plant eaters. This gave them a source of food that they alone could get to.

Because *Saturnalia*'s long neck was so useful, its relatives and descendants became some of the most common plant-eating animals in the Late Triassic and Early Jurassic worlds.

Plateosaurus
"Broad lizard"

Length: over 26 feet (about 8m)
Diet: plants

Plateosaurus looks at first like *Saturnalia*. In many ways it wasn't very different in shape from the small Brazilian dinosaur. However, *Plateosaurus* had a major difference: it was much larger.

Why did the prosauropods become so large? There are two main reasons: competition with other plant eaters, and defense against meat eaters. When *Saturnalia* first appeared, it was about the

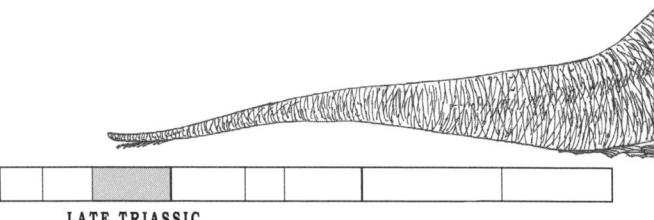

LATE TRIASSIC

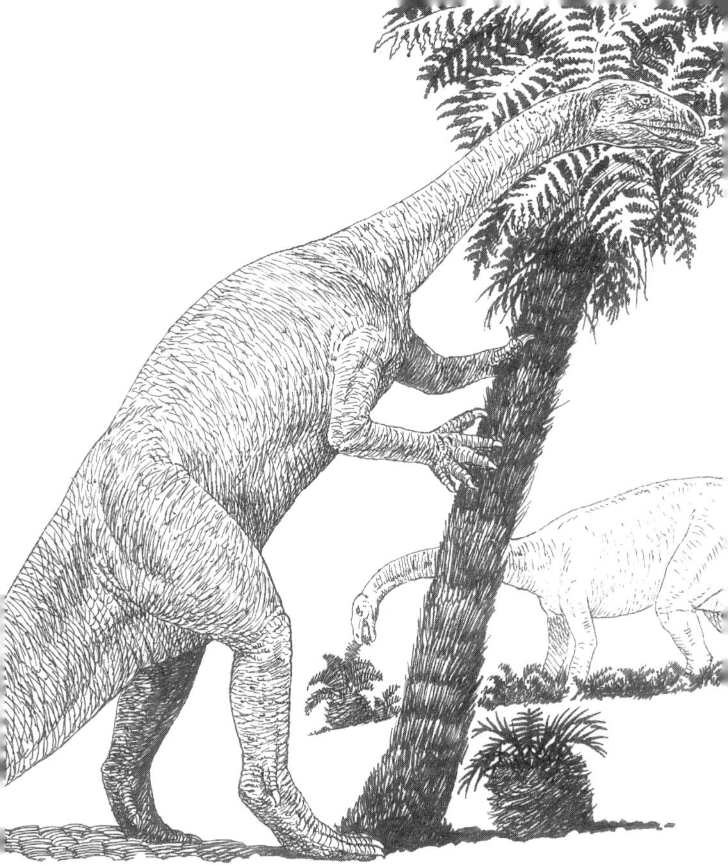

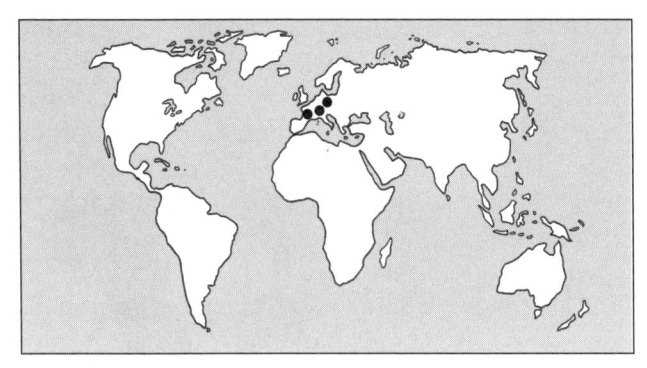

FOUND IN GERMANY, SWITZERLAND, FRANCE

same size as other plant-eating dinosaurs, and smaller than some. However, by growing larger and larger, the prosauropods were able to feed higher and higher into the trees, eating leaves that no other animal could reach. Also, by becoming larger, the prosauropods were better able to defend themselves from an attacking meat eater.

By the time *Plateosaurus* had evolved, prosauropods had become the biggest animals that lived on land up to that time, and were therefore reasonably safe. Some very large meat-eating relatives of crocodiles and early meat-eating dinosaurs may have attacked a sick or injured or young *Plateosaurus*, but a full-grown adult prosauropod may have been left alone most of the time. These dinosaurs seem to have traveled in small herds, walking across the landscape of Triassic Europe looking for plants to eat.

Plateosaurus is the best known of all prosauropods. These new giant prosauropods were some of the most common large animals of the early part of the Age of the Dinosaurs.

Shunosaurus
"Shuno reptile"

Shuno is the old name for the Sichuan province of China.

Length: about 33 feet (10m)
Diet: plants

As time went by, the prosauropods became larger and larger. Eventually they were so large they were too big to walk around on just two legs. Their forelimbs became heavy and straighter, and the fingers of their hands became so short and stubby they weren't able to hold anything.

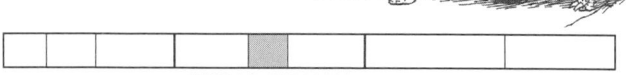

MIDDLE JURASSIC

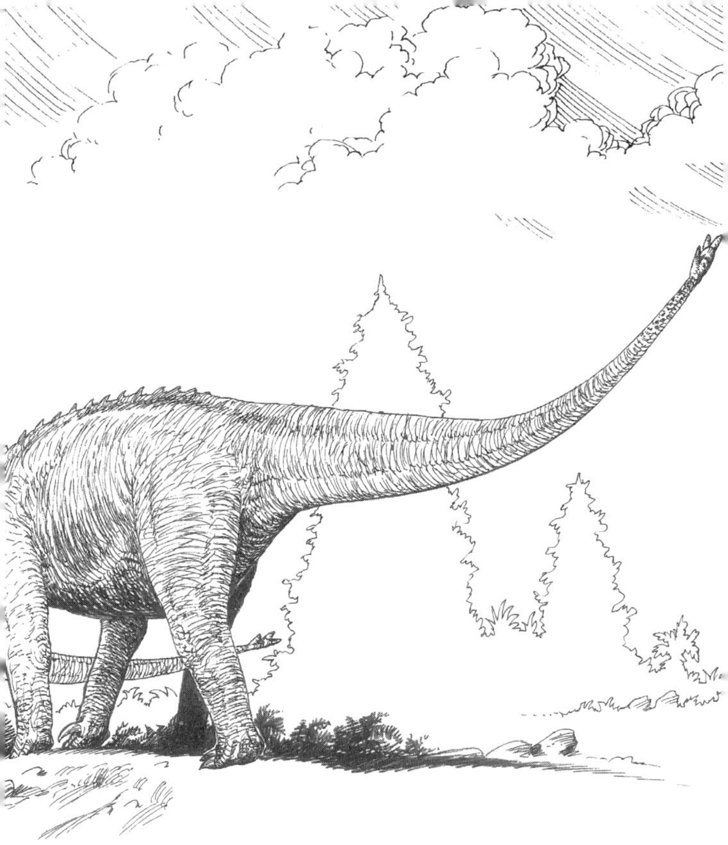

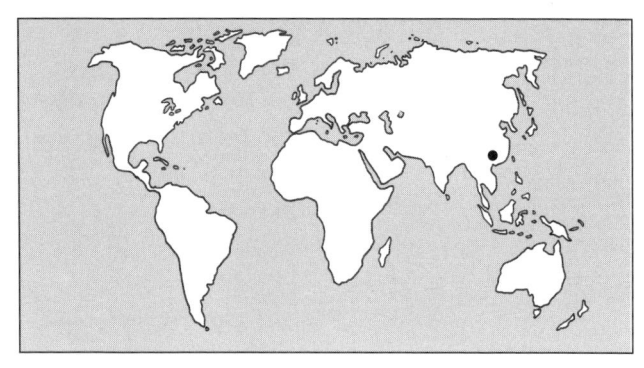

FOUND IN CHINA

These dinosaurs had evolved into the first true **sauropods** (lizard feet).

One of the best known of all the early sauropods was *Shunosaurus* of China. It had, like all sauropods: a very small head, long neck, large fat body with four strong legs, and a long tail. Its tail was unusual in that it ended with a bony club, rather like the tail of some ankylosaurs. Like those armored dinosaurs, *Shunosaurus* probably used it to clobber attacking meat-eating dinosaurs.

Of course, the tail club was not *Shunosaurus*'

only defense. The earlier prosauropods were too large to be attacked by the predators of their time. Because of this, the predators themselves evolved new larger and more advanced forms. In response, the descendants of the prosauropods—such as *Shunosaurus*—became larger still. This "arms race" between sauropodomorphs and predators continued throughout the Mesozoic Era.

Mamenchisaurus
"Mamen Ferry reptile"

Mamen Ferry is a place in China.

Length: about 86 feet (about 26m)
Diet: plants

China was home to many different types of sauropod. *Mamenchisaurus* was one of a group of Chinese sauropods with extraordinarily long necks. Sauropods had become larger and larger partly as a defense against meat eaters, and partly so they

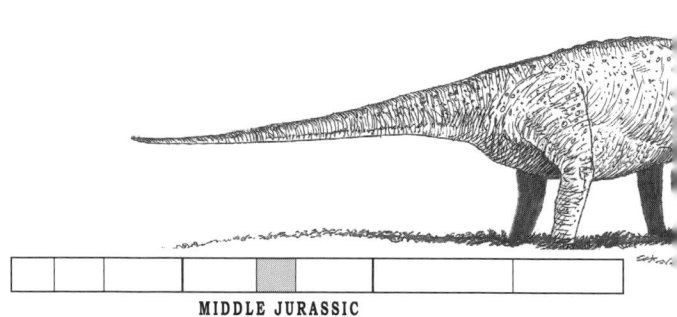

MIDDLE JURASSIC

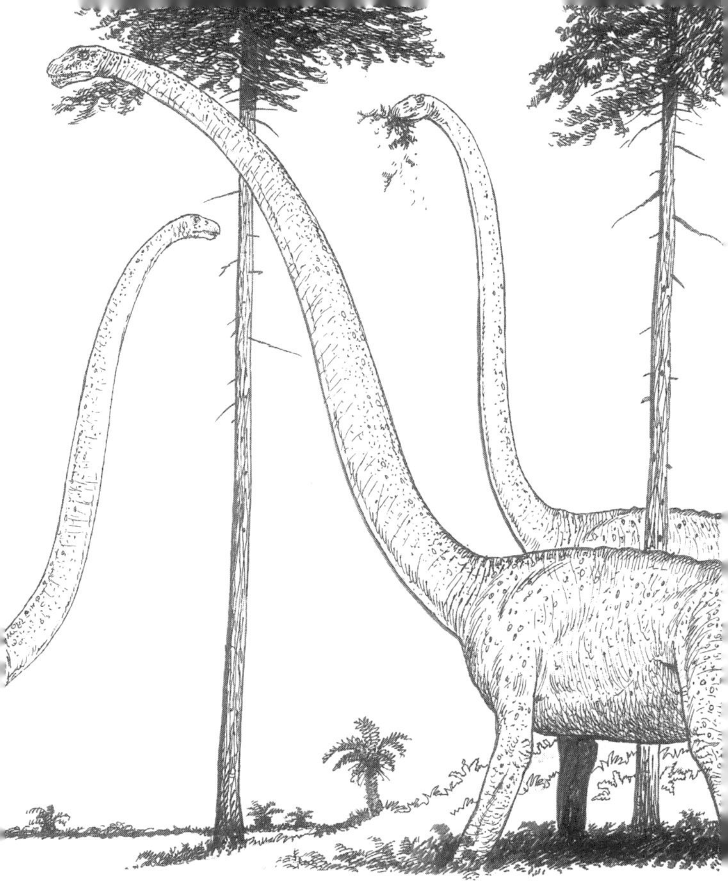

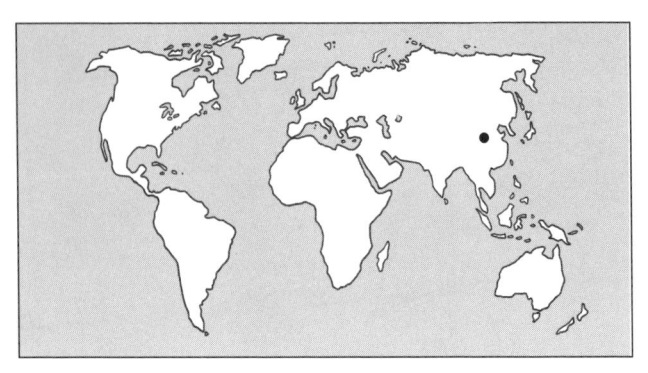

FOUND IN CHINA

could feed higher in the trees. Different branches of the sauropod group found different ways of reaching the highest parts of trees.

Mamenchisaurus was part of a group of sauropods known only from China. It had the longest neck of any animal—almost 35 feet (11m) long! It could stretch this long neck up into the trees where it could munch on the leaves. Its body was heavy, keeping its weight close to the ground.

Why isn't this particular type of sauropod found outside China? Maybe because during the

Middle and Late Jurassic periods, China was its own large island. If these super-long-necked dinosaurs evolved after China separated from the other lands, they wouldn't have been able to migrate to other continents.

Jobaria
"Jobar"

Jobar was a mythical creature from the legends of the Toureg people of northern Africa.

Length: over 69 feet (21m)
Diet: plants

Jobaria was only recently discovered by paleontologists exploring in the northern African country of Niger.

A very "average" sauropod, *Jobaria* was not exceptionally big. Its head didn't have any special

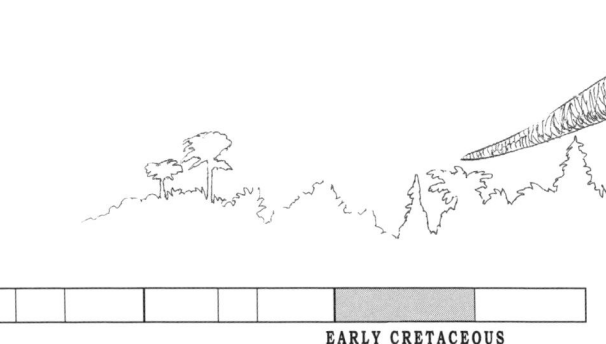

EARLY CRETACEOUS

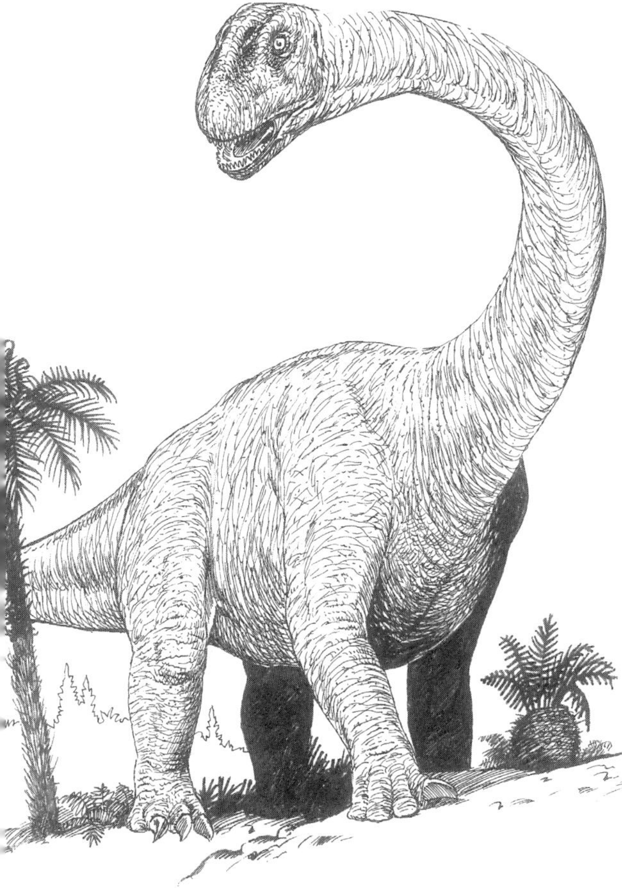

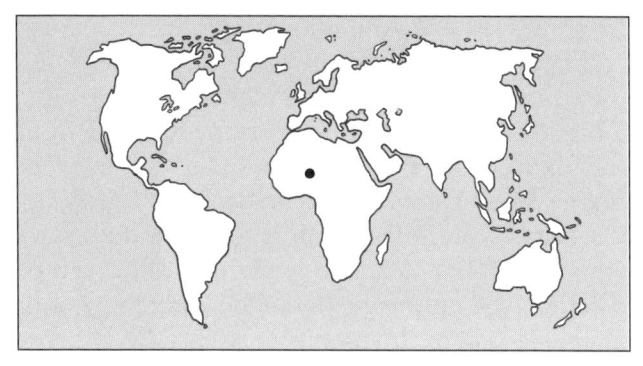

FOUND IN NIGER

features; its tail was not whip-shaped or club-like. Like the more advanced sauropods, its hand was shaped like a column, and its nostrils were large and further back on its head than *Shunosaurus* and *Mamenchisaurus*. *Jobaria* seems more advanced than those dinosaurs, but it was less specialized than the sauropods that were common in the Late Jurassic and the Cretaceous Epochs.

How can it be that a primitive dinosaur is found later than more advanced sauropods? Sometimes a particular primitive body plan can be successful in some places, even though more specialized forms evolved in other parts of the world. Even today, there are animals and plants found in some lands that survive with almost no change from long ago, while the same types died out in other places. One example is the tuatara: this relative of the lizards is still found alive today in the island country of New Zealand, while the same type of creature died out long ago in the rest of the world. Scientists call such animals or plants "living fossils." It seems that *Jobaria* was a kind of "living fossil" in the Early Cretaceous Epoch, surviving in northern Africa while the same type of sauropod had already died out elsewhere.

Diplodocus
"Double beam"

This referred to the shape of the bones on the underside of the tail.

Length: about 94 feet (28 m)
Diet: plants

LATE JURASSIC

Diplodocus is one of the most famous and most completely known of these dinosaurs. It is found in the famous Morrison Formation of the American West.

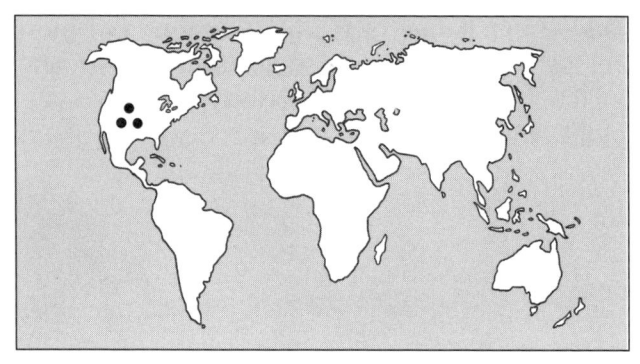

FOUND IN COLORADO, WYOMING, AND UTAH, U.S.

There are two groups of sauropods that were more advanced than *Jobaria*. *Diplodocus* and its kin were one of these groups. Their skulls were long and low; their teeth were shaped like pencils and placed only at the very front of the snout. Their nostrils perched on the top of the head. They also had very short forearms for a sauropod.

The neck of *Diplodocus* was very long (although not quite as long as that of *Mamenchisaurus*). Its tail was extremely long, too, possibly the longest of any dinosaur. It was shaped like a whip, and some scientists think that it was used to smack at attacking predators (the way much smaller lizards do today). Skin impressions of *Diplodocus* show that it (and possibly its relatives) had a series of small triangular bumps of skin and scales running in a ridge down its back and tail.

Diplodocus and its relatives probably had a different way of reaching up high into the trees than *Mamenchisaurus*. With their shorter forearms, they had less weight in the front of the body than most sauropods. Some paleontologists think that these dinosaurs could rear up on their hind legs to reach extremely high into the trees. They might have used their tail as an extra "leg" to help support their weight.

Apatosaurus
"Deceptive reptile"

Length: more than 76 feet (23 m)
Diet: plants

Apatosaurus was a close relative of *Diplodocus*. They lived in the same region at the same time. For many decades *Apatosaurus* was also known as *Brontosaurus*.

LATE JURASSIC

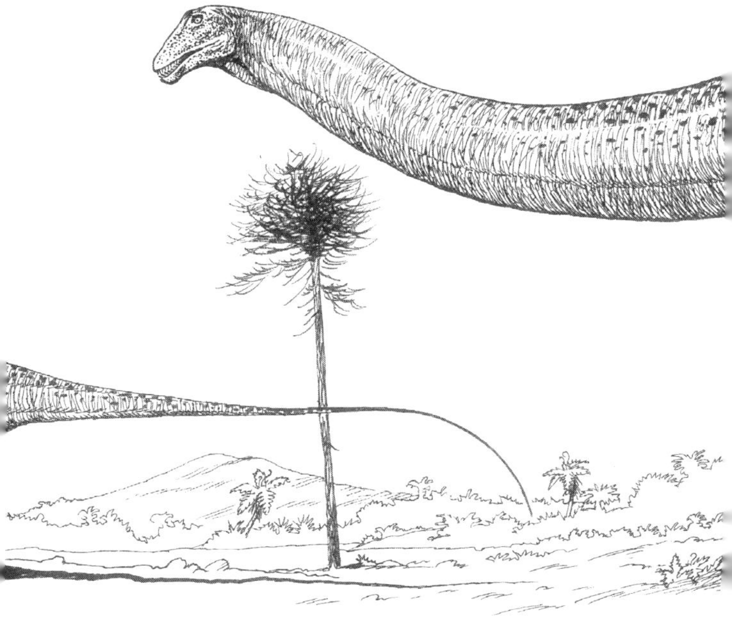

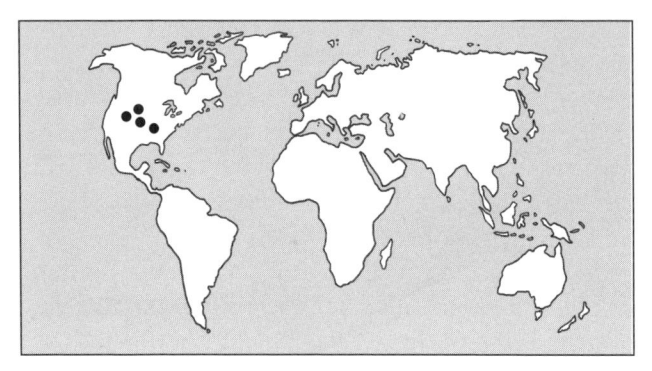

Found in Colorado, Wyoming, Utah, and Oklahoma, U.S.

How is it that this dinosaur had two names? When a paleontologist discovers a fossil, the skeleton of the creature is seldom complete. Even so, the partial skeleton might be different from all other dinosaurs currently known, so it is given a new name. Later another fossil may be found that is also thought to be from some new kind, and it too is given its own name.

This happened with *Apatosaurus*. In 1877 paleontologist Othniel Charles Marsh described a partial skeleton of a giant sauropod, and gave it the name *Apatosaurus*. Two years later he named a second skeleton, which was much more complete, *Brontosaurus* ("thunder lizard"). Later, scientists realized that both names had been given to the same type of dinosaur! Because no dinosaur could have two different names, only one name could be chosen. Which one should be used?

Scientists have a set of rules about the naming of plants and animals, including extinct plants and animals. One of those rules is that if a type of animal or plant has been given more than one name, the first name it was given shall be the true name. So, even though "*Brontosaurus*" was a more exciting and popular name, the true name of this dinosaur was *Apatosaurus*.

Apatosaurus was very similar to *Diplodocus* in most features, but it was much stockier, with a much thicker neck and very strong arm and leg bones. Perhaps it didn't rear up into the trees to feed, but used its stronger body to push the trees over. Unfortunately, we can't tell about this from the types of material (bones, teeth, footprints, eggs) that are found as fossils.

Amargasaurus
"La Amarga reptile"

La Amarga is the formation where it was found.

Length: 43 feet (about 13m)
Diet: plants

One of the smallest and most bizarre of all the sauropods, *Amargasaurus* had a strange double-sail running down its spine.

EARLY CRETACEOUS

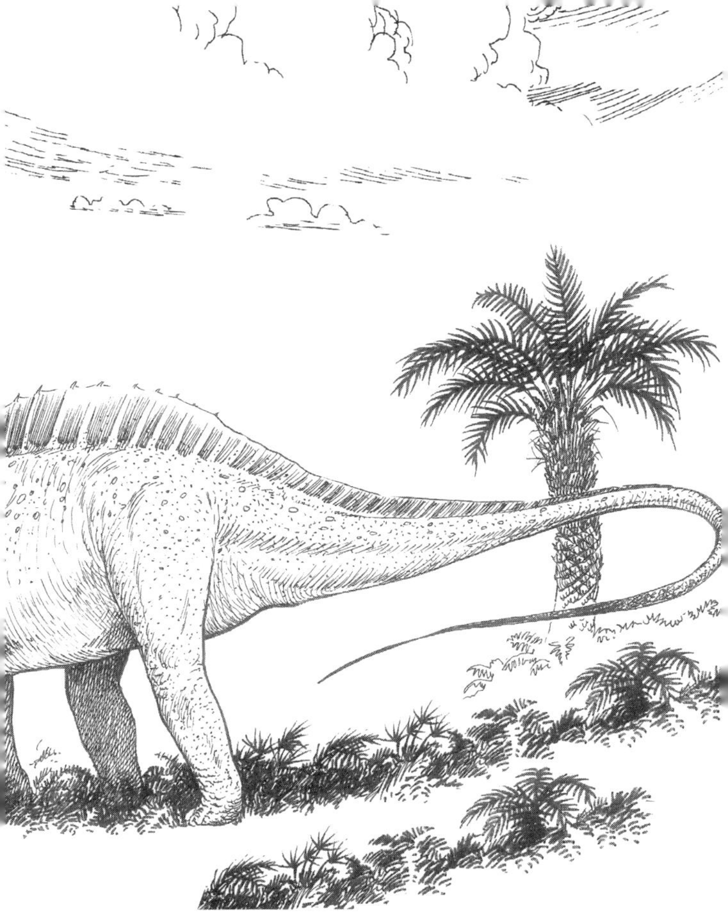

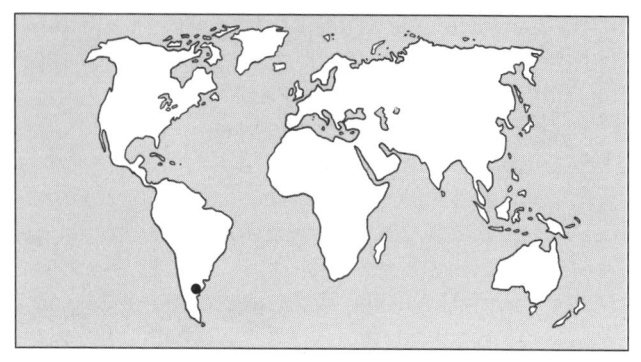

FOUND IN ARGENTINA

Amargasaurus was descended from *Dicraeosaurus* ("forked reptile") or one of its relatives. That sauropod, from the Late Jurassic Epoch, lived at the same time as *Diplodocus* and *Apatosaurus*. It was similar to these two dinosaurs, but smaller—only 36 feet (11m) long. Like *Diplodocus* it had a long skull with pencil-shaped teeth and very short forearms. Its tail seems to have been somewhat whip-like, but nowhere near as long as that of *Diplodocus*. However, there were some differences. The neck of *Dicraeosaurus* was fairly short for a sauropod, and the spines on its back were much taller than those of other Jurassic sauropods.

Amargasaurus looked very much like *Dicraeosaurus*. It had spines on its back with a deep split down the middle, but in A*margasaurus* they were much taller, which made the spines in front of its hips form a sort of double sail: one row of spines down the right side of the back, and one row down the left.

The sails may have been a kind of defense—used to scare off an attacking predator by making the dinosaur look much larger than it really was. Or maybe the sails were brightly colored, attracting other *Amargasaurus*. Perhaps they cooled down the body when the animal turned into the wind. They may have served all these functions, the way the ears of the modern African elephant scare off attackers, signal to other elephants, and cool the animal in the tropical heat.

Camarasaurus
"Chambered reptile"

Length: over 59 feet (18m)
Diet: plants

Camarasaurus is the most common dinosaur found in the Morrison Formation of the Late Jurassic Epoch of the American West.

Diplodocus, *Apatosaurus*, and *Amargasaurus* are typical of the long-skulled, short-armed branch of the advanced sauropods. *Camarasaurus* was one of the most primitive of the other group

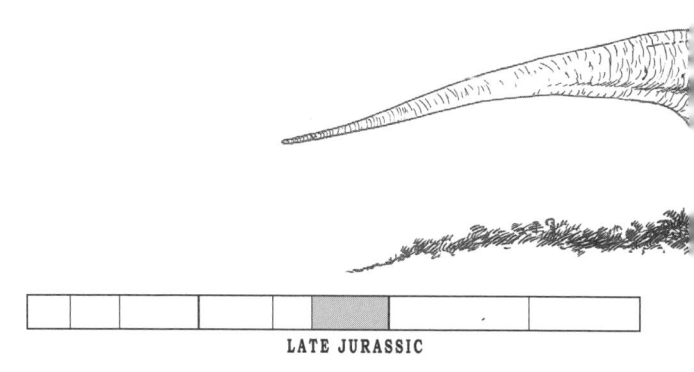

LATE JURASSIC

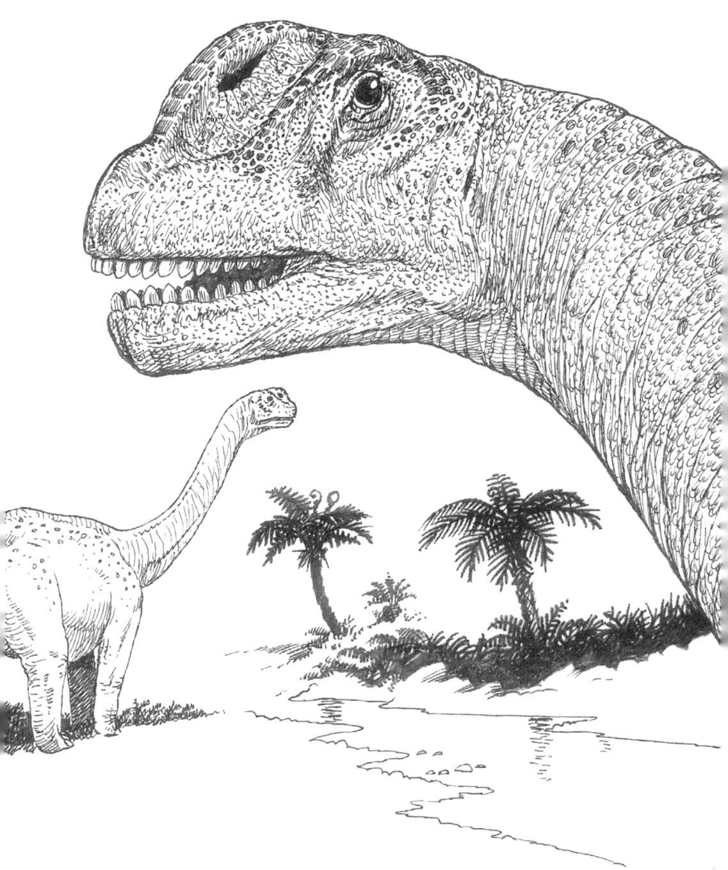

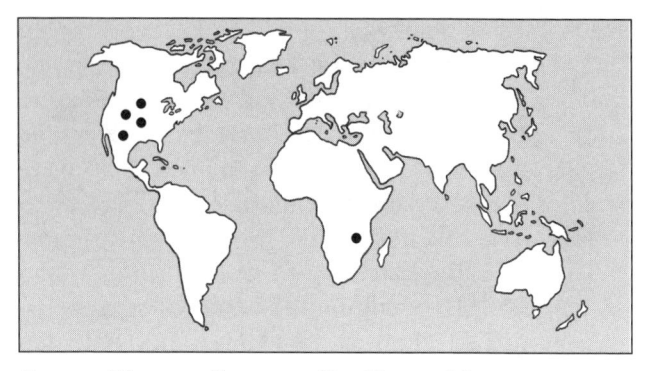

Found in Wyoming, Colorado, New Mexico, Montana, and Utah, U.S.; possibly Zimbabwe, Africa

of sauropods. These dinosaurs all had extremely big nostrils—the openings for their nostrils were even bigger than their eye sockets!—and very long bones in their hands. Their teeth were very thick and shaped like fat spoons, very different from the pencil-teeth of *Diplodocus* and its kin.

In the world today giant mammals (like elephants and rhinos) have babies that are pretty big: a baby elephant is bigger than almost anything else on the plains of Africa. So we might expect the babies of giant sauropods to be even bigger than baby elephants. In fact, they were much smaller. The biggest sauropod eggs known are only about the size of a basketball. Even the largest dinosaurs came from babies that were smaller than a German shepherd dog!

How long would it take a dinosaur to grow from such a tiny hatchling to an adult bigger than an elephant? By studying the bones of sauropods, paleontologists think it took dinosaurs only ten years or so to go from hatching to full size. Dinosaurs of all sorts seem to have been very fast growers!

Brachiosaurus
"Arm reptile"

Length: about 79 feet (24m)
Diet: plants

Brachiosaurus was long thought of as the largest of all dinosaurs. Although bigger dinosaurs have been found, it does seem to have been one of the tallest. Its head was 40 feet (12m) or more above the ground. Some fossils of *Brachiosaurus* were once thought to be a dinosaur called "*Ultrasauros*," but paleontologists now think that this

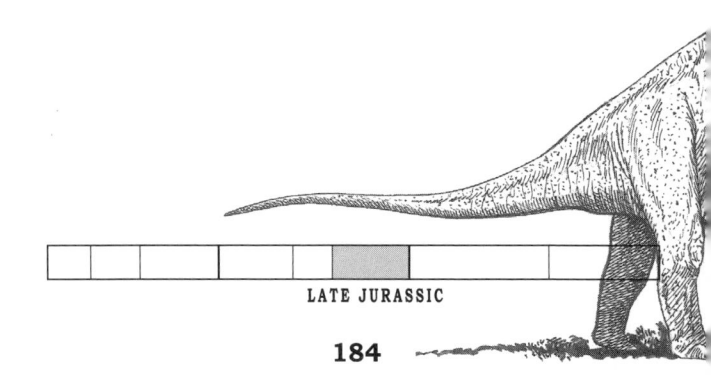

LATE JURASSIC

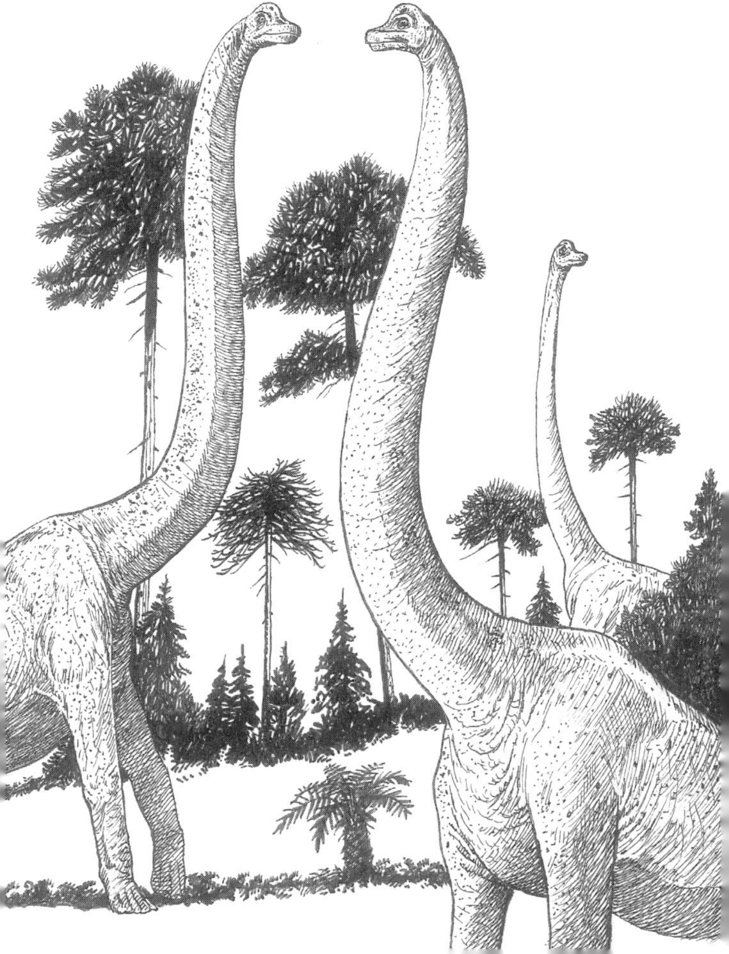

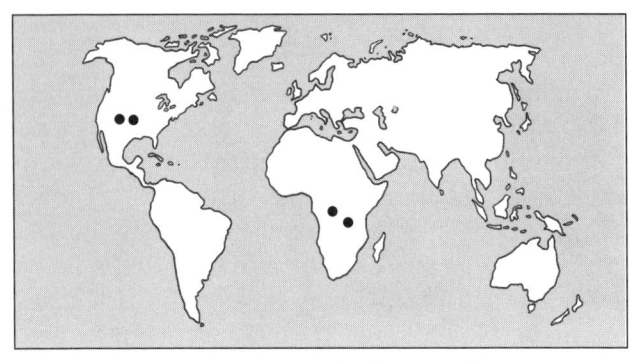

FOUND IN COLORADO AND UTAH, U.S.; TANZANIA; ZIMBABWE

was simply a very much larger specimen of the true *Brachiosaurus*.

In most dinosaurs the front legs are shorter than the back legs. In some sauropods, like *Camarasaurus*, they were equal in length. *Brachiosaurus* is special in that its front legs were actually longer than the hind legs. In addition, the spines of its backbone were very tall, to support the weight of its extremely long neck. *Brachiosaurus* was thus built "uphill." This is yet another way the sauropod could reach high into the trees.

The nostrils of *Brachiosaurus* were very large, and placed on a bump on top of the head. Once paleontologists thought that *Brachiosaurus* spent most of its time underwater, snorkeling by sticking only this bump above water. However, had it done that, the great pressure of the water would have crushed the lungs of the dinosaur. Instead *Brachiosaurus* probably spent most of its time on land. The big nostrils may have had a fleshy sac on them, which could be inflated to make loud noises.

Dinosaurs like *Brachiosaurus* were common in many parts of the world in the Early Cretaceous Epoch.

Argentinosaurus
"Argentina reptile"

Length: perhaps 100 feet (30m)
Diet: plants

Argentinosaurus is possibly the largest dinosaur known to science. Sometimes people think that giant sauropods were found only in the Late Jurassic Epoch. In fact, the largest of all sauropods came from the Late Cretaceous Epoch of Argentina.

LATE CRETACEOUS

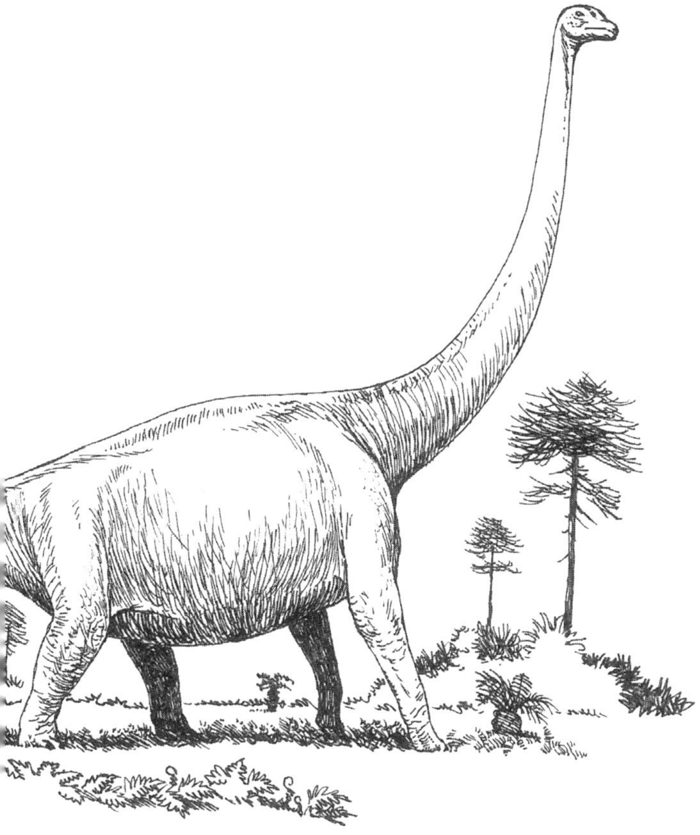

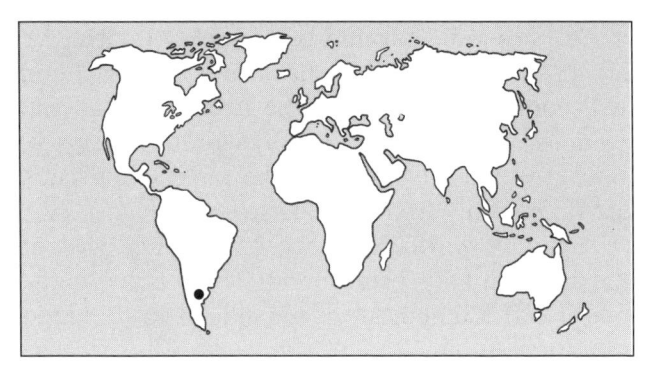

FOUND IN ARGENTINA

Argentinosaurus was one of a group called **titanosaurs** ("titanic reptiles"), which were common in the Cretaceous Period, especially in South America, India, and Madagascar. Their skulls were something like that of *Brachiosaurus*. Some had spoon-shaped teeth like *Brachiosaurus* and *Camarasaurus*; others had pencil-shaped teeth like *Diplodocus*. Their hips were very broad.

One problem with studying giant dinosaurs is that it is hard to find complete skeletons. In order to make a complete fossil, the skeleton of a dead animal has to be covered very quickly to preserve all the bones. It is rare that a big enough flood will come along to cover the body of an animal completely before scavengers begin to feed on it. Because of this, almost all the largest dinosaurs are known only from partial skeletons.

Argentinosaurus is no exception. Only parts of the skeleton have been found. These bones show that it was a titanosaur of gigantic size. It is hard to figure out how long this dinosaur was, because the neck and tail can be shorter or longer in different types of sauropods. Nevertheless, the size of the backbones and leg bones show that this was an immense animal, weighing between 80 and 100 tons. This is as much as a herd of elephants! In comparison, the largest known specimens of *Brachiosaurus* were probably only 55 to 60 tons. *Seismosaurus* and *Supersaurus*, the giant relatives of *Diplodocus*, were probably much longer than *Argentinosaurus,* but most of this length was in their long necks and whip-like tails. They, too, weighed "only" 55 to 60 tons.

Saltasaurus
"Salta reptile"

Salta is a province of Argentina.

Length: over 36 feet (about 11m)
Diet: plants

Not all titanosaurs were as gigantic as *Argentinosaurus*. *Saltasaurus*, one of the last of this group, was not much bigger than the first sauropods. It is very unusual because it had body armor!

During the Late Cretaceous Epoch titanosaurs were very common in many parts of the world.

LATE CRETACEOUS

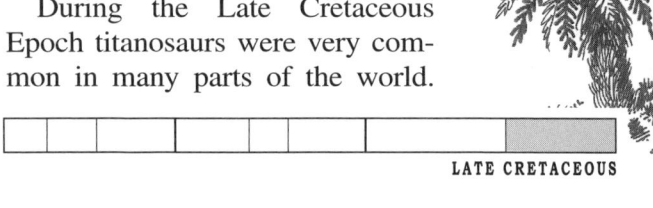

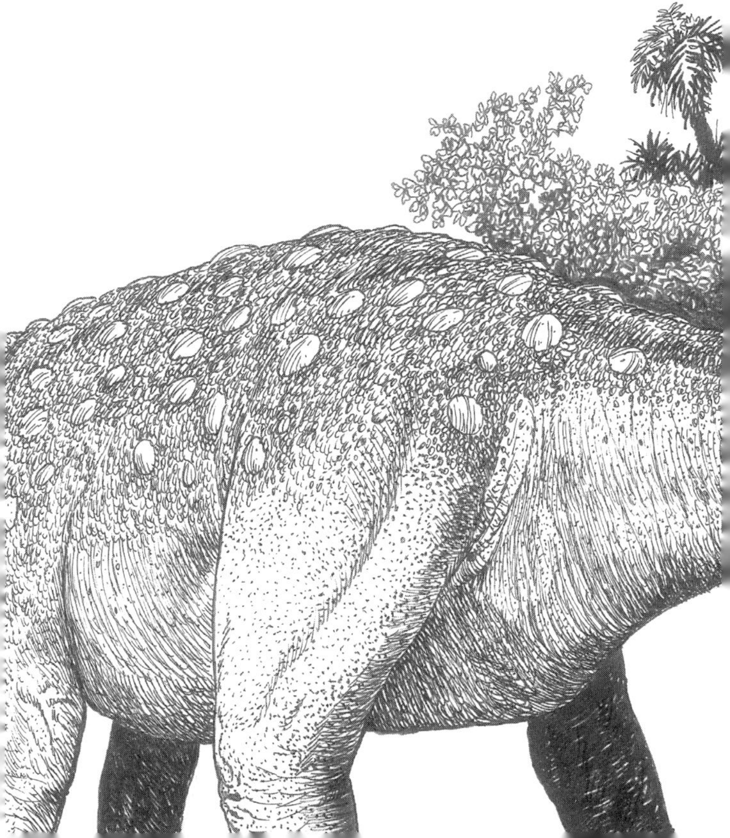

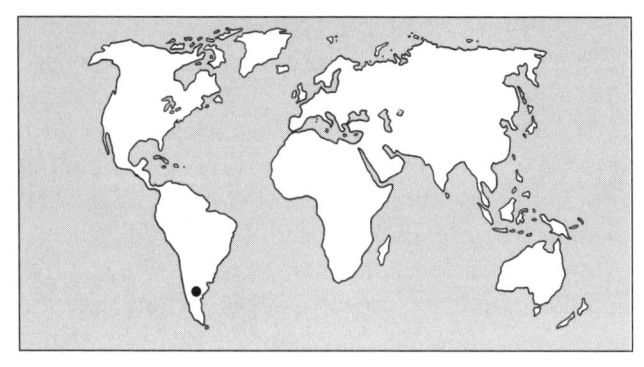

FOUND IN ARGENTINA

They were found in Mongolia, China, throughout Europe, and Australia. In South America, India, and Madagascar titanosaurs were the most common dinosaurs around.

At the very end of the Age of Dinosaurs one type, called *Alamosaurus*, moved up from South America into the American West.

Titanosaurs evolved into different sizes and specialties. Some were very large, others smaller. Some had very slender legs; others had legs that were thick and heavy. *Saltasaurus* was a small, stocky-legged titanosaur. When it was discovered, paleontologists were surprised to find that it had armor plates on its back!

Before this the only dinosaurs known to have lots of armor on their back were thyreophoran ornithischians, such as the ankylosaurs. Now that armored sauropods had been discovered, paleontologists went back to their museums to look at fossils found in previous digs. Many of the titanosaur skeletons had been found near armor plates. Because no one had ever imagined armored sauropods, these earlier discoveries were thought to be from some unknown kind of ankylosaur. However, it now seemed that these armor plates were actually from titanosaur sauropods.

Despite having armor on their back, scientists think that titanosaurs like *Saltasaurus* may have been the most agile of all the sauropods. Their backbones were very flexible. This might mean that titanosaurs were better able to move fast and make better turns than earlier types of sauropod. However, no paleontologist thinks that any sauropod, even titanosaurs, were among the fastest of dinosaurs! Instead, they think that these were just the last and most advanced of the long line of sauropodomorphs.

Some titanosaurs, such as *Alamosaurus* in the American West, *Magyarsaurus* in Hungary and Romania, and *Titanosaurus* in India, were around at the very end of the Age of Dinosaurs.

·9·
THEROPODS, THE BIRDLIKE MEAT EATERS

The last major group of dinosaurs is the **theropods** (beast feet). They are called "beast feet" because many of them had curved toe claws ending in sharp points, something like meat-eating birds and mammals today. Many theropods had teeth shaped like steak knives—flat on each side with a row of bumps or **serrations** running up the front and back of each tooth. Like the serrations on a steak knife, the serrations on the theropod tooth helped it cut through meat.

Theropods are commonly called meat-eating dinosaurs. It is true that all the meat-eating dinosaurs known to paleontology are theropods, but many sorts of theropods actually ate things other than meat. In fact, several sorts of theropods lost their teeth and evolved beaks instead!

Some theropods are among the most primitive of all dinosaurs: they had not changed much from the common ancestor of all dinosaurs. They were about 3⅓ feet (1m) long, ran only on their hind legs, and had grasping hands. In fact, all theropods, no matter how big they got, could run only on their back legs. Many of them had very good grasping hands, although some had hands that were so small they were practically useless! In one group of theropods, the hands evolved into wings!

Theropods had many specializations. They had hollow bones that were strong but lightweight. Almost all of them had a special extra joint in their lower jaw, which helped them hold on better to struggling victims. Except for the most primitive theropods (*Eoraptor* and *Herrerasaurus*), they had a special type of collarbone. Where most animals have two separate collarbones (you can feel yours on the front of your chest, just below your shoulders), the collarbones of theropods were fused into a single bone. This single bone is called a "wishbone."

Only one group of animals alive today has a wishbone: the birds. Paleontologists have discovered many details of anatomy that show that birds are the specialized descendants of theropod dinosaurs! Remember, scientists decide if an animal is a dinosaur or not by whether it is the descendant of the most recent common ancestor of *Megalosaurus* and *Iguanodon*. Any creature that is a descendant of that common ancestor is considered a dinosaur. Since birds are descendants of that common ancestor, paleontologists now consider modern birds a type of dinosaur!

This sounds strange, but over the years many discoveries have shown that the bird skeleton is just a modified version of a theropod dinosaur skeleton. Also, recent discoveries of fossils in China show that many sorts of theropod dinosaur actually had simple feathers. Other than birds, these theropod dinosaurs are the only animals known to have had feathers.

Among the first dinosaurs, theropods have been found on every continent. Most types died out by the end of the Age of Dinosaurs—except for the birds that live today, which are a surviving group of theropod dinosaur.

FAMILY TREE OF THEROPODS

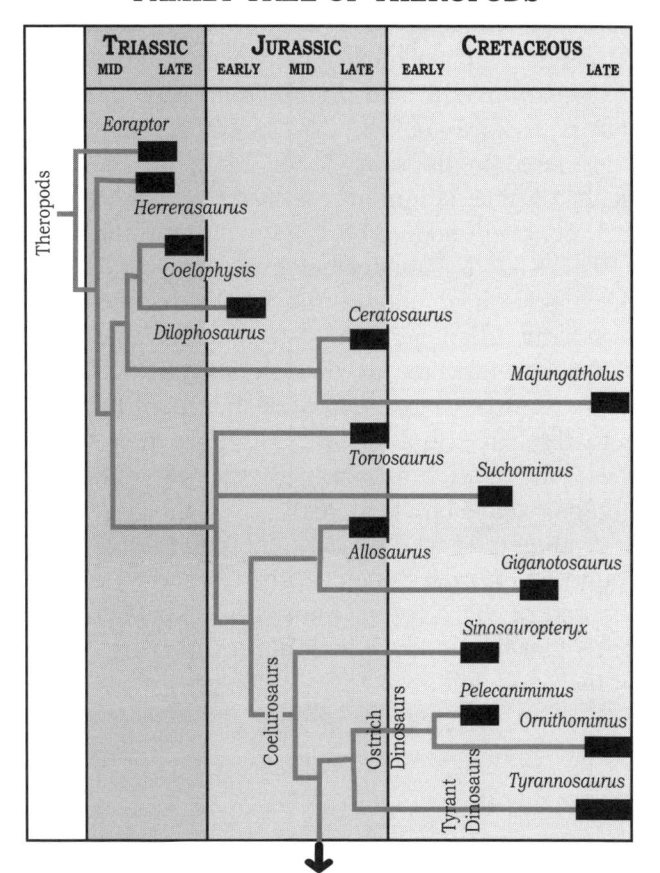

FAMILY TREE OF THEROPODS (continued)

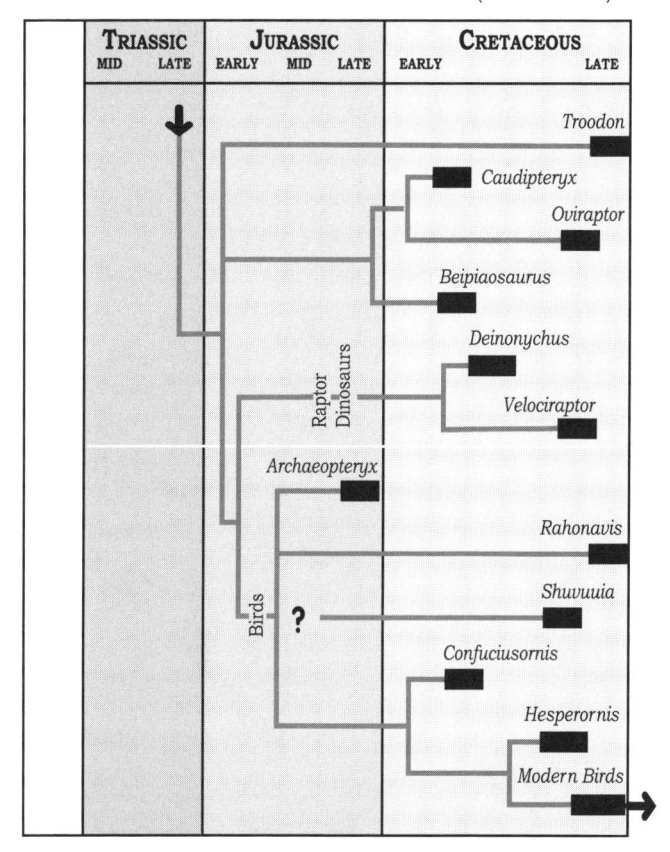

	TRIASSIC		JURASSIC			CRETACEOUS	
	MID	LATE	EARLY	MID	LATE	EARLY	LATE

- Troodon
- Caudipteryx
- Oviraptor
- Beipiaosaurus
- Deinonychus
- Velociraptor
- Raptor Dinosaurs
- Archaeopteryx
- Rahonavis
- Shuvuuia
- Birds
- Confuciusornis
- Hesperornis
- Modern Birds

Eoraptor
"Hunter of the dawn"

Length: about 3⅓ feet (1m)
Diet: meat (small animals)

Eoraptor is one of the most primitive dinosaurs ever discovered. It is our best evidence of what the common ancestor of all dinosaurs looked like.

LATE TRIASSIC

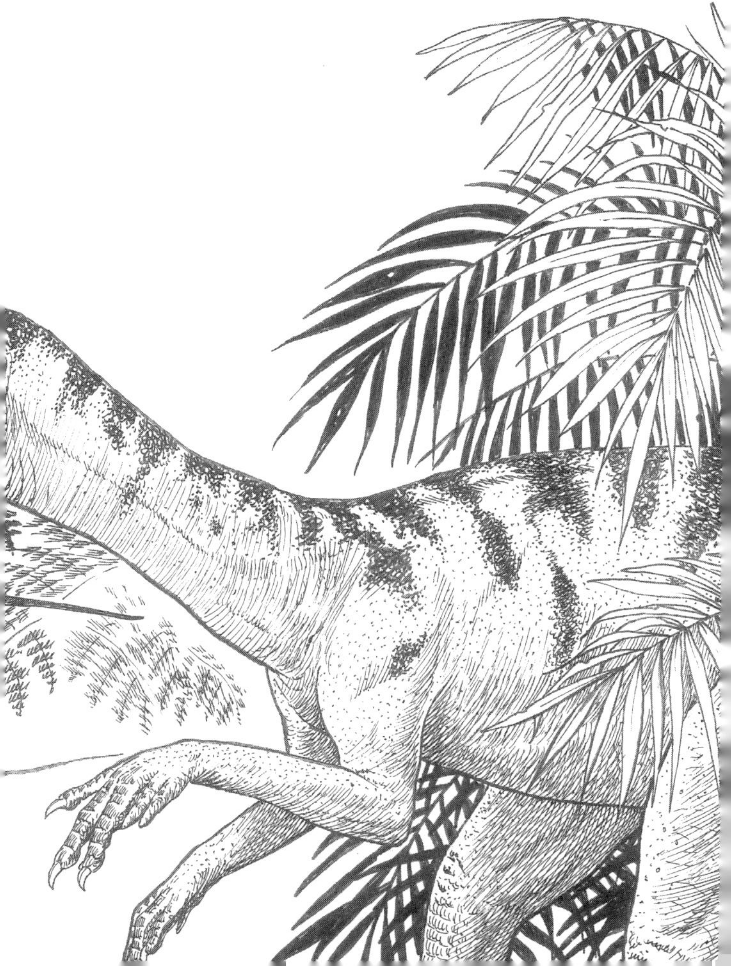

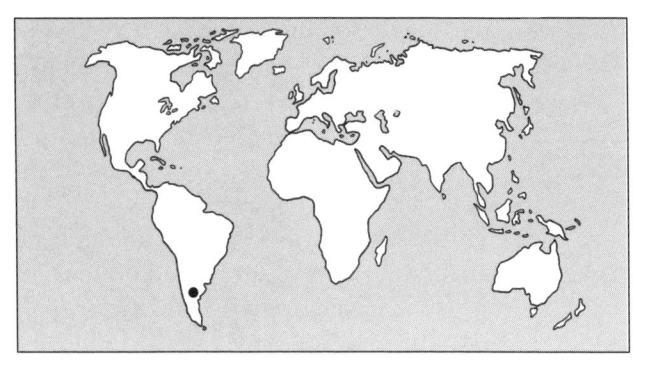

FOUND IN ARGENTINA

Scientists had long thought that ornithischians, sauropodomorphs, and theropod dinosaurs all came from a single common ancestor. Because all three groups were known to be around by the Late Triassic Epoch, paleontologists realized that their common ancestor had to have lived in the earliest part of the Late Triassic Epoch or even earlier.

While searching in rocks from this period in Argentina, paleontologists uncovered the skeleton of a very primitive dinosaur. Its sharp teeth showed that it was a meat eater, so they named it

Eoraptor, the hunter of the dawn of the Age of Dinosaurs. It was clearly a dinosaur, but it had very few features to show to which group of dinosaur it belonged. Because of its very hollow bones, scientists decided it was a very early theropod dinosaur.

It turns out that *Eoraptor* came too late in time to be the actual common ancestor of all dinosaurs: other groups of dinosaur were already around when it lived. Still, its skeleton gives us clues on how the earliest dinosaurs lived.

Like most early dinosaurs *Eoraptor* was a two-legged runner. It had hands that were good for grasping food. It was small enough to hide from the larger theropod *Herrerasaurus* (see page 206) and even bigger land-living relatives of crocodiles, which were the top meat eaters of its world.

Eoraptor probably ate many sorts of small animals: little mammal-ancestors and lizards, insects, fish, and the eggs of other reptiles.

Herrerasaurus
"Herrera's reptile"

Named after Don Vittorio Herrera, a rancher and guide who found the site where Herrerasaurus was uncovered.

Length: over 13 feet (4m)
Diet: meat

Herrerasaurus lived in the same place and time as little *Eoraptor*. It was larger and more powerful, a hint of the giant predators to come.

LATE TRIASSIC

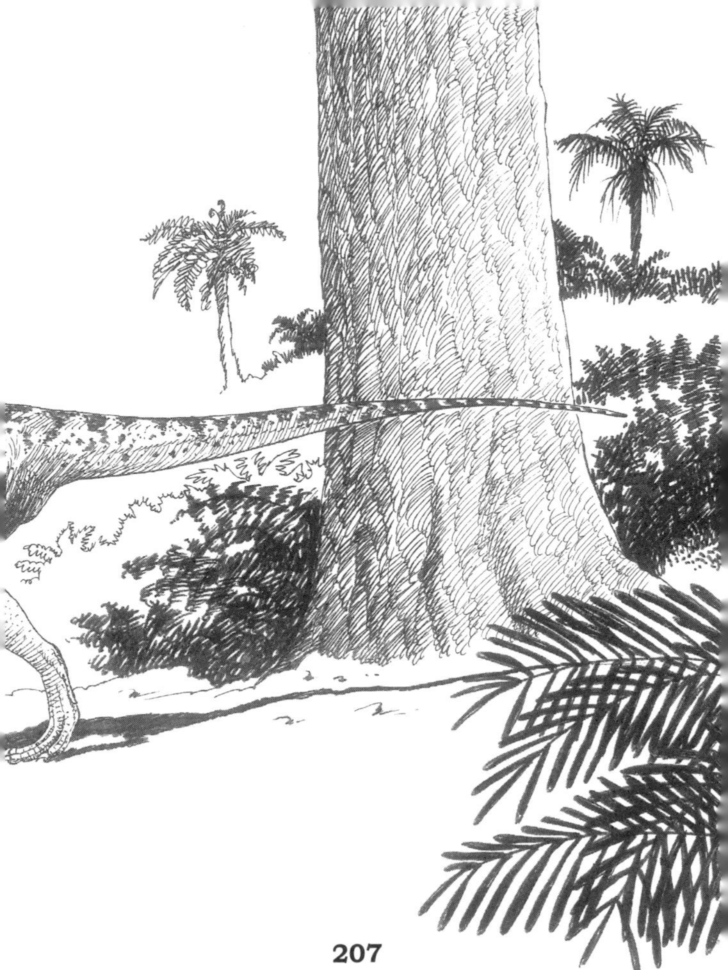

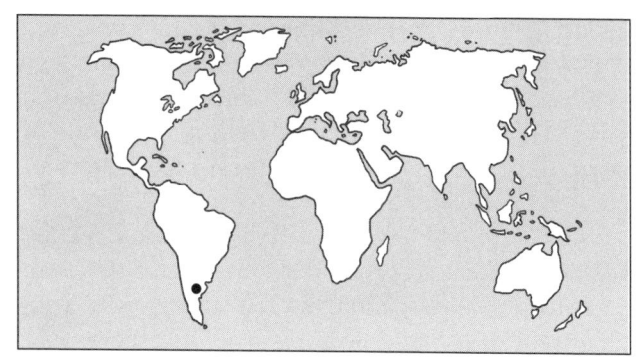

FOUND IN ARGENTINA

Little *Eoraptor* probably couldn't attack animals much bigger than lizards and mammals. Its larger and more advanced relative, *Herrerasaurus*, would have been able to go after animals its own size or maybe even larger. *Herrerasaurus* had a powerful skull with a special joint in its lower jaw. This joint was a kind of "shock absorber" to help it hold on to struggling prey. *Herrerasaurus* was the first theropod with this kind of jaw, and almost all the later ones had it, too.

The hands of *Herrerasaurus* were long and

ended in strong grasping fingers. It could grab and clutch animals it was trying to eat. It had long legs to chase after other animals, and to help it run away from the giant land-dwelling relatives of crocodiles, which were the largest meat eaters of the Late Triassic world.

Herrerasaurus and its relatives passed on the jaw joint, the long grasping hands, and the long legs to their descendants, the more advanced theropods of the rest of the Age of Dinosaurs.

Primitive theropods like *Herrerasaurus* were found in many places in the Late Triassic Epoch. But by the end of that epoch, these primitive theropods had disappeared, replaced by their more specialized descendants.

Coelophysis
"Hollow form"

Length: about 13 feet (4m)
Diet: meat (small animals)

Among the first of the more advanced theropods, *Coelophysis* is one of the best known of all Triassic dinosaurs.

Coelophysis was long and skinny. Although it grew to be around the same length as *Herrerasaurus*, it was much lighter. Most of its length

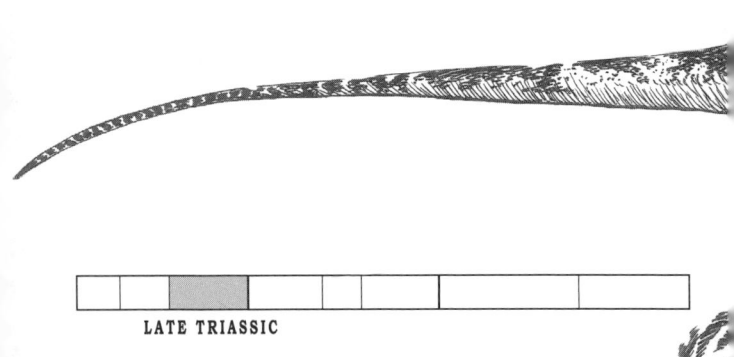

LATE TRIASSIC

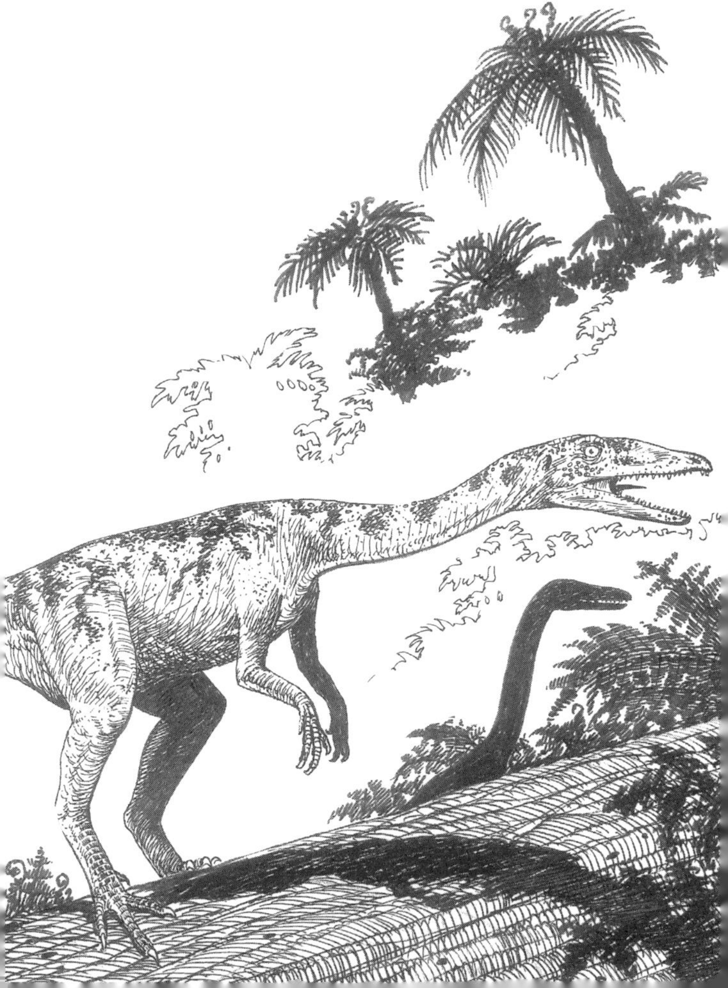

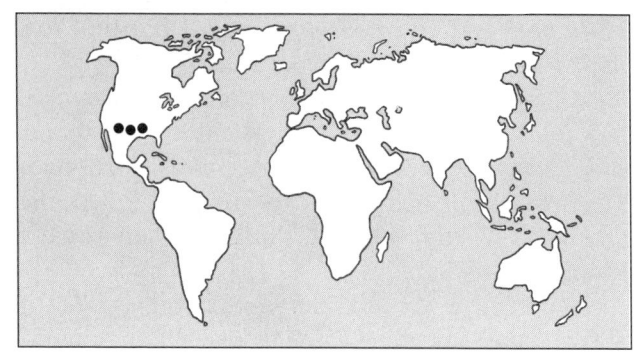

FOUND IN NEW MEXICO, ARIZONA, AND TEXAS, U.S.

was in its skinny neck and tail. Its skull was long and low and filled with small sharp teeth. *Coelophysis* and all later theropods lost their pinky (in *Eoraptor* and *Herrerasaurus* this finger was small, but it was still there). Its legs were longer and skinnier than in *Eoraptor* and *Herrerasaurus*, and it was probably one of the fastest dinosaurs of its age. The foot of *Coelophysis* and later theropods was like the foot of a bird. Its first toe was very small and short, so that it walked only on the middle three toes

(*Eoraptor* and *Herrerasaurus* had a big first toe, and so walked on four toes).

Coelophysis and its relatives are now known to be the earliest dinosaurs with a wishbone. Scientists are not sure what these early wishbones were used for. Maybe they helped brace the shoulders when *Coelophysis* and its relatives were holding on to a victim.

The small teeth of *Coelophysis* suggest that it ate mostly smaller animals: early mammals, lizards, small dinosaurs, and so on. After the Early Jurassic Epoch this kind of meat eater became rare.

Dilophosaurus
"Double-crested reptile"

Length: about 20 feet (over 6m)
Diet: meat

Dilophosaurus was a larger, more powerfully built relative of *Coelophysis*. It was one of the first big theropod predators.

At the end of the Late Triassic Epoch most of the other groups of big animals—the protomammals and the crocodile-relatives—died out. No one is quite sure of the

EARLY JURASSIC

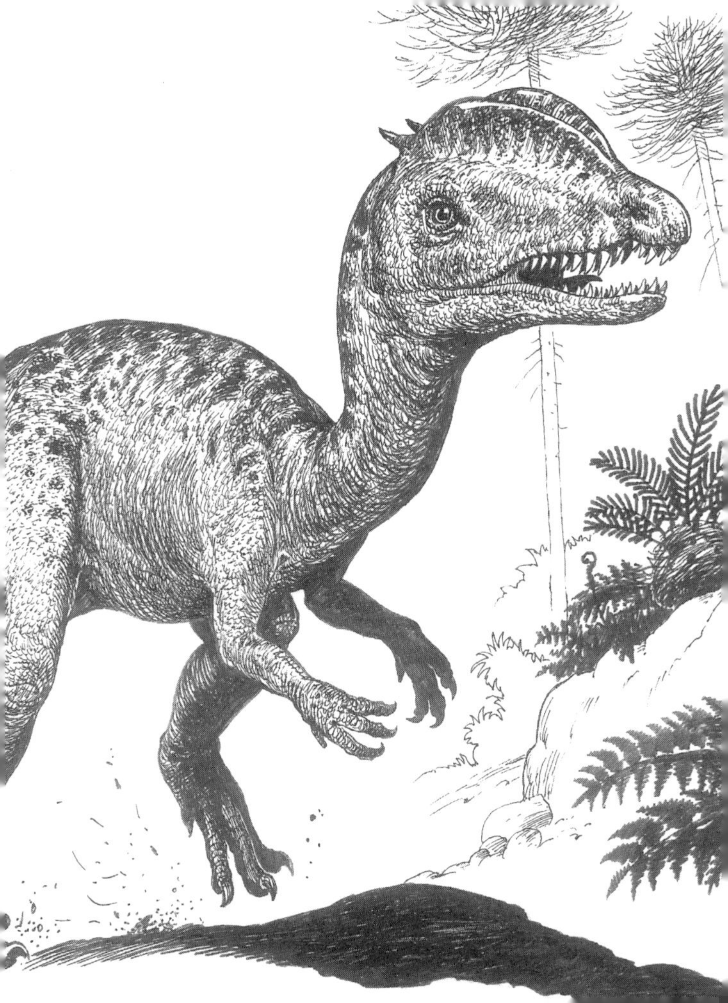

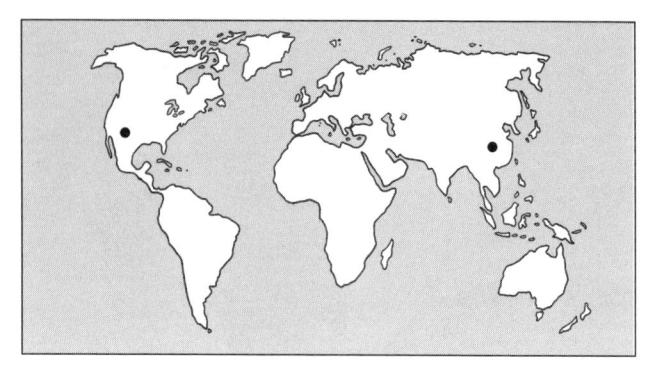

FOUND IN CHINA; ARIZONA, U.S.

reason, although there was a lot of volcanic activity at this time. Whatever the reasons, dinosaurs survived as the main group of big land animal. And theropods became the top group of meat eaters at the beginning of the Early Jurassic Epoch. *Dilophosaurus* was one of these new larger theropods.

In most features *Dilophosaurus* was simply a larger version of *Coelophysis*. However, its skull was bigger and its neck was shorter. Its teeth were very big, and it probably ate bigger animals than

Coelophysis did. It's probably no coincidence that thyreophorans (like *Scutellosaurus* and *Scelidosaurus*) began to show up when *Dilophosaurus* and its kin appeared. These armored dinosaurs probably evolved their armor and (later) their larger size to protect themselves against the newer, larger theropods.

Dilophosaurus is called the "double-crested reptile," because of the pair of thin ridges on the top of its head, one on the left side and one on the right. The crests were probably used as a signal to others of its own kind. They were much too thin to have been used as a weapon.

Some movies and books say that *Dilophosaurus* could spit poison and had a big frill on its neck. But to date there is no evidence of poison grooves in its fangs or a frill around its neck.

Ceratosaurus
"Horned reptile"

Length: about 20 feet (over 6m)
Diet: meat

Ceratosaurus was one of the most distinctive of all theropods. It had a narrow flat "horn" on its snout.
    Ceratosaurus was one of the predators found in

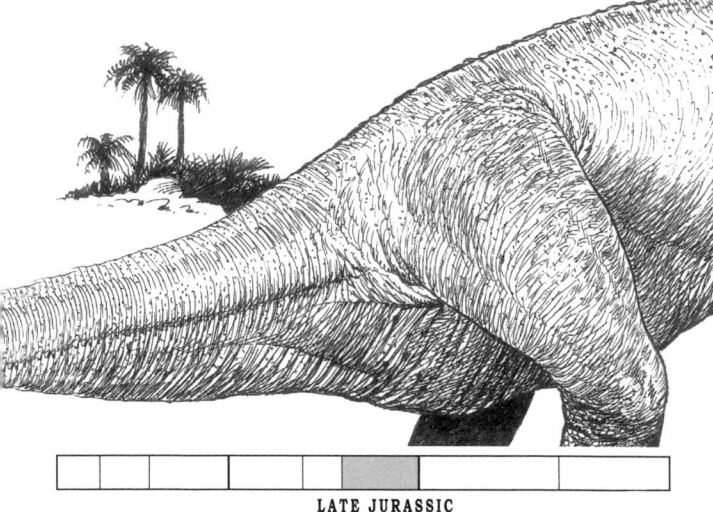

LATE JURASSIC

219

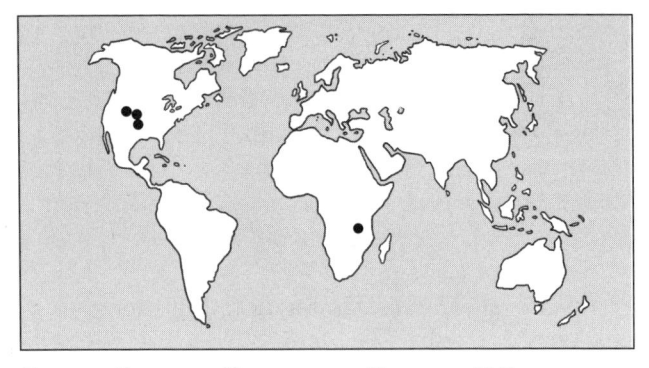

Found in Colorado, Utah, possibly Oklahoma, U.S.; possibly Tanzania, eastern Africa

the Morrison Formation of the Late Jurassic Epoch of the American West. In the details of its backbones, hips, and legs it was similar to the earlier *Coelophysis* and *Dilophosaurus*; in other ways it was more like *Majungatholus* and its relatives.

Ceratosaurus had a tall, powerful skull full of large teeth. It had a shorter, stronger neck than *Coelophysis* and *Dilophosaurus*. Its arms were short, and its four fingers were probably too short to do much grasping. *Ceratosaurus* probably went after dinosaurs its own size or smaller, slicing big hunks of meat out of its prey with its strong jaws. It seems to have been the only theropod with bony armor—a simple row of small knobs running down the back. The narrow horn in the center of its snout was probably too weak to have been a weapon, and was probably used as a kind of display to other *Ceratosaurus*.

Ceratosaurus was not the only big theropod in its environment. The larger *Torvosaurus* and *Allosaurus* were also around at the time, as were little meat eaters, too. How could so many different types of meat eaters live together?

If we look at some places in the modern world, like the Serengeti Plains of Africa, we can find lions, leopards, cheetahs, spotted hyenas, hunting dogs, and jackals all living side by side. It may be that all the different Morrison theropods also lived together, each hunting in its own way, and trying to steal from kills made by the other.

Majungatholus
"Majunga dome"

Majunga is the place in Madagascar where it was found.

Length: about 23 feet (over 7m)
Diet: meat

Majungatholus was one of a group of bizarre relatives of *Ceratosaurus*. When parts of its skull were first discovered, paleontologists thought it was actually a dome-headed pachycephalosaur!

This dinosaur was discovered on the island of

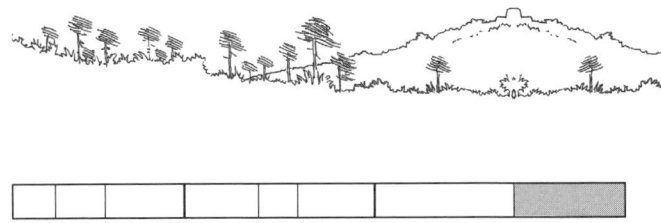

LATE CRETACEOUS

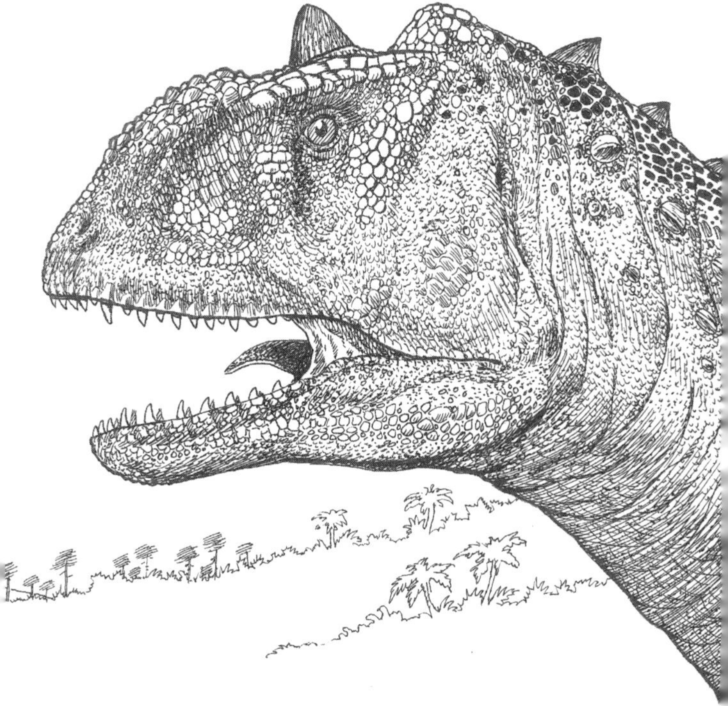

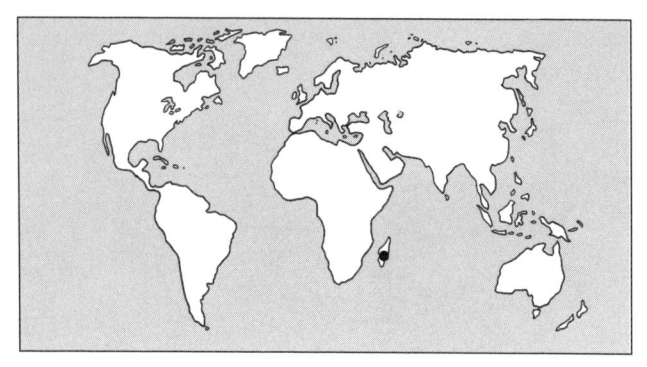

FOUND IN MADAGASCAR

Madagascar. Paleontologists found the top of its head, in which the bones were all fused together with a small dome in the middle. Because no dinosaurs other than pachycephalosaurs were known to have skull domes, scientists thought that this fossil came from that group of ornithischians. However, after the rest of the skull was uncovered, paleontologists recognized that it was really a theropod.

Majungatholus had a mouthful of short, sharp teeth in its strong, deep skull. The dome on its head might have been used in pushing matches, like those of pachycephalosaurs.

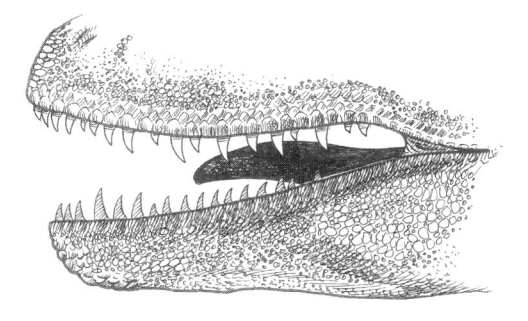

TEETH OF MAJUNGATHOLUS

Dinosaurs very similar to *Majungatholus* lived throughout the southern parts of the world during the Late Cretaceous Epoch. They all had deep skulls with many bones fused together and very unusually shaped backbones. Their arms were all very short.

Why were all these strange theropods common in the southern continents, but not elsewhere during the Late Cretaceous Epoch? This has to do with the changing pattern of continents during the

Age of Dinosaurs. During the Late Jurassic Epoch much of the world was still connected by land, so different groups of dinosaurs could walk all over the world. As the continents moved away from each other, seas formed between lands that were once connected, isolating them. The southern continents (South America, Africa, Antarctica, Australia, what is now the island of Madagascar, and what is now India) were still joined together

GONDWANA

in a land mass scientists call **Gondwana.** Here, a theropod that was related to *Ceratosaurus* evolved features of *Majungatholus* and its kin, and spread throughout these southern lands. When Gondwana broke apart, descendants of this common ancestor evolved into *Majungatholus*, *Carnotaurus*, and the rest.

Wherever *Majungatholus* and its close relatives are found, titanosaur sauropods are the most common plant-eating dinosaurs. Although it is unlikely that theropods could kill a full-grown titanosaur, they probably could hunt younger sauropods. Perhaps the later titanosaurs evolved their armor to defend against attacks by *Majungatholus* and its kin.

Torvosaurus
"Savage reptile"

Length: about 33 feet (over 10m)
Diet: meat

Torvosaurus was a large, heavy built theropod from the Late Jurassic Morrison Formation of the American West. It had very powerful forelimbs ending in huge claws. It was closely related to *Megalosaurus* from the Middle Jurassic Epoch of England.

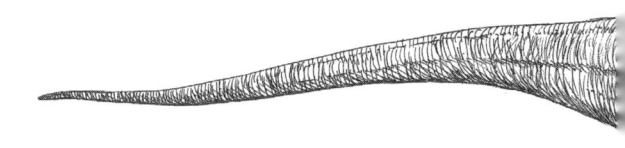

For many decades only two types of large theropod were known from the Morrison Formation: horned *Ceratosaurus* and the more advanced

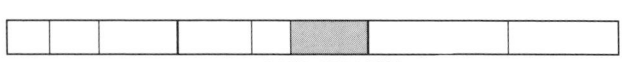

LATE JURASSIC

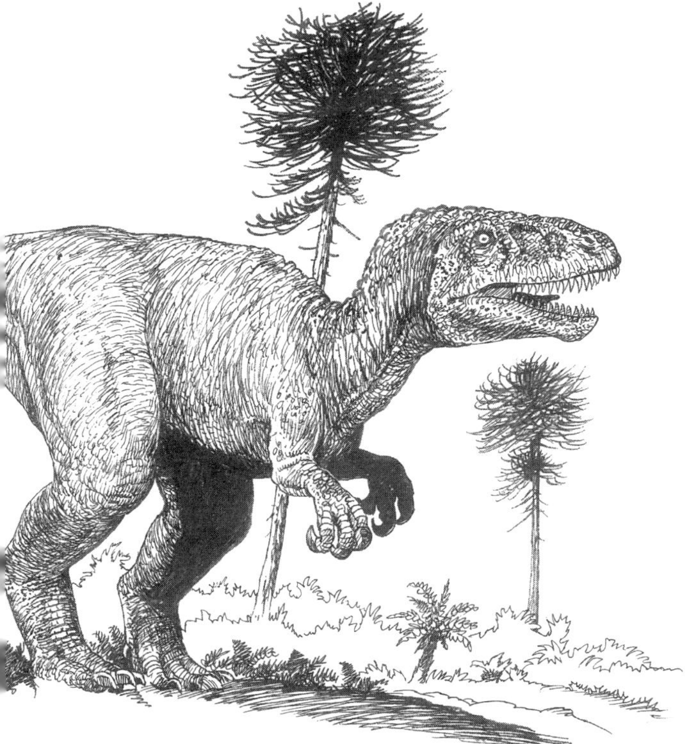

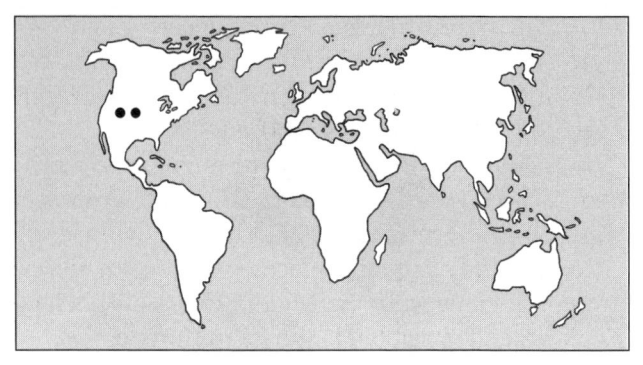

FOUND IN COLORADO, UTAH, U.S.

Allosaurus. However, fossil remains began to be discovered of another big meat eater, one with very strong arms and short but powerful forearms. The hands of this dinosaur, which had only three fingers, ended in gigantic claws like the talons of eagles. As more of the skeleton was found, paleontologists realized that this was a new type of large theropod dinosaur. It was named *Torvosaurus*, the "savage reptile."

This new theropod was bigger than *Ceratosaurus*. Compared to the more graceful *Allo-*

saurus, *Torvosaurus* was a brute; its arms and legs were shorter and stockier. It probably wasn't able to hunt such fast or agile prey as *Allosaurus*, but instead went after slower dinosaurs.

In many ways *Torvosaurus* resembles the theropod *Megalosaurus* (see page 21). *Megalosaurus* was one of the first fossil dinosaurs known to science, and only bits and pieces of it are known at present. It came from the Middle Jurassic Epoch of England, and possibly elsewhere in Europe.

Although it doesn't look like it at first, *Torvosaurus* was probably more closely related to birds than the theropods already mentioned. For example, like birds, *Torvosaurus* and other, more advanced theropods had only three fingers; *Coelophysis*, *Ceratosaurus*, and more primitive meat eaters had four. Its tail was stiffer than the tails of *Coelophysis* and *Ceratosaurus*, like the tails of early birds. Its teeth were all in front of its eye sockets, as in early birds, but unlike the teeth of *Coelophysis* and *Ceratosaurus* (which run underneath the eye socket). Although *Torvosaurus* was not a direct ancestor to birds, it was more closely related to birds than it was to *Ceratosaurus*.

Suchomimus
"Crocodile mimic"

Length: about 36 feet (11m)
Diet: meat (especially fish)

Most theropods had teeth shaped like steak knives. One group of Cretaceous theropods evolved cone-shaped teeth and long narrow snouts. These were probably fish eaters.

EARLY CRETACEOUS

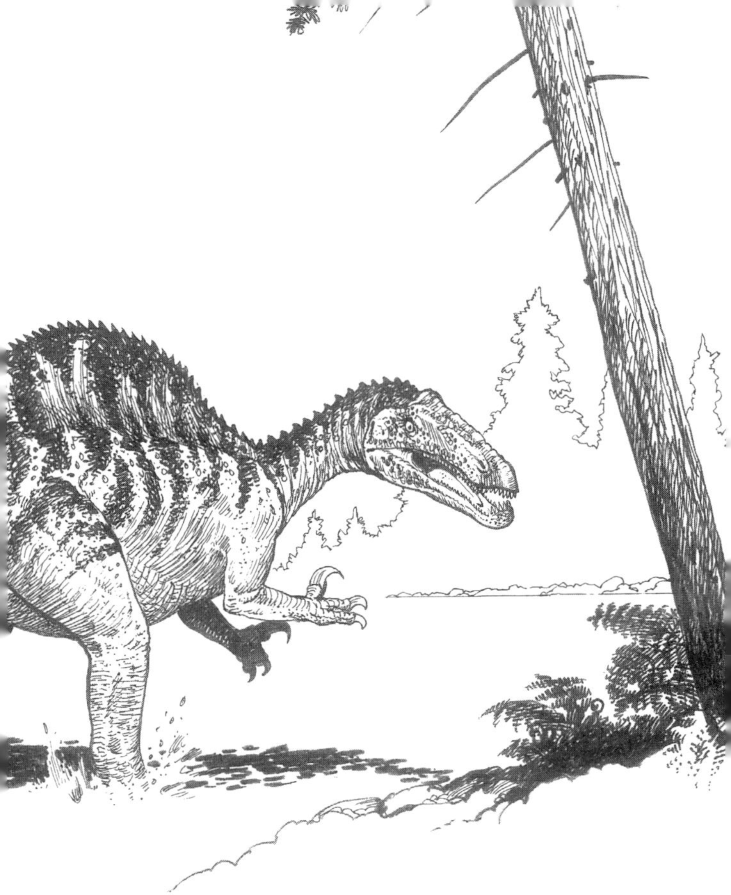

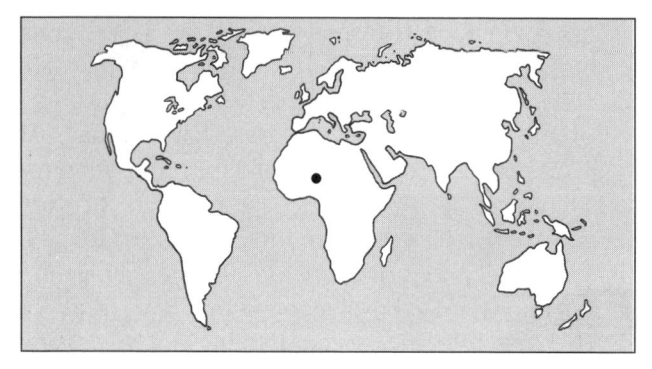

FOUND IN NIGER

Suchomimus probably had an ancestor that looked a lot like *Torvosaurus*. Like that Jurassic dinosaur, *Suchomimus* had a very short but strong forearm and a three-fingered hand with very big claws. However, the skull of *Suchomimus* was very different from *Torvosaurus*. It was long, low, and narrow. Its teeth were shaped like cones, similar to the teeth of modern crocodiles and alligators. In fact, its head looked something like the head of a crocodile, which is why it was named *Suchomimus*, the "crocodile mimic."

Why would a theropod have a head and teeth like those a crocodile? It turns out that when *Suchomimus* was alive, its northern African home was very different from the desert it is today. At that time this land was full of lakes and streams, and in these waters lived great numbers of very large fish, some of them up to 10 feet (3m) long! It is very likely that *Suchomimus* was a fish-eating theropod. It may have stood along the shore or waded out into the water, looking for a passing fish. When one would come by, *Suchomimus* could dip its huge snout into the water and grab the fish with its strong jaws and teeth. Perhaps it used its big claws to help pull the fish onto the shore.

Suchomimus would have been able to go after land animals, like other dinosaurs, too. After all, modern crocodiles and alligators eat land mammals as well as fish—otherwise, people wouldn't have to worry about these modern reptiles!

Allosaurus
"Other reptile"

Length: almost 40 feet (up to 12m)
Diet: meat

Allosaurus was the most common meat-eating dinosaur in the Late Jurassic Morrison Formation of the American West.

No giant theropod is known from more skeletons and in more detail than *Allosaurus*. In one quarry in Utah the remains of at least 44 different *Allosaurus* were found mixed together! The teeth of *Allosaurus* are the most common remains of theropods found in the Late Jurassic of the American West.

Allosaurus is also known from Portugal in Europe, where nests

LATE JURASSIC

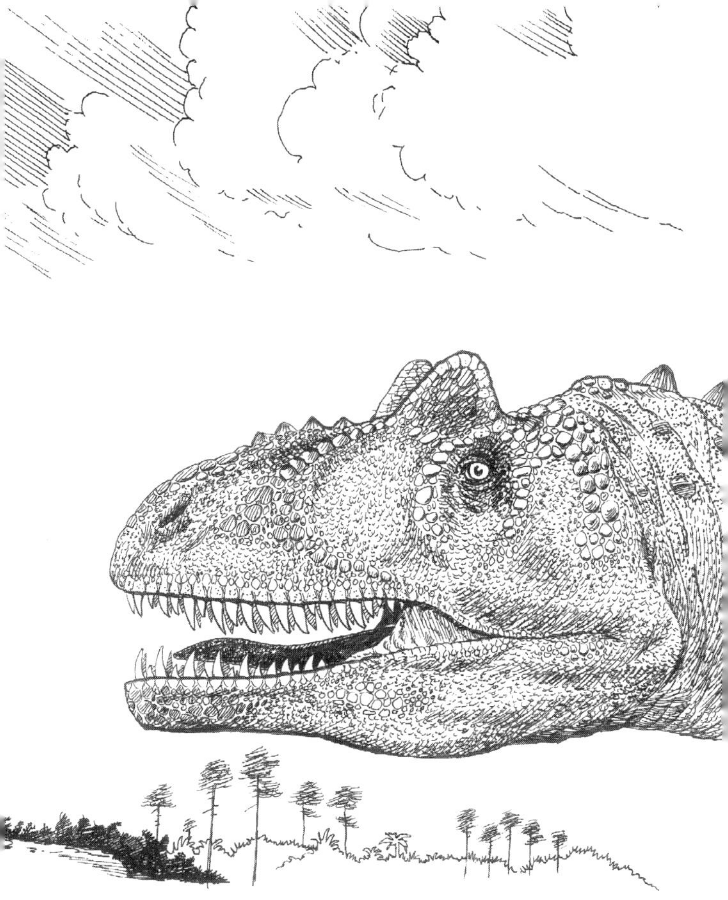

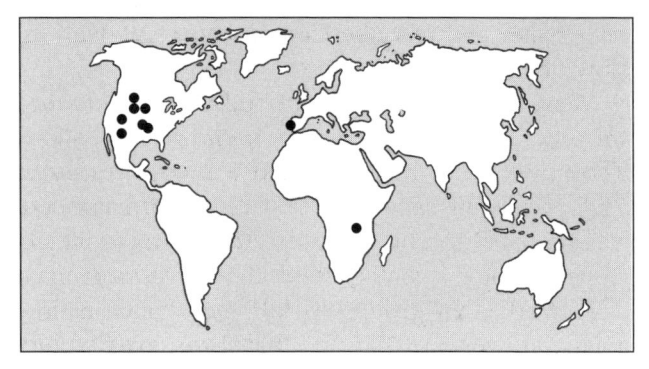

Found in Wyoming, Colorado, Utah, New Mexico, Montana, South Dakota, Oklahoma, U.S.; Portugal; possibly Tanzania, eastern Africa

of *Allosaurus* eggs, including the bones of unhatched babies, have been found. Back in the Late Jurassic Epoch, Europe and North America were still connected by land, so *Allosaurus* could walk from one region to another.

Allosaurus grew much larger than *Ceratosaurus*, and a little longer than *Torvosaurus*. More slender than *Torvosaurus*, *Allosaurus* was probably faster and more agile. While *Torvosaurus* could probably only hunt slow prey, *Allosaurus* could chase after faster animals like *Camptosaurus* as well as slow ones.

Many bones of big sauropods, like *Camarasaurus*, *Diplodocus*, and *Apatosaurus*, show *Allosaurus* tooth marks. Could a lone *Allosaurus* attack an adult sauropod? A full-grown sauropod was probably too big for even *Allosaurus* to attack alone, so some scientists think that *Allosaurus* may have worked in groups to kill these plant-eating giants. However, it may be that *Allosaurus* would only go after sick and injured sauropods, so that it would not risk being killed by a strong and healthy plant eater. *Allosaurus* may even have waited for sick and injured sauropods to die before feeding on their carcasses. We may never know for sure.

Allosaurus had a pair of triangular horns just in front of its eyes, and a pair of crests down its nose. Many of its close relatives also had some kinds of decoration on their heads. *Cryolophosaurus* of the Early Jurassic Epoch of Antarctica, for instance, had a tall forward-facing ridge on the top of its skull, while *Monolophosaurus* of the Middle Jurassic Epoch of China had a very tall crest running down the center of its head.

Giganotosaurus
"Giant southern reptile"

Length: over 46 feet (14m)
Diet: meat

Bigger than *Tyrannosaurus*, *Giganotosaurus* is the largest theropod known today. This gigantic relative of *Allosaurus* lived around the same time and place as the largest of all dinosaurs, the titanosaur sauropod *Argentinosaurus*.

For many decades paleontologists thought *Tyrannosaurus* was the largest meat-eating dinosaur. Then the remains of a new giant meat eater were discovered in Argentina, in rocks that dated back to the very beginning of the Late Cretaceous Epoch, the same age as the rocks containing fossils of the mighty *Argentinosaurus*. The skull of this

LATE CRETACEOUS

241

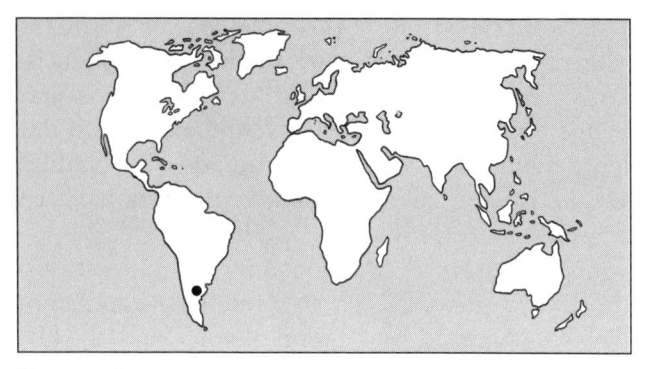

FOUND IN ARGENTINA

new dinosaur, which they named *Giganotosaurus*, was an amazing 6 feet (1.8m) long, and full of huge, sharp teeth.

It did not have the specialized features found in *Majungatholus* and its kin, the most common predators in Late Cretaceous South America. It was also different from *Tyrannosaurus* and the tyrant dinosaurs. Although it also had short arms, they were more strongly built than those of tyrant dinosaurs, and might still have had three fingers. Its legs were shorter and bulkier than those of tyrant dinosaurs, so it probably wasn't as fast a runner. Also, its teeth were shaped like flat steak knives, not thick like the teeth of tyrant dinosaurs. While *Giganotosaurus* was around, almost all the large plant eaters were sauropods. So, unlike *Tyrannosaurus*, *Giganotosaurus* did not have to chase after fast prey.

Giganotosaurus was one of the last of the *Allosaurus* relatives. In the southern continents they disappeared as *Majungatholus* and its kin became more common. In the northern continents tyrant dinosaurs replaced the older giants.

Sinosauropteryx
"Chinese feathered reptile"

Length: just over 3⅓ feet (1m)
Diet: meat (small animals)

Sinosauropteryx was a primitive member of the most advanced group of meat eaters, the **coelurosaurs** (hollow-tailed reptiles).

Not all theropods were giant predators.

EARLY CRETACEOUS

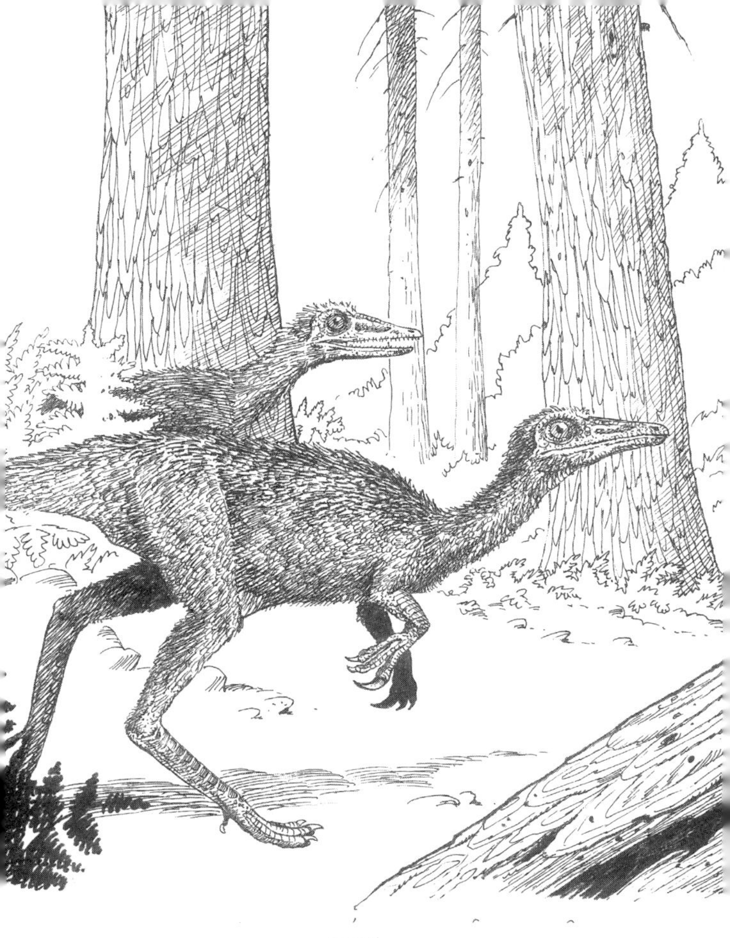

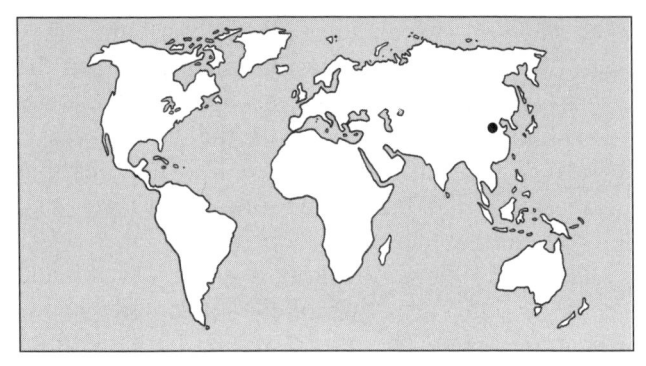

Found in China

Many (but not all) coelurosaurs were little. They had long grasping three-fingered hands and bigger brains than other types of dinosaur, and were probably smarter and more agile. Most amazing of all, new discoveries show that most—perhaps all—kinds of coelurosaurs had feathers!

We don't normally think of dinosaurs with feathers! In the modern world the only animals with feathers are birds. However, the feathers of birds had to come from some previous kind of animal.

For many decades paleontologists had known

that skeletons of coelurosaurs showed that they were the most likely ancestors of birds. Even the most primitive coelurosaurs, like the 3⅓-foot (1m)-long *Compsognathus* of the Late Jurassic Epoch of Germany and France, had features that were more like birds than like *Allosaurus* and more primitive theropods.

Then, in 1996 an amazing discovery was made in the Yixian Formation of the Early Cretaceous Epoch of China. The mud that later hardened into the rock of the Yixian Formation was made of grains so small that it preserved many little details that are normally lost when an animal becomes fossilized. The Yixian was famous for preserving the remains of the feathers of primitive birds, the patterns on the backs of Cretaceous insects, and other details. But, in 1996 the skeleton of a small dinosaur very similar to the older *Compsognathus* was discovered in the Yixian. Around the skeleton of this little theropod were the impressions of primitive feathers!

Scientists named this dinosaur *Sinosauropteryx*, the "Chinese feathered reptile." Although it was feathered, it was clearly not a bird. Instead it was a primitive coelurosaur, most likely a close relative of *Compsognathus*. This was the first discovery of feathers on a group of coelurosaurs other than birds, but it wasn't the last!

What would a dinosaur do with feathers? The arms of *Sinosauropteryx* were short but were not wings, so it couldn't use these feathers to fly. In fact, the feathers were only simple hair-like structures, and wouldn't have made good wings anyway. However, birds use their feathers for many things besides than flying. Feathers keep their bodies warm, protect their eggs when the bird is brooding on its nest, and are a form of decoration. Perhaps *Sinosauropteryx* used its feathers for some of these purposes, or perhaps all of them. There may have even been some other uses we haven't thought of yet.

Sinosauropteryx and its relative *Compsognathus* were very primitive coelurosaurs, while birds are the most specialized of this group of theropods. Paleontologists believed that because feathers are such special structures, it is unlikely that they would have evolved more than once in the history of life. So, if *Sinosauropteryx* had feathers, and birds had feathers, then they most likely had a common ancestor that also had feathers. That common ancestor would have passed these feathers on to all its descendants.

Since then, every time a more advanced coelurosaur than *Sinosauropteryx* has been found in the Yixian Formation, it has had feathers. So, strange as it seems, it appears likely that all coelurosaurs were feathered, or at least had feathered ancestors!

Pelecanimimus
"Pelican mimic"

Length: 8¼ feet (up to 2.5m)
Diet: meat (small animals, especially fish), maybe some plants?

Like a pelican, *Pelecanimimus* had a pouch underneath its throat where it could carry food.

The coelurosaurs that were more advanced than *Sinosauropteryx* branched into many different, specialized groups. One branch is the ostrich dinosaur. Like their namesakes, these dinosaurs had small heads with big eyes at the ends of long necks. Their legs were very long, which made ostrich dinosaurs probably the fastest dinosaurs of the Mesozoic Era. Unlike ostriches, though, ostrich dinosaurs had long arms ending in three-fingered hands and long bony tails.

EARLY CRETACEOUS

251

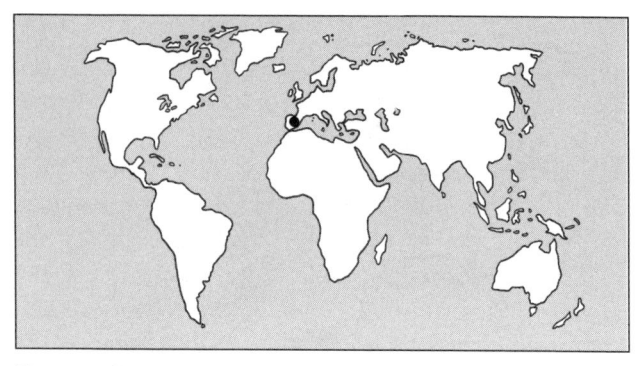

FOUND IN SPAIN

Pelecanimimus is the oldest known and the smallest known ostrich dinosaur. Most ostrich dinosaurs were toothless, but *Pelecanimimus* had 220 very small teeth. What could it have been eating with all those teeth? They were too small to rip apart the flesh of larger animals. *Pelecanimimus* may have gone after small land animals, such as mammals, lizards, and frogs. Because *Pelecanimimus* lived in a region with lakes and lagoons, some paleontologists think it may have eaten a lot of fish as well.

However, the diet of *Pelecanimimus* might have been more than the meat of small animals. The shape of the teeth of this ostrich dinosaur was something like the leaf-shaped teeth of prosauropods and ornithischians. Like these dinosaurs it might have eaten some plants, too.

Ostrich dinosaurs were very common in Asia and North America during the Late Cretaceous Epoch.

Ornithomimus
"Bird mimic"

Length: over 14 feet (about 4.3m)
Diet: meat, eggs, plants?

Ornithomimus means "bird mimic": it looked like an ostrich, but had long arms and a long tail. Along with the other ostrich dinosaurs, it was probably among the fastest dinosaurs of the Cretaceous world. It had a toothless beak like modern birds.

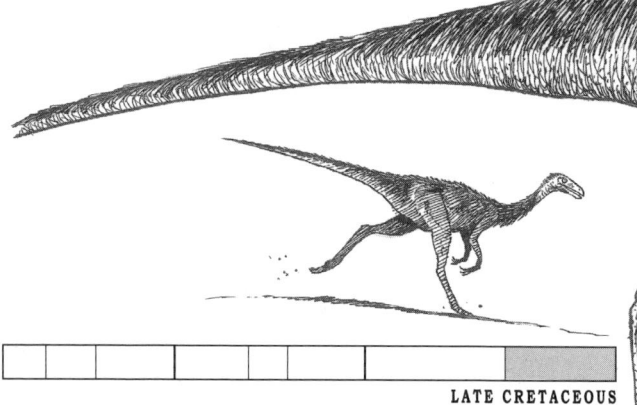

LATE CRETACEOUS

255

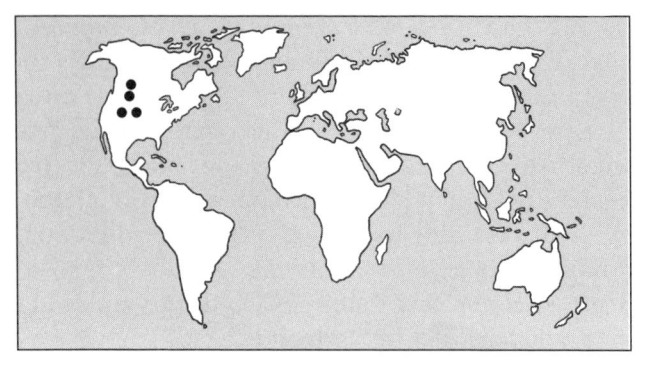

Found in Colorado, Utah, Montana, U.S.; Alberta, Canada

After *Pelecanimimus*, the ostrich dinosaurs began to lose their teeth. Primitive *Harpymimus* of the Early Cretaceous era of Mongolia had only twenty tiny teeth or so in its lower jaws; all the later ostrich dinosaurs lacked teeth altogether.

Because they had only toothless beaks, no one is quite sure what they ate. Some think they ate mostly meat, while others have suggested a diet of eggs. Still others think that plants were their main food. It is possible that, like the modern ostrich, they ate all these foods.

The hands of *Pelecanimimus*, *Ornithomimus*, and the other ostrich dinosaurs were different from other coelurosaurs. Although they had three fingers, like most other coelurosaurs, all the fingers were the same length, and not built for clutching. Instead they formed a sort of clamp, with all the fingers facing the same direction. Some paleontologists think they used this kind of hand to clamp onto branches, so they could bring fruit and leaves closer to their beaks.

The eyes and brains of ostrich dinosaurs were quite large, perhaps to help them see where they were headed while running at high speed. Their legs were very long and very slender, and their feet had a special sort of shock absorber, so that they could run fast without getting tired.

Most paleontologists don't think that ostrich dinosaurs were mostly running after their prey. They think these dinosaurs were probably running to keep from becoming prey! They lived at the same time and in the same places as *Tyrannosaurus* and the other tyrant dinosaurs, which also had the same type of long legs and shock-absorbing feet.

Tyrannosaurus
"Tyrant reptile"

Length: up to 43 feet (13m)
Diet: meat

Tyrannosaurus was the last of the giant meat-eating dinosaurs, one of a branch of giant coelurosaurs called tyrant dinosaurs. It is the most famous of all of them, and the largest.

Paleontologists once thought that *Tyrannosaurus* was a descendant of *Allosaurus* and its kin. However, details of the skeleton show that tyrant dinosaurs were actually very large meat-eating coelurosaurs, closer to ostrich dinosaurs, raptors, and birds than to *Allosaurus*. Like other coelurosaurs, tyrant dinosaurs had large brains. In fact, even though

LATE CRETACEOUS

259

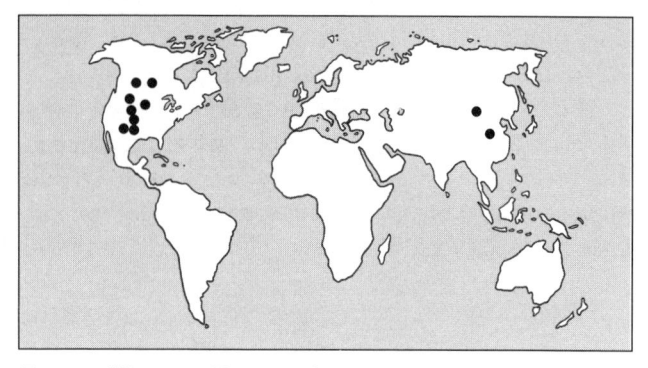

Found in Wyoming, Montana, South Dakota, Colorado, Texas, New Mexico, U.S.; Alberta, Saskatchewan, Canada; China; Mongolia

Giganotosaurus and *Carcharodontosaurus* were larger, *Tyrannosaurus* had a brain that was twice as big!

The skulls of tyrant dinosaurs were wider in back than those of *Allosaurus*. Because of this, the eyes of the tyrant dinosaurs faced further forward, so they could more easily focus on things in front of them. Also, because their skulls were wide in the back, they had bigger and stronger neck muscles.

The roof of their mouth was covered by bone, unlike the jaws of *Allosaurus* and its kin.

The teeth of tyrant dinosaurs also differed from those of most meat eaters. They were not shaped like steak knives. Instead they were as long and thick as a fat banana, and the serrations did not run exactly up the front and back. They would not have

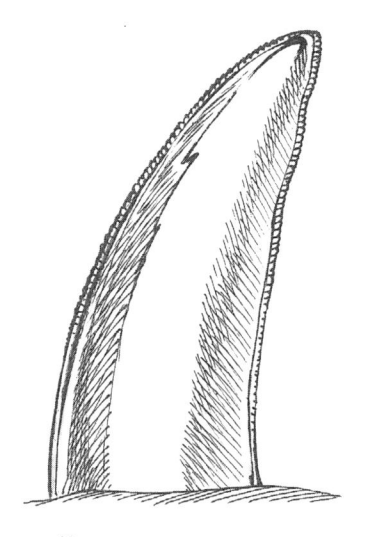

TYRANNOSAURUS TOOTH

been very good for slicing through meat, but they were so strong they could crush bones. They could also hold the flesh of their victims as the powerful neck of *Tyrannosaurus* tore big chunks of meat from its prey.

Tyrannosaurus and its relatives are famous for having very small arms. In fact, their arms were so short they could not even reach their mouth. Also, tyrant dinosaurs had only two fingers. What would tyrant dinosaurs do with such tiny arms?

It is not likely that *Tyrannosaurus* used its arms while hunting. Its jaws were much better suited for that. Instead the little arms might have helped hold on to the bodies of its victims while the jaws did their work. Or, if an adult *Tyrannosaurus* still had the feathers of its ancestors on its arms, it might have used them to signal other tyrants. Even today birds that have lost the ability to fly will signal each other with their otherwise useless wings. Right now, though, this is just speculation.

A few paleontologists think that tyrant dinosaurs were too slow to be hunters, but instead only scavenged from carcasses. However, all tyrant dinosaurs had very long and slender legs and the same kind of shock-absorbing feet found in ostrich dinosaurs. In fact, the hind limbs of tyrant dinosaurs and ostrich dinosaurs are so similar that early paleontologists thought that *Tyrannosaurus* legs were from some kind of giant *Ornithomimus*! So all tyrant dinosaurs were probably faster than the big plant-eating dinosaurs they lived with. Small tyrant dinosaurs might have even been able to run fast enough to catch large ostrich dinosaurs.

Troodon
"Wounding tooth"

Length: about 10 feet (up to 3m)
Diet: meat, eggs, plants?

Troodon was a mystery to paleontologists for a long time. When only its teeth were known, they thought it was some kind of Cretaceous lizard. Later scientists thought these leaf-shaped teeth looked like those of pachycephalosaurs, and some people used to use the name "*Troodon*" for the dome-headed dinosaur *Stegoceras*! Eventually, with better fossils,

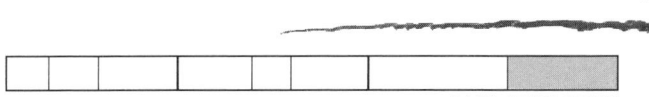

LATE CRETACEOUS

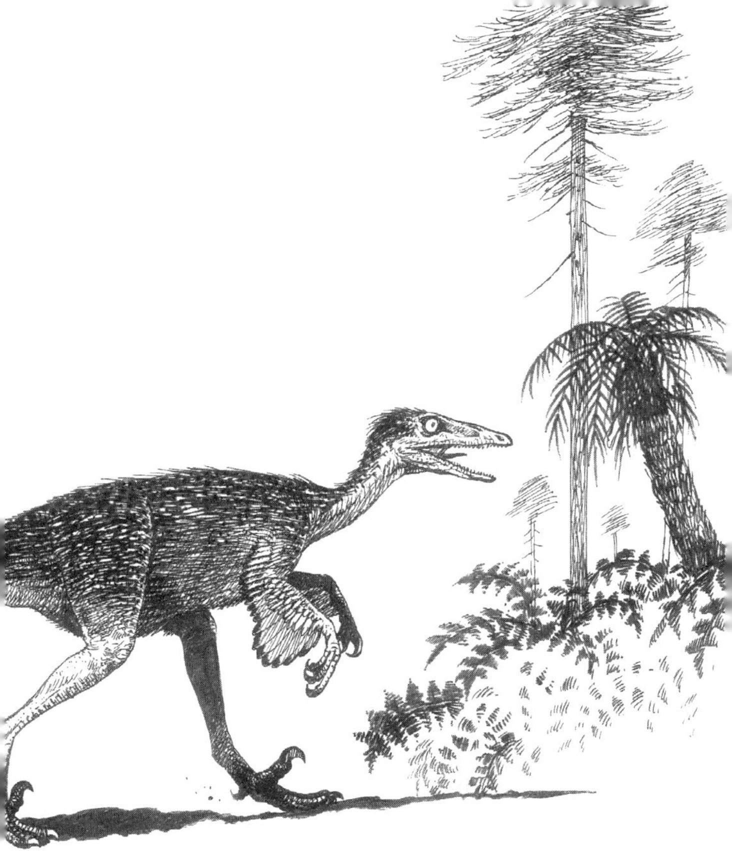

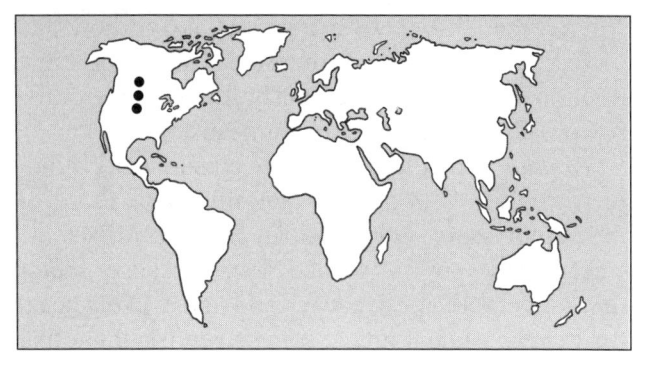

Found in Montana, Wyoming, U.S.; Alberta, Canada

they realized that *Troodon* was actually a kind of coelurosaur.

When the braincase of *Troodon* was discovered, scientists were surprised. At that time most paleontologists thought of dinosaurs as being small-brained animals. In an ornithischian or a sauropodomorph, the size of the brain compared to the size of the body was quite small. When the size of *Troodon*'s brain was compared to its body, however, it was found to be similar to those of today's primitive mammals and birds. Although this didn't suggest that *Troodon* was a genius, it did show that at least some kinds of dinosaur had a lot more brainpower than was previously thought. The same has proven true for other coelurosaurs.

Troodon's diet continues to puzzle paleontologists. Some of its features are similar to those of raptor dinosaurs. For example, it has a retractable sickle claw on its second toe. Because raptor dinosaurs were meat eaters, and most likely used their claws while hunting, some scientists think that *Troodon* was a meat eater, too. On the other hand, the shape and size of the teeth of *Troodon* are similar in some ways to the teeth of ornithischian and prosauropod dinosaurs, suggesting that they might have eaten some meat. Perhaps *Troodon* ate all kinds of food, just as bears or raccoons do today.

The arms of *Troodon*, unlike those of most other advanced coelurosaurs, were short. Their wrists had a special bone in them that let the hands fold up close against the body. This way the long arms could be tucked out of the way while it was running. *Troodon*'s legs and feet were similar to those of ostrich dinosaurs and it had the special shock-absorber feet that helped it run faster.

Caudipteryx
"Feather tail"

Length: 4 feet (over 1.2m)
Diet: plants, meat?

Caudipteryx was another of the dinosaurs found in the Yixian Formation of the Early Cretaceous Epoch of China. On its arms and its tail it had long feathers.

A few paleontologists think that *Caudipteryx* was some kind of flightless bird, like a prehistoric turkey, because the feathers on its

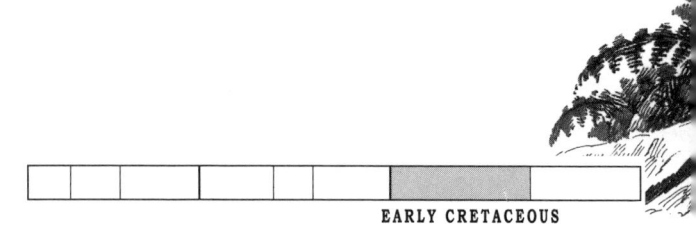

EARLY CRETACEOUS

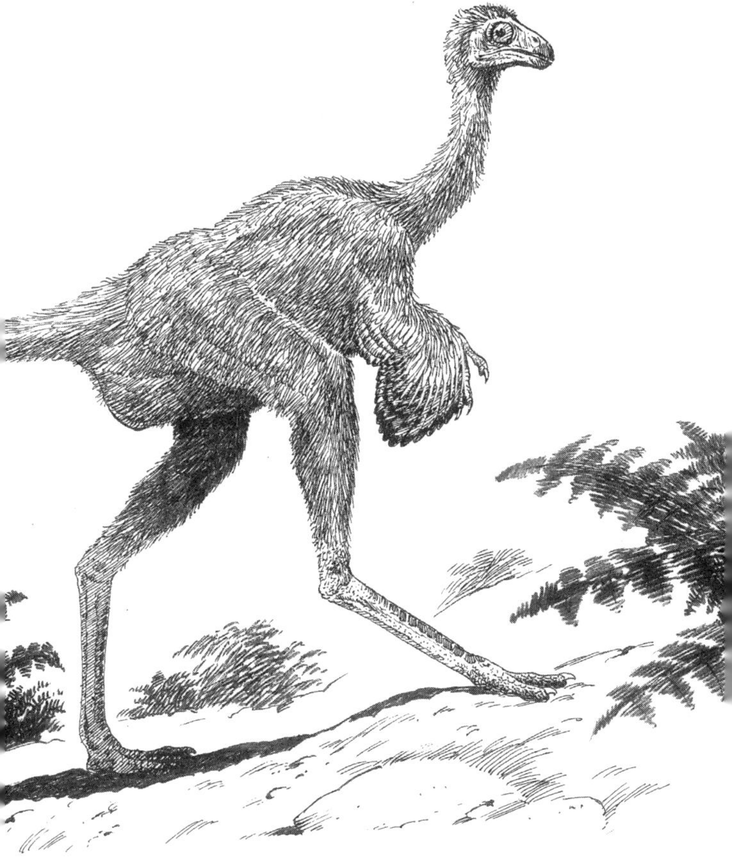

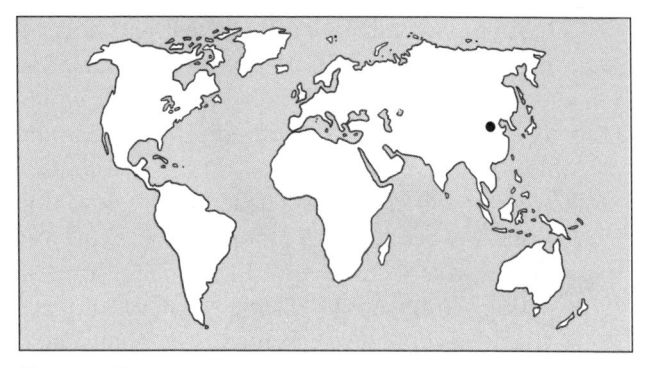

FOUND IN CHINA

arms and tail look more like the feathers of birds than those of *Sinosauropteryx*. However, the skeleton of *Caudipteryx* shows that it was a closer relative of *Oviraptor* than of birds.

What use would the long, broad feathers on the short arms and tail of *Caudipteryx* serve? Some have suggested that they were mostly decorations. Others have thought that they might have been used to protect its nest while it was brooding. Recently scientists have discovered fossils showing that various types of coelurosaurs, such as *Troodon* and *Oviraptor*, would lie on their nest and cover it with their arms and tail. If these dinosaurs had longer feathers, like those of *Caudipteryx*, it would help to keep those eggs covered. Both ideas are possible.

Caudipteryx had a small head with a few tiny teeth in its lower jaw. The shape of the skull and the little peg-like teeth are not like those of typical meat-eating dinosaurs. Some paleontologists think that *Caudipteryx* was mostly a plant eater, using its little beak to bite off bits of plants that the gizzard stones in its belly would grind up. However, it might also have eaten small mammals, fish, lizards, amphibians, and the like.

The bones of another small bird-like dinosaur, called *Microvenator*, were found in the Early Cretaceous rocks of Montana many years before *Caudipteryx* was discovered. *Microvenator* also seems to be related to *Oviraptor*. Unfortunately, because *Microvenator* was not found in the fine-grained mud like the Yixian, we may never know for sure if the little Montana dinosaur also had long feathers on its arms and tail.

Oviraptor
"Egg thief"

Length: over 11½ feet (up to 3.5m)
Diet: meat, plants, eggs?

One of the strangest looking of all the branches of the coelurosaur family tree was *Oviraptor* and its relatives.

Like ostrich dinosaurs, these theropods had

LATE CRETACEOUS

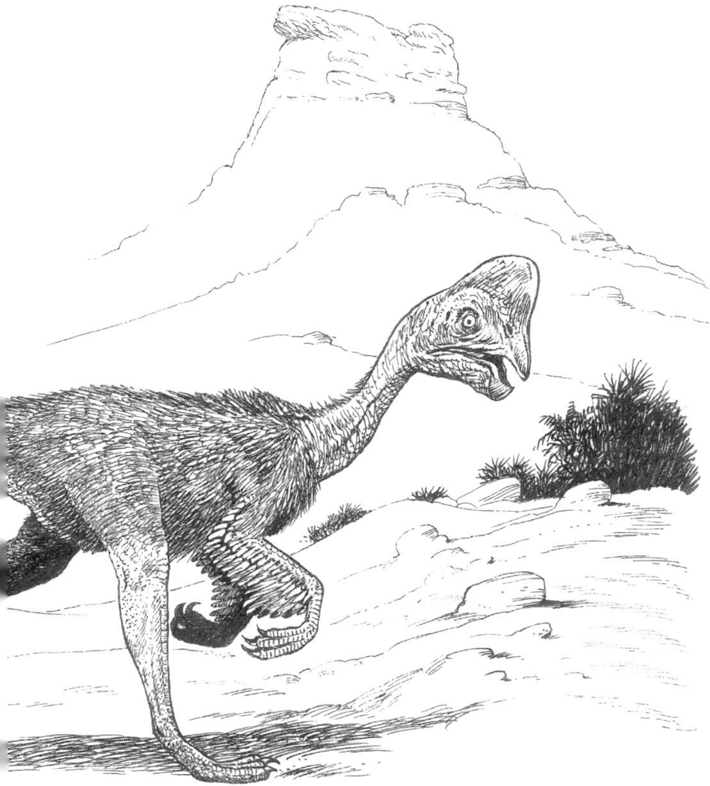

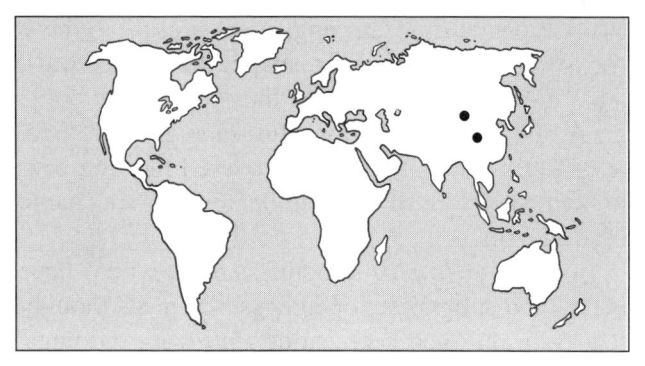

FOUND IN MONGOLIA; CHINA

toothless beaks, but unlike ostrich dinosaurs, their heads did not look much like those of birds. Instead, they had short boxy skulls with deep jaws, and, in some cases, tall crests on the top. *Oviraptor* had, long arms with big hands that it could fold up against its body.

The name *Oviraptor* means "egg thief." It got this name because of a famous misunderstanding. In the sandstones of Mongolia where *Oviraptor* was found, the most common kind of dinosaur was *Protoceratops*, the little ceratopsian. Also, many types of dinosaur eggs were present in these rocks. Most of them were shaped like long ovals, and paleontologists thought they must have come from the most common dinosaur in the area, *Protoceratops*. Later they uncovered the first ever known skeleton of *Oviraptor* among the same kind of eggs.

Because *Oviraptor*'s toothless beak would have been good at breaking open eggs, scientists thought that *Oviraptor* had been eating *Protoceratops* eggs. Almost seventy years later other paleontologists found out that this was a mistake. Inside one of the eggs that people had thought were *Protoceratops* eggs was the skeleton of a baby *Oviraptor*. It turned out these were *Oviraptor* eggs, and not *Protoceratops* eggs after all!

Since then other skeletons of *Oviraptor* have been found with their nests. These fossils reveal that *Oviraptor* covered its eggs in the nest, protecting them from the heat of the day, the cold of desert nights, or from true egg eaters.

What was the true diet of *Oviraptor*? It's hard to tell. Many different foods have been suggested: eggs, meat, plants, and shellfish.

Beipiaosaurus
"Beipiao reptile"

Beipiao is a city in China.

Length: about 7⅓ feet (up to 2.2m)
Diet: plants

Beipiaosaurus was another feathered coelurosaur found in the Early Cretaceous Yixian Formation of China. It is one of the oldest and most primitive examples of a very strange branch of the coelurosaurs.

Beipiaosaurus had a jaw full of teeth that looked more like those of a prosauropod than

EARLY CRETACEOUS

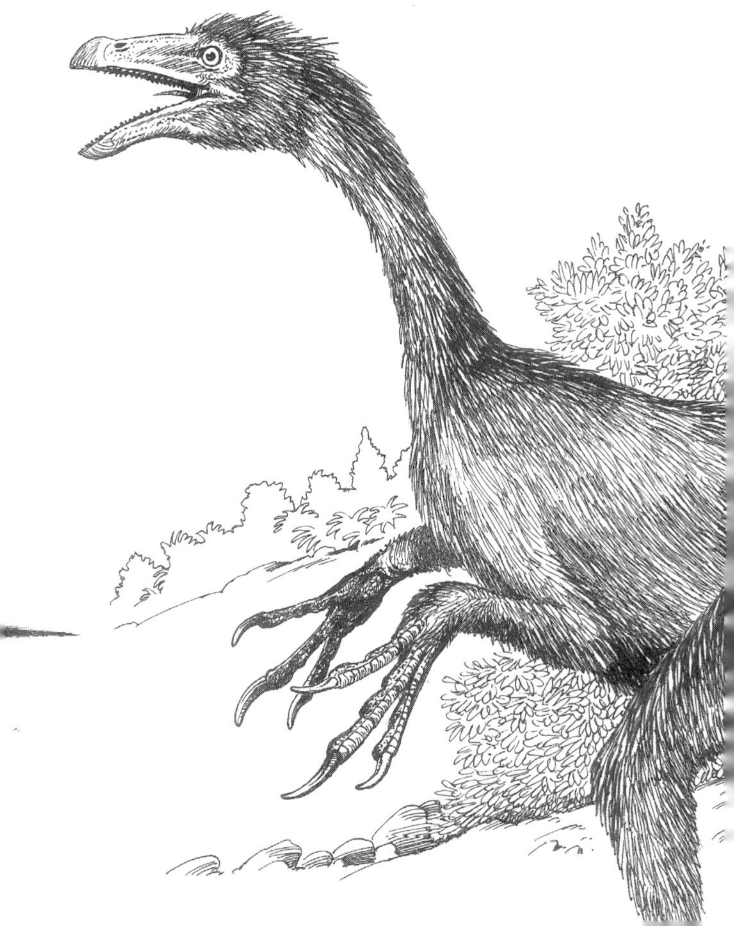

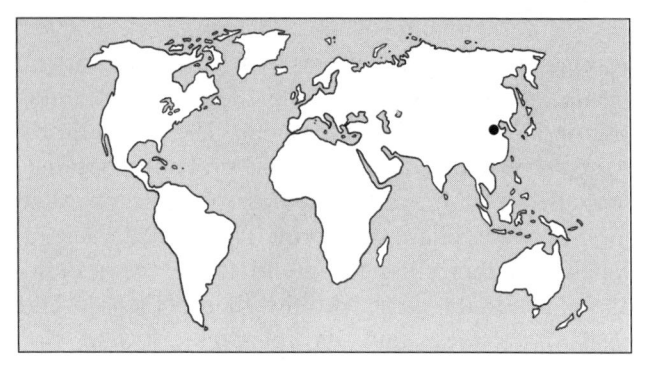

FOUND IN CHINA

those of a theropod. It probably ate only plants. The rest of its skeleton, though, showed that it was a theropod. It had a three-fingered hand with the special folding wrist joint and a foot where only three toes touched the ground. Along its arms were long, simple hair-like feathers.

In this weird branch of coelurosaur, the pubis bone in the hips points backwards, like in ornithischian dinosaurs. As in ornithischian dinosaurs this backwards-pointing bone helped make more room for a big gut that would digest all the plants it ate.

The descendants of *Beipiaosaurus* were even stranger looking than it was. They had very small heads at the ends of long necks, more like sauropodomorphs than theropods. Their hind limbs were very short for theropods, probably because they had become slow-moving plant eaters that didn't have to chase their prey. Their feet shrank so much that their first toe could touch the ground again, like in the most primitive theropods.

Beipiaosaurus and its relatives all had big claws on their hands. In the case of its giant *Tyrannosaurus*-sized relative, Late Cretaceous *Therizinosaurus* of Mongolia, these claws were almost 3⅓-feet (1m)-long! Why should plant-eating dinosaurs have big claws?

Perhaps they used their claws and strong arms to break down tree branches so they could eat the leaves. Another possible use for big claws would be defense. *Beipiaosaurus* and its relatives would be too heavy to run fast from meat-eating theropods, but they could use their powerful claws to strike out at attackers. After getting slashed by these big claws, any predator would think twice before going after *Beipiaosaurus* again.

Deinonychus
"Terrible claws"

Length: about 10 feet (up to 3m)
Diet: meat

The discovery of *Deinonychus*, the first raptor dinosaur known from more than just a few bones, changed the way scientists think about dinosaurs.

EARLY CRETACEOUS

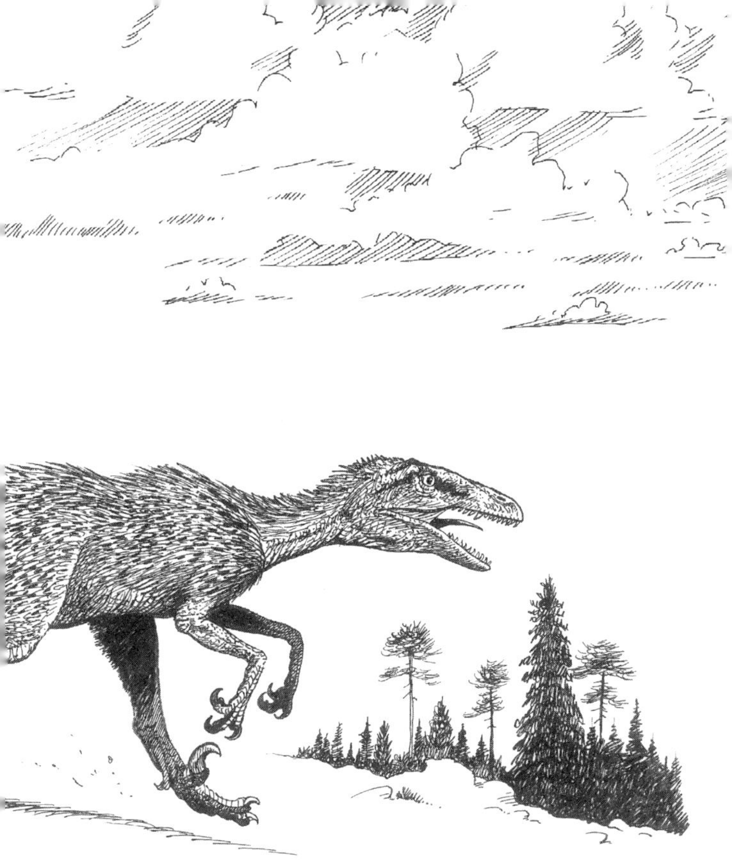

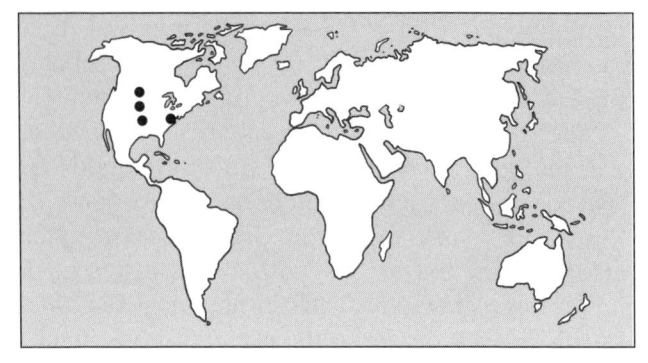

FOUND IN: MONTANA, WYOMING, OKLAHOMA, POSSIBLY MARYLAND, U.S.

Before *Deinonychus* was discovered, many paleontologists thought of dinosaurs as being slow-moving and stupid, more like land-living crocodiles than fast, agile hunters. In the 1960s John Ostrom of Yale University found some of the first skeletons of a new type of small coelurosaur. It had jaws full of sharp curved teeth, and long grasping arms with the special folding joint now known in many types of coelurosaur. Its tail was unusual: it had long, stiffening, bony rods for most of its length, similar to the tail of the ornithopod *Hypsilophodon* and its relatives. Like those small ornithopods, *Deinonychus* probably used that stiff tail to make fast turns while running.

The most unusual thing about *Deinonychus* was the bones of its foot. Like most theropods, its first toe was so short it didn't reach the ground. Its third and fourth toes were like those of other coelurosaurs, but its second toe was different. It had a huge claw, very curved and very flat side-to-side. It was similar to the claws of lions, tigers, and other big cats; and, like cats' claws, it could

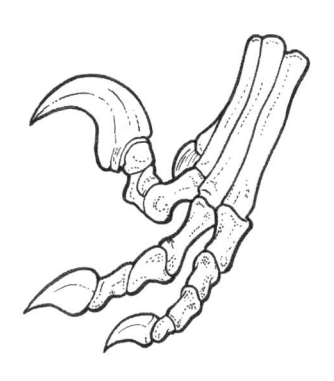

DEINONYCHUS FOOT BONES

be retracted upwards so that *Deinonychus* would not break it while running.

This suggested to Ostrom that *Deinonychus* was an agile, fast hunter, something like a big cat. It could leap on a victim (like the ornithopod *Tenontosaurus*) and use its big foot claw to tear and rip at the sides of the prey, just as a lion might when it attacks a big antelope. Because paleontologists often found the remains of more than one *Deinonychus* with the bones of a single *Tenontosaurus*, Ostrom suggested that the smaller theropod used teamwork, hunting as a gang to attack the much larger plant eater.

That's how *Deinonychus* changed what people thought about the way some dinosaurs attacked. Instead of being slow-moving land crocodiles, they seemed to be quick and cunning hunters. But there were other surprises in store in the skeleton of *Deinonychus*.

The hip bones of *Deinonychus* showed that its pubis bone pointed backwards. This was a little like the hips of ornithischian dinosaurs, but unlike them, *Deinonychus* was no plant eater. However, there was another creature that had hips just like those of

Deinonychus: the early bird *Archaeopteryx*. Ostrom then compared more details in the skeletons of *Deinonychus* and *Archaeopteryx*, and found that they were incredibly similar. He suggested that *Deinonychus* and other raptor dinosaurs were the closest of all known dinosaurs to the ancestors of birds.

Velociraptor
"Swift hunter"

Length: about 6½ feet (up to 2m)
Diet: meat

Velociraptor was a famous meat-eating dinosaur. It was small (only as heavy as a greyhound dog) but fierce. In Mongolia, a skeleton of *Velociraptor* and *Protoceratops* were found together— the arms of the hunter were holding on to the ceratopsian's head, and the sickle-like claw was inside the neck of the much heavier *Protoceratops*!

LATE CRETACEOUS

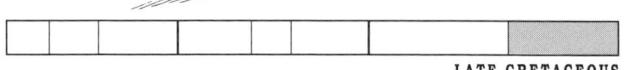

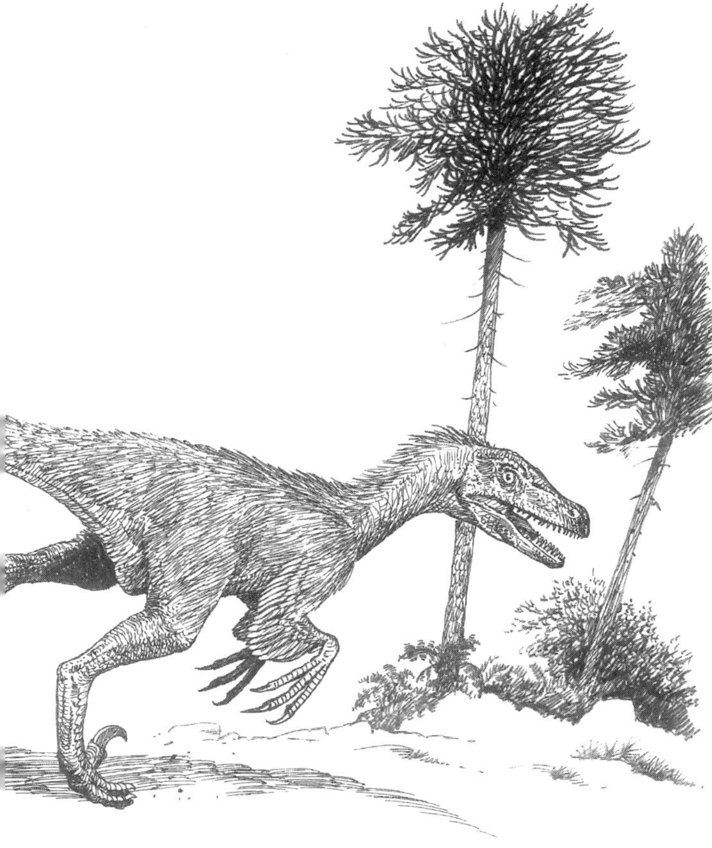

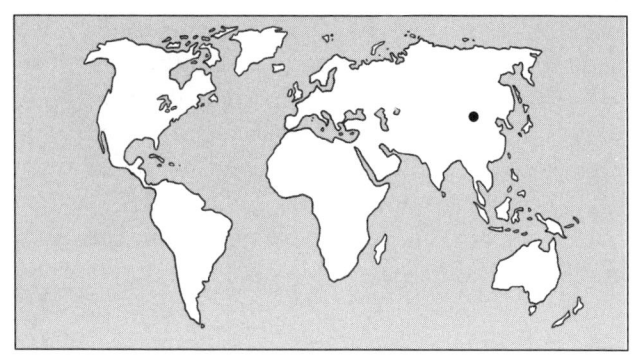

FOUND IN MONGOLIA

Although the first skeleton of this little Mongolian dinosaur had been found long before Ostrom found *Deinonychus*, *Velociraptor* was only known from a skull and bits and pieces of a skeleton—not enough to realize how special it was. After *Deinonychus* was found, paleontologists began to recognize that *Velociraptor* was a smaller relative of that American dinosaur. In fact, they gave *Deinonychus*, *Velociraptor*, and their whole branch of the coelurosaur family tree the nickname "raptor dinosaurs" in honor of this Mongolian predator.

Velociraptor was basically a smaller version of *Deinonychus*: it had the same long, grasping arms, backwards-pointing hip bone, sickle-shaped claw on its foot, and extra-stiff tail. Like *Deinonychus*, *Velociraptor* seemed to have attacked animals much bigger than itself.

Other raptor dinosaurs are known to paleontology. *Saurornitholestes* of the Late Cretaceous Epoch of North America is very similar to *Velociraptor*; some paleontologists think they are the same dinosaur. Perhaps most interesting is *Sinornithosaurus* from the Early Cretaceous Yixian Formation of China. This little raptor, even smaller than *Velociraptor*, has been found to have been covered with feathers. In fact, many paleontologists now think that all raptor dinosaurs were covered with feathers, including famous *Velociraptor* and *Deinonychus*.

Archaeopteryx
"Ancient wing"

Length: about 20 inches (about 0.5m)
Diet: meat?

One of the most famous dinosaurs, *Archaeopteryx* is also the most famous early bird. Its fossils have been found with feather impressions. Because it is such an early, primitive bird, paleontologists recognize that it was closely related to *Deinonychus* and *Velociraptor*.

Few discoveries in paleontology have caused as much of a stir as *Archaeopteryx*. When it was first found, it showed something very remarkable: a combination of the features of modern birds and of primitive reptiles. Like modern birds it had feathers, a three-fingered hand, a backwards-pointing first toe placed at the bottom of the foot, a backwards-pointing pubis, and a wishbone. Unlike modern birds, but like other reptiles, it had

LATE JURASSIC

separate fingers with claws rather than a hand that was fused together; individual tailbones all the way to the tip, instead of a fused mass of bones at the end; and teeth in its jaws instead of a toothless

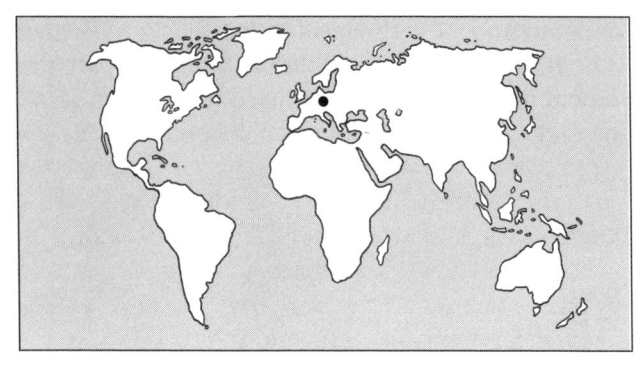

FOUND IN GERMANY

beak. Even though most scientists regarded it as a true bird, it showed clearly that birds had evolved from some kind of reptile.

With the discovery of many kinds of extinct reptiles, scientists now have a good idea about where birds came from. Many of the features that were once known only in birds, like feathers, a three-fingered hand, and wishbones, are now known to be present in advanced theropods, particularly coelurosaurs. In fact, the only creatures that have the exact combination of features found in

Archaeopteryx are raptor dinosaurs. Paleontologists do not think that *Archaeopteryx* is a direct descendant of raptor dinosaurs, but that *Archaeopteryx* (and later birds) and raptor dinosaurs all evolved from the same common ancestor. The branch with the raptor dinosaurs became ferocious predators with huge sickle claws and an extra-stiff tail. The branch with *Archaeopteryx* and later birds evolved longer and stronger feathers on the arm, and a special ability found in no other dinosaur—the ability to fly!

Some scientists think that *Archaeopteryx* could only live on the ground, so that flight began from the ground up. Others think that *Archaeopteryx* must have lived in trees, so that flight began with earlier tree-dwelling dinosaurs gliding from branch to branch. In fact, *Archaeopteryx* looks as if it would have been equally at home on the ground, running after lizards and mammals, and up in the trees, using its backwards-pointing first toe to hold on to branches. We may never know exactly how flight began, but whether it was from the ground up or the trees down, fossils show us clearly that birds are just one of the many branches of the coelurosaur dinosaurs.

Rahonavis
"Bird that menaces from above"

Length: about 20 inches (around 0.5m)
Diet: meat?

Rahonavis was a primitive bird, about the size of a modern crow. Its skeleton was very similar to that of *Velociraptor*: it even had a little sickle claw. Scientists think that, if it was a meat eater, it might have flown on top of its victims and attacked them with its clawed feet.

At present only a single skeleton of *Rahonavis* has been found, and this is missing most of its front end. Even so, it gives us hints about the weird kinds of bird that lived alongside (and over the heads of!) other dinosaurs.

LATE CRETACEOUS

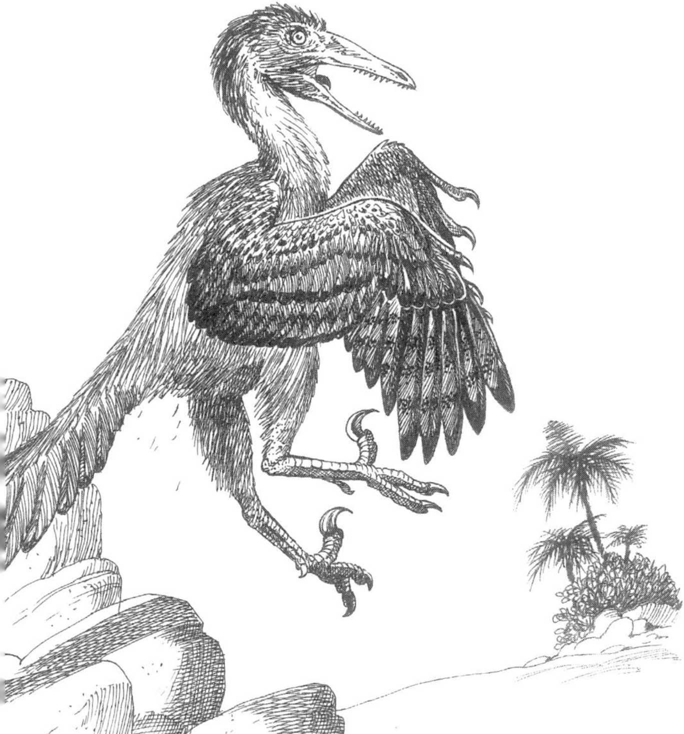

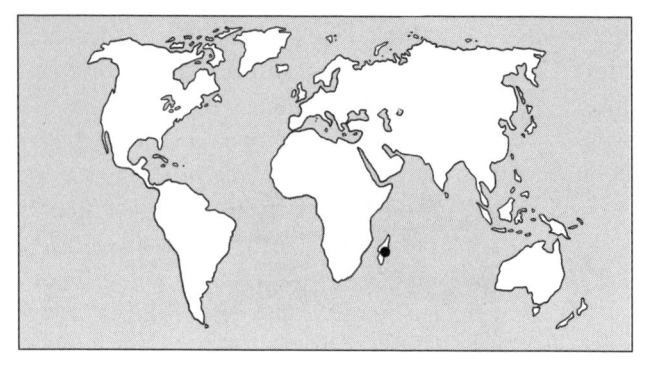

FOUND IN MADAGASCAR

Rahonavis lived at the same time and place as the theropod *Majungatholus*. The skeleton of the little coelurosaur looks something like *Archaeopteryx*, but it has sickle-claws on its feet like the raptor dinosaurs. Paleontologists wish they had more of the skeleton of this creature so that they could figure out more details about how it lived, what it ate, and so on.

Should *Rahonavis* be called a dinosaur or a bird?

Once scientists had to make a decision about

questions like this. Back then they regarded "birds" and "dinosaurs" as different types of creatures, even if they recognized that birds were actually the descendants of dinosaurs. Now, however, they don't have to make that choice. Once an animal is part of one group, it and its descendants will always be part of that group. Because birds are the descendants of dinosaurs, they are still part of the dinosaur family. So, *Rahonavis* is a dinosaur *and* a bird!

Shuvuuia
"Bird"

Length: about 3 feet (up to 0.9m)
Diet: insects? plants?

Shuvuuia and its relatives are extremely weird-looking dinosaurs. Their arms are very short and have only one big claw. Their legs are built for fast running. They may, in fact, be a bizarre group of early birds.

Bits and pieces of the skeleton of *Shuvuuia* or one of its close relatives were found

LATE CRETACEOUS

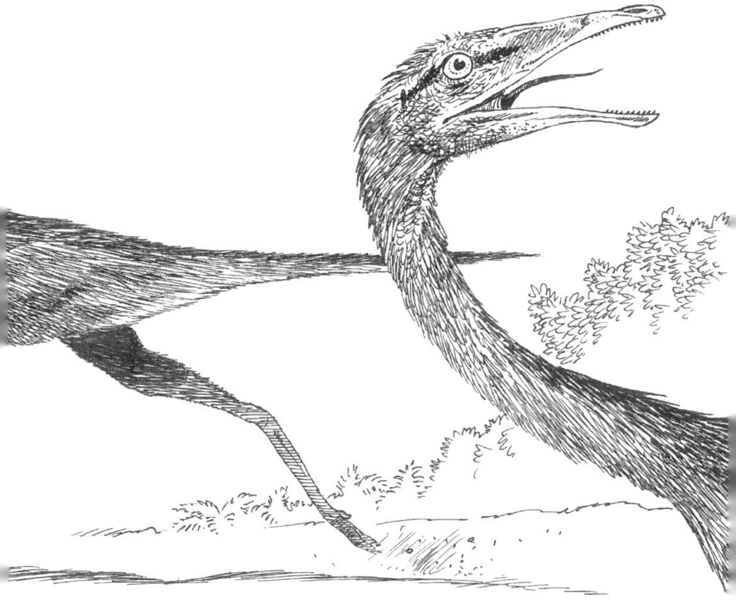

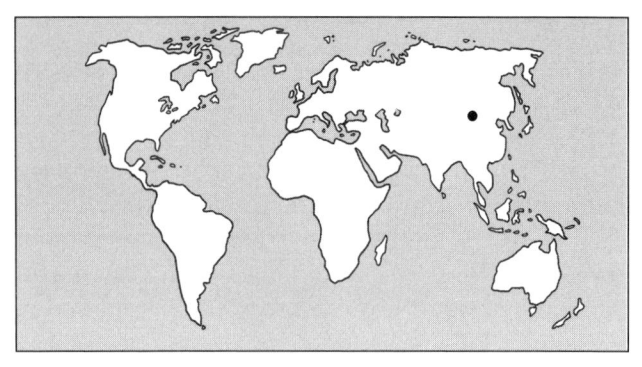

FOUND IN MONGOLIA

long ago in the deserts of Mongolia. However, it wasn't until seventy years later that enough remains of these remarkable little dinosaurs were found to figure out what the whole animal looked like.

Like ostrich dinosaurs, *Shuvuuia* and its kin had a small head on a long neck and only tiny teeth in their jaws. They had backwards-pointing hip bones. Their arms were very short but extremely strong, and their hands had only one working finger (their thumb), which ended in a big claw. Their legs were long and good for running, and *Shuvuuia* and a few of its relatives even had a special shock-absorbing foot, like that found in tyrant and ostrich dinosaurs.

No one is quite certain how *Shuvuuia* lived. It probably didn't hunt big animals, but it may have chased small lizards and mammals. Some scientists think it might have eaten ants and other insects. Its long legs would have been very useful in running away from predators; in fact, it lived in the same deserts as *Velociraptor*, so it certainly needed some way to escape.

Paleontologists are still unsure about where *Shuvuuia* and its relatives fit in the family tree of coelurosaurs. Some think they are close relatives of the ostrich dinosaur, while others think that they are actually a type of early bird. Wherever they belong among the theropods, they are clearly among the strangest creatures that lived in the Mesozoic world!

Confuciusornis
"Confucius bird"

Named for the ancient Chinese philosopher.

Length: about 6 inches (15cm)
Diet: plants? insects?

Confuciusornis was a primitive Chinese bird. In some ways it was more like modern birds than *Archaeopteryx*. Its jaws didn't have any teeth, and its tail ended with most of the bones fused together into a short stump. Like *Archaeopteryx*, but unlike modern birds, though, it still had separate fingers, which ended with claws. Some *Confuciusornis* had a pair of

EARLY CRETACEOUS

FOUND IN CHINA

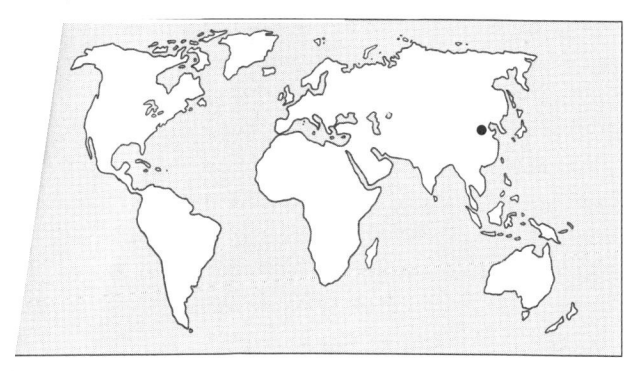

long feathers coming from its tail, but some didn't; maybe the ones with long tail feathers were adult males, and the ones without were babies and females.

Like *Sinosauropteryx*, *Caudipteryx*, *Beipiaosaurus*, *Sinornithosaurus*, and other coelurosaurs found in the Yixian Formation, *Confuciusornis* fossils are surrounded by the impressions of feathers. However, unlike the smaller feathers on the arms of other types of coelurosaurs, those on the wings of *Confuciusornis* were big enough to help it fly! With its grasping hands and feet, *Confuciusornis* probably

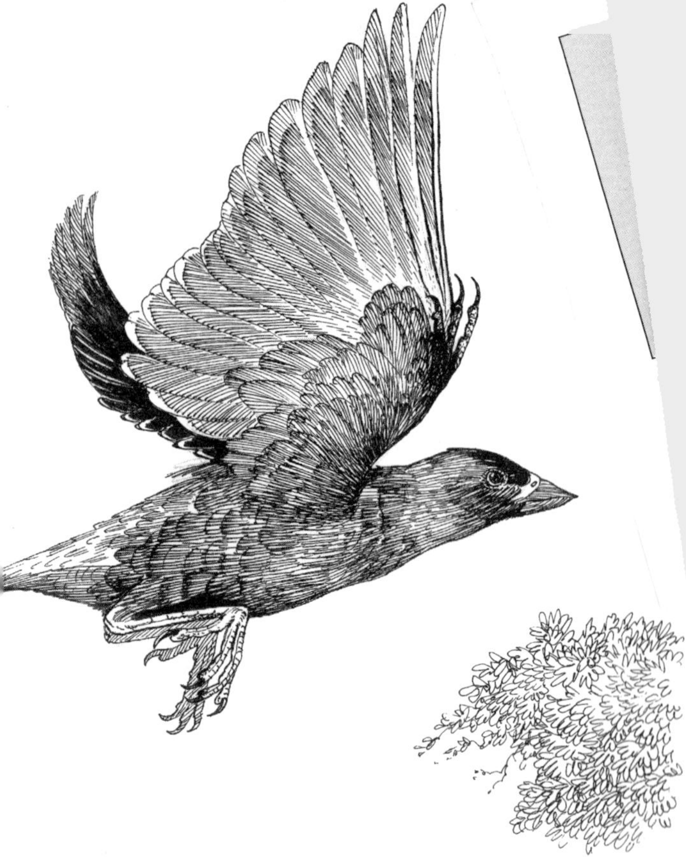

clambered around in the trees of ancient China, using both flight and climbing to get away from its hungry, but land-bound, coelurosaur relatives.

Although the beak of *Confuciusornis* didn't have any teeth, paleontologists do not think it was very closely related to modern birds. Other birds from the Age of Dinosaurs had skeletons more like modern birds, but still had teeth. In these other birds, the fingers lost their claws and were fused together. Also, the breastbones of these other birds had a big ridge or keel down the middle. As with modern birds, this keel was where the strong flying muscles were attached.

No one is quite sure what *Confuciusornis* ate. Maybe it ate fruit: in fact, some of the oldest fruit plants known to science come from the same Yixian Formation! Maybe they used their beaks to crack open seeds. Possibly they ate insects or small mammals or lizards or amphibians. Until paleontologists find the remains of a meal in the belly of a *Confuciusornis* skeleton, we can only guess.

Hesperornis
"Western bird"

Length: about 5 feet (up to 1.5m)
Diet: fish

Many older dinosaur books say that there were no sea-going dinosaurs. While it is true that the dolphin-like ichthyosaurs, the long-necked plesiosaurs, and the sea lizards called mosasaurs were not dinosaurs at all, we now know that one type of dinosaur did live in the water: the sea bird *Hesperornis*.

In the modern world, not all birds fly. Some, like ostriches and kiwis, live all their life on the ground. Others, like penguins, spend a lot of their time in the water.

The same was true in the Late Cretaceous Epoch. Some birds, like *Patagopteryx* of Argentina and *Gargantuavis* of France, were strictly ground birds. *Hesperornis* was a swimming bird.

LATE CRETACEOUS

307

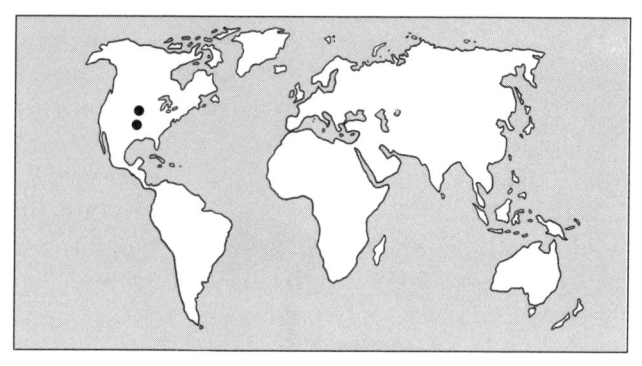

Found in Kansas, Nebraska, U.S.

Not only had the wings of *Hesperornis* shrunk up—all the bones below the elbow had disappeared. Its legs stuck out of the back of its body, and its feet had become flippers. It was quite a large bird, up to 5 feet (1.5m) long. It probably went on shore only for brief periods, and to lay its eggs.

Like most Mesozoic birds, *Hesperornis* still had teeth in its beak. It probably fed on the many fish that lived in the shallow seas that covered the middle parts of North America back in the Late Cretaceous Epoch. *Hesperornis* would have had to keep a watch out for some of the marine reptiles with which it shared the oceans of Kansas, like the 33-foot (10m) -long sea lizard *Tylosaurus*.

Why should birds become sea animals? Even today many kinds of birds—gulls, albatrosses, frigate birds, puffins, and so on—get most of their food from the sea. This was also true in the Mesozoic Era. Some of the fish-eating birds of the Cretaceous Period would spend a lot of time down in the water as well as flying above it. The descendants of some of these birds spent so much time in the water that their wings began to shrink. Eventually, this led to the wingless sea bird *Hesperornis*.

• 10 •
MODERN BIRDS

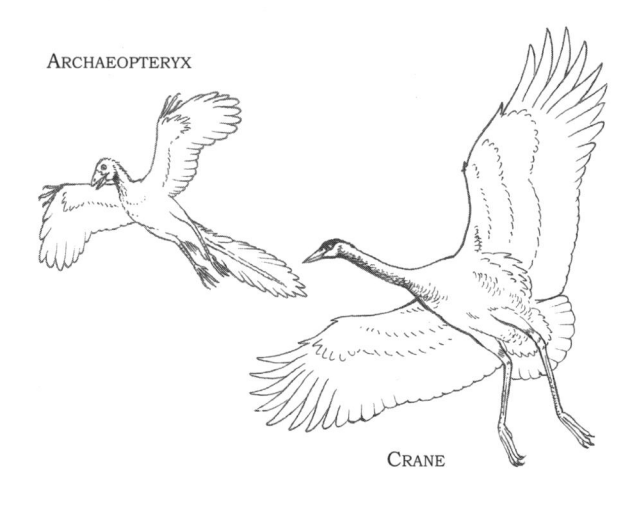

ARCHAEOPTERYX

CRANE

Most people don't think of birds as being dinosaurs, but fossils show that they are. We now know that many dinosaurs other than birds also had feathers. Just as bats are still mammals—even though they fly—birds are still dinosaurs. Of all the groups of dinosaurs, only modern toothless birds survived the great extinction at the end of the Cretaceous Period.

Modern birds have several features in common. They all have toothless beaks. They all have "hands" in which the fingers are fused together, tails where the bones at the end are all fused into a single piece (as in *Confuciusornis* and later birds), feet with the first toe located at the bottom and facing backwards (as in *Archaeopteryx*), pubis bones in the hips that face backwards (as in the raptor dinosaurs), special folding joints in the wrist to let the hand fold against the body (as in *Oviraptor*), feathers (as in *Sinosauropteryx*), wishbones (as in *Coelophysis*), hollow bones (as in *Eoraptor*), and legs that are held directly underneath the body (as in *Lagosuchus* and other primitive dinosaur relatives). As you can see, many of the features that make birds special in the modern world were just passed on from their earlier dinosaur ancestors.

Modern-type birds were already present at the end of the Age of Dinosaurs. Although their fossils are only fragments, possible Late Cretaceous parrots, ducks, loons, and others have been found alongside their bigger dinosaur relatives.

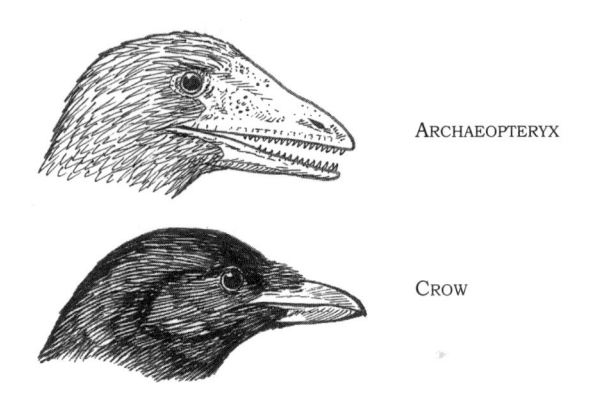

ARCHAEOPTERYX

CROW

Although dinosaurs like *Triceratops*, *Anatotitan*, and *Tyrannosaurus* would look out of place in the modern world, these smaller dinosaurs probably looked a lot like their modern descendants. Not all dinosaurs were strange giants!

· 11 ·
THE WORLDS OF THE DINOSAURS

Not all dinosaurs lived in the same place and at the same time. The first dinosaurs appeared almost 235 million years ago, and the last dinosaurs (other than birds) died out 65 million years ago. In fact, the last of the giant dinosaurs, like *Tyrannosaurus* and *Triceratops*, live much closer to you in time than to earlier dinosaurs like *Stegosaurus* and *Apatosaurus*, and more than twice as close to you as to the earliest dinosaurs like *Herrerasaurus* and *Saturnalia*!

Scientists divide the long ages of the Earth into different sections. The last 545 million years are divided into three big sections, called **eras**:

The Paleozoic Era
The Mesozoic Era
The Cenozoic Era

The Paleozoic Era

The first of these, called the **Paleozoic** (ancient life) **Era,** lasted from 545 to 251 million years ago. During the Paleozoic Era, the first animals with backbones—primitive fish—appeared. Much later, plants, then arachnids and insects, and finally the first amphibians moved onto the land. By the latter part of the Paleozoic, vertebrates with shelled eggs, including protomammals and true reptiles, were common.

The Mesozoic Era

The next section of time, the **Mesozoic (middle life) Era,** lasted from 251 to 65 million years ago. It was during this period that the great dinosaurs dominated the land. The Mesozoic Era is divided into three sections: first the **Triassic Period,** then the **Jurassic Period,** and finally the **Cretaceous Period.** During the Mesozoic Era, many types of reptile returned to the sea; flying reptiles called **pterosaurs** and birds took to the air; and the first mammals and the first flowers and fruit plants appeared.

The Cenozoic Era

After the Mesozoic came the **Cenozoic** (recent life) **Era,** which began 65 million years ago and continues today. During the Cenozoic Era furry warm-blooded mammals became a major group of land animals and grasslands began to cover large sections of the Earth. During the last two million years great sheets of ice moved down from the poles and from the mountains to cover huge areas, only to retreat again.

Throughout these eras it wasn't just animals and plants that were changing. The surface of the Earth is divided into huge sections called **plates** that move slowly against each other. The folding and crumpling of these plates formed the great mountain chains. As the plates collided and separated, the continents themselves joined and then broke apart. The levels of the seas changed through time. At some periods shallow seas covered large parts of the land, and other times the land was high and dry.

All these changes acting together—animals, plants, land, and water—mean that as time goes by the world looks very different. Let us take a look at some of the different worlds in which the dinosaurs lived.

The Triassic Period

The **Triassic Period** ran from 251 to 205 million years ago. The word "Triassic" means "three-part," so called because this Period is divided into three sections: the **Early Triassic Epoch,** the **Middle Triassic Epoch,** and the **Late Triassic Epoch.**

THE EARLY TRIASSIC EPOCH

During the Early Triassic Epoch all the continents of the world had collided to form a single super-landmass. This supercontinent is called **Pangaea** (all lands). Because all the lands were joined, land animals from one part of the world could move with ease to any other part of the world. Protomammals were the most important group of animals on land.

THE MIDDLE TRIASSIC EPOCH

During the Middle Triassic the surface of the land became drier. Because true reptiles can deal with dry conditions better than mammals and their ancestors, reptiles became more important. The relatives of the ancestors of crocodiles evolved into many forms: huge meat eaters, armored plant eaters, and more. Under the shadow of these creatures the tiny ancestors of the dinosaurs appeared: small running two-legged reptiles, such as *Lagosuchus*. These dinosaur-ancestors ran around on legs held directly under their body.

THE LATE TRIASSIC EPOCH

In the Late Triassic true dinosaurs appeared. Early ornithischians, early sauropodomorphs, and early theropods became common and were found all over the world. Theropods like *Eoraptor*, *Herrerasaurus*, and *Coelophysis* hunted smaller animals, but there were bigger predators among the crocodile relatives that hunted the theropods. Early ornithischians like *Pisanosaurus* were among the smaller but faster plant eaters. Early prosauropods like *Saturnalia* became the first plant eaters that could feed from higher up than the ground; later prosauropods like *Plateosaurus* became the largest animals on land.

Other new creatures appeared: the first turtles, the first lizards, the first crocodiles, and the first mammals. Some reptiles began to return to the sea; among these were the **ichthyosaurs** (fish reptiles), which spent their entire life in the water and evolved bodies that looked a lot like dolphins. Other reptiles developed long wings and became flying reptiles called **pterosaurs** (winged reptiles).

During the last few million years of the Late Triassic Epoch, many of the earlier types of animals began to die out. The last of the protomammals and the last of the crocodile-relatives disappeared. No one is quite certain why these groups died, but when they were gone, the mighty dinosaurs were the rulers of the land.

The Jurassic Period

The **Jurassic Period** lasted from 205 to 144 million years ago. It is named after the Jura Mountains on the border of France and Switzerland. Like the Triassic Period, the Jurassic Period is divided into three sections: the **Early Jurassic Epoch,** the **Middle Jurassic Epoch,** and the **Late Jurassic Epoch.**

THE EARLY JURASSIC EPOCH

The dinosaurs of the Early Jurassic Epoch were very similar to those of the Late Triassic. The most primitive theropods, like *Eoraptor* and *Herrerasaurus*, had died out, and theropods very similar to *Coelophysis* were the most common meat eaters. Some of these, like *Dilophosaurus*, became the largest meat eaters on land. Prosauropods were the most common large plant eaters. Small ornithopods, like *Heterodontosaurus,* became common. The first thyreophorans, like *Scutellosaurus,* appeared. Because the armor of these little dinosaurs didn't protect them against large theropods, thyreophorans quickly evolved into bigger and heavier forms like *Scelidosaurus.*

In the seas a new group of reptile appeared—the long-necked **plesiosaurs.** Pterosaurs continued to fly in the skies. New sorts of mammals appeared.

The supercontinent Pangaea began to break apart. Down the middle, between what is now the eastern part of North America and the western part of Africa, a big rift formed. Volcanoes burst into the sky, and water rushed in to fill the rift. As this rift grew, it began to become an ocean. The Atlantic Ocean had been born.

THE MIDDLE JURASSIC EPOCH

During the Middle Jurassic Epoch dinosaurs continued to become larger and more specialized. True sauropods like *Shunosaurus* and *Mamenchisaurus* appeared, able to feed high in the trees. Powerful meat eaters evolved, so that thyreophorans evolved into stronger forms. The first stegosaurs like *Huayangosaurus* appeared.

THE LATE JURASSIC EPOCH

The Late Jurassic Epoch was the Golden Age of the Dinosaurs. The best fossils from the time were found in the Morrison Formation of the American West. Huge sauropods like *Camarasaurus*, *Diplodocus*, *Apatosaurus*, and *Brachiosaurus* became common, as did advanced stegosaurs like *Stegosaurus*. New forms of ornithopod, like *Camptosaurus*, developed. Hunting these plant eaters were large theropods like *Ceratosaurus*, *Torvosaurus*, and *Allosaurus*. Coelurosaurs became common as small theropods, and some of these evolved into early birds such as *Archaeopteryx*.

Sharing the skies with the first birds were the

short-tailed pterosaurs called **pterodactyls.** The pterodactyls of the Jurassic Period were mostly small, with wingspans of only 5 feet (1.5m) or less. In the seas ichthyosaurs and plesiosaurs were common, as were sea-going crocodiles.

As the Atlantic Ocean widened, the continents began to spread apart. However, a connection between the lands of the dinosaurs still existed. Because of this, dinosaurs in Africa, Europe, and North America were all still similar.

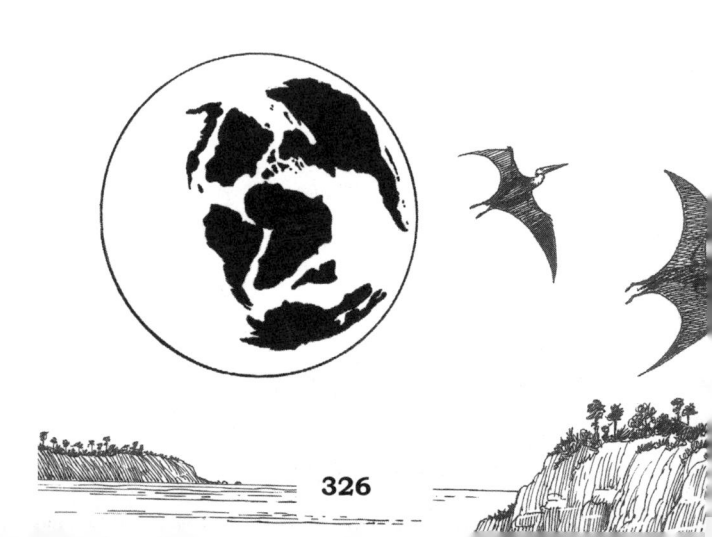

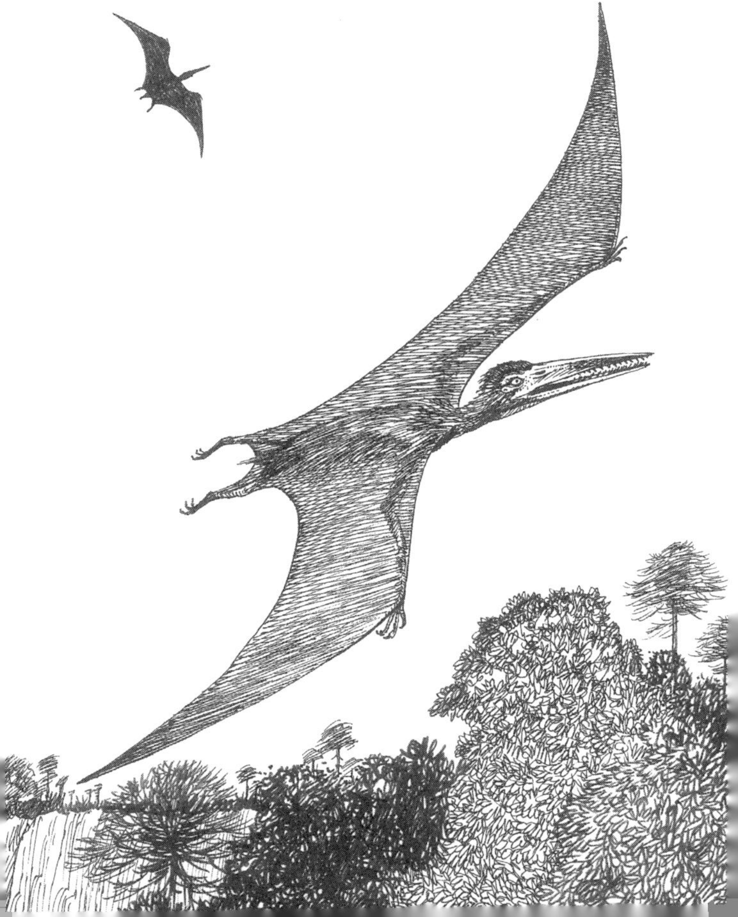

The Cretaceous Period

The great **Cretaceous Period** lasted from 144 to 65 million years ago. The word "Cretaceous" means "chalk"; during this time chalk (a type of limestone) was deposited in the many warm, shallow seas that covered much of the Earth. The Cretaceous Period is divided into only two sections: the **Early Cretaceous Epoch** and the **Late Cretaceous Epoch.**

THE EARLY CRETACEOUS EPOCH

During the Early Cretaceous Epoch sauropods were still common, but ornithopods like *Hypsilophodon*, *Tenontosaurus*, *Muttaburrasaurus*, *Iguanodon*, *Altirhinus*, and *Ouranosaurus* became the most common plant eaters around. Stegosaurs became very rare and finally disappeared, but ankylosaurs such as *Gastonia* replaced them. Raptor dinosaurs like *Deinonychus* became common predators. In Asia early ceratopsians like *Psittacosaurus* and many new types of coelurosaur such as *Sinosauropteryx*, *Caudipteryx*, *Beipiao-*

saurus, raptors, and more advanced birds like *Confuciusornis,* evolved. In Africa, Europe, and South America crocodile-mimic theropods such as *Suchomimus* were found.

The oldest known flowering and fruiting plants appeared in this time. These plants used flowers to attract insects that helped them pollinate, and fruit to attract animals (like mammals or dinosaurs) to help spread their seeds.

Mammals began to become more specialized. Pterodactyls became gigantic: some grew to wingspans of 39 feet (12m) or more! Ichthyosaurs became rare, but plesiosaurs survived. Modern types of fish, clam, and snail evolved in the seas.

During the Early Cretaceous the spreading Atlantic Ocean separated the continents even more. Because of this, dinosaurs in one land became more differentiated from those of other lands. The areas in the south (South America, Africa, Antarctica, Australia, India, and Madagascar) formed the supercontinent **Gondwana** (see page 226), while those of the north (North America, Europe, and Asia) formed **Laurasia.** Sea levels began to rise and flood parts of the land.

THE LATE CRETACEOUS EPOCH

The Late Cretaceous Epoch was the age of the most advanced giant dinosaurs. At the beginning of the epoch the largest dinosaurs of all time—titanosaur sauropods like *Argentinosaurus*—appeared. In South America and other Gondwana lands titanosaurs were the main group of plant eaters and weird new theropods such as *Majungatholus* were the main meat eaters. In the north a land connection between Asia and western North America allowed many types of dinosaur to migrate, including club-tailed ankylosaurids, dome-headed pachycephalosaurs, horned ceratopsians, duckbills, tyrant dinosaurs, and some other coelurosaurs.

MAP OF LATE CRETACEOUS EPOCH

During the latter part of the Late Cretaceous Epoch, a diverse group of dinosaurs lived in western North America: ankylosaurs like *Edmontonia* and *Ankylosaurus*, pachycephalosaurs like *Stegoceras* and *Pachycephalosaurus*, true horned ceratopsians like *Einiosaurus* and *Triceratops*, duckbills like *Hypacrosaurus* and *Anatotitan*, and coelurosaurs like *Ornithomimus*, *Tyrannosaurus*, *Troodon*, and others. In Asia relatives of these dinosaurs were common: pachycephalosaurs like *Homalocephale*, ceratopsians like *Protoceratops*, and coelurosaurs such as *Oviraptor*, *Velociraptor*, and *Shuvuuia*. In Gondwana the armored titanosaurs like *Saltasaurus* were the main plant eaters, and carnivores like *Majungatholus* the main meat eaters.

In the seas of the Late Cretaceous the ichthyosaurs had disappeared, but plesiosaurs were still common. These were joined by sea turtles (some up to 13 feet [4m] long), swimming birds like *Hesperornis*, and sea-going lizards called **mosasaurs.** Giant pterodactyls continued to fly through the skies. Modern-style birds and mammals appeared. In fact, if you were to go back in a time machine to the end of the Cretaceous Period, most of the animals and plants would look similar to modern animals and plants (at least, until you saw a giant dinosaur or pterodactyl passing by).

• 12 •
WHERE DID THE DINOSAURS GO?

EXTINCTION

The boundary between the Mesozoic Era and the Cenozoic Era represents a time when many groups of animals and plants died out, or became **extinct.** Something happened at the end of the Cretaceous Period to make many creatures disappear.

Victims of this **extinction** include types of shellfish, such as coiled shelled relatives of octopi and squids, giant scallops, and giant cone-shaped clams. The last of the plesiosaurs and mosasaurs died out in the seas. In the air the last of the pterosaurs died out. On land the surviving land dinosaurs became extinct: the last thyreophorans, pachycephalosaurs, ceratopsians, ornithopods, sauropods, and most of the theropods (from giant predators like *Majungatholus* and tyrant dinosaurs to ostrich dinosaurs and *Oviraptor* to raptor dinosaurs) disappeared. Among the birds, all types with teeth died out.

What happened to these creatures? Some earlier ideas, like disease or attacks by alien hunters in flying saucers, don't make much sense, because there isn't any evidence for them. However, at least three big changes were taking place in the world at the end of the Late Cretaceous Epoch that might have brought about the end of the Age of Dinosaurs.

The shallow seas that once covered many parts of the world began to drain into the deeper oceans. When water covered the land, the climate was mild—winters were not too cold, and summers were not too hot. Warm temperatures were found from the poles to the equator. When the shallow seas drained back into the deep oceans, the climate on land became harsher. Winters became colder and summers hotter. Many types of plants that needed certain weather to grow died out, and the animals (including dinosaurs) that ate them either died or had to migrate.

Toward the very end of the Late Cretaceous

Epoch the volcanoes of the world became more numerous. A gigantic series of volcanoes erupted in western India, covering huge areas with lava. Volcanoes emerged in the Rocky Mountains of the American West. These volcanoes threw huge amounts of ash and dust high up into the air. This ash and dust blocked some of the sunlight coming to the Earth. The temperatures became cooler, and plants began to grow more slowly without enough sunlight. Life became harder for plant-eating animals on land and in the sea.

Finally, a great disaster occurred. An asteroid, maybe 6 to 10 miles (10 to 15km) across, crashed to Earth in what is now Mexico's Yucatan Peninsula. This blast carved a huge crater about 120 miles (200km) across, and sent powerful blasts and giant tidal waves around the world. More important, the blast threw a fantastic amount of ash and dust high up into the air. Because the high atmosphere was filled with ash and dust, almost no sunlight could reach the surface of the Earth. Plants died on land and sea without the life-giving sunlight. Many plant eaters on land and in the sea starved to death, and after a last final feast many meat eaters began to starve. When the ash and dust settled, the world had changed.

Scientists know that all these changes occurred. Some think that any one of them would have been enough to bring an end to the Mesozoic Era; others think that only all three in combination were enough to change the world. Whatever the cause, the great extinction at the end of the Cretaceous Period saw the dawn of a new world.

SURVIVAL

Not everything in the world died out at the end of the Cretaceous Period, however. Every living thing in the world today, from algae to daisies to redwood trees, from corals to clams to insects, from sharks to trout to frogs, from turtles to snakes to crocodiles, and from platypi to kangaroos to cats and dogs and horses and people, all had ancestors that survived the draining of the continents, the giant volcanoes, and the asteroid impact.

Some may have survived because they could hibernate or because they could live on just a little food. Others may simply have been lucky, living in corners of the world that were not as strongly affected. However they survived, they came out after the dust settled and continued to grow, thrive, and evolve into the animals and plants of the Cenozoic Period.

When most people think of dinosaurs, they think about creatures that are huge and terrifying and extinct. As we have seen, though, scientists regard dinosaurs as any descendant of the most recent common ancestor of *Iguanodon* and *Megalosaurus*. Not all of these dinosaurs were huge (like tiny *Sinosauropteryx*) or terrifying (like peaceful *Hypsilophodon*). And not all dinosaurs are extinct.

Sometimes people say they see a sauropod in the jungles of Africa or a ceratopsian in Australia. However, these sightings always turn out to be mistakes or fakes. What is more interesting, though, is that just about every person alive *has* seen a living dinosaur. In fact, most of us have eaten several!

As we have seen, birds are a type of coelurosaur, and thus are a type of dinosaur. Any time you see an ostrich in a zoo, a hummingbird feeding at a flower, a flight of geese in the sky, or a chicken on your dinner table, you are seeing a modern dinosaur. The age of the giant dinosaurs may be long over, but dinosaurs survive!

GLOSSARY

Ancestors. The populations or species from which a group descended

Ankylosaurids. Ankylosaurs with club tails.

Ankylosaurs. Heavily armored dinosaurs, a type of thyreophoran

Cenozoic Era. The Age of Mammals, 65 million years ago to the present

Ceratopsians. Horned dinosaurs, a type of marginocephalian

Coelurosaurs. The most bird-like theropod dinosaurs

Common ancestry. Two or more groups that have a particular population or species as the same ancestor

Cretaceous Period. The third and last Period of the Mesozoic Era, from 144 to 65 million years ago

Descendants. All the organisms that came from a particular ancestor

Dinosauria. The formal name of dinosaurs as a group

Evolution. Descent with modification

Extinction. The disappearance of all members of a species or larger group of organisms

Fossils. The remains of an organism or traces of its behavior preserved in rock

Gondwana. An ancient supercontinent, composed of the modern continents South America, Africa, India, Antarctica, and Australia

Ichthyosaurs. Dolphin-shaped marine reptiles of the Mesozoic Era

Jurassic Period. The second and middle Period of the Mesozoic Era, from 200 to 144 million years ago

Laurasia. An ancient supercontinent, composed of the modern continents North America, Europe, and Asia (except for India)

Marginocephalians. Ridge-headed dinosaurs, including the pachycephalosaurs and ceratopsians; a type of ornithischian

Mesozoic Era. The Age of Reptiles, from 251 to 65 million years ago

Mosasaurs. Sea-going lizards of the Cretaceous Period

Nodosaurids. Shoulder-spined ankylosaurs

Ornithischian. Bird-hipped, beaked, herbivorous dinosaurs, including thyreophorans, ornithopods, and marginocephalians

Ornithopods. Ornithischian dinosaurs with special jaw structures

Pachycephalosaurs. Dome-headed dinosaurs, a type of marginocephalian

Paleontologists. Scientists who study ancient life

Paleozoic Era. The period of time between 545 and 251 million years ago

Pangaea. An ancient supercontinent, composed of all the modern continents fused together

Plates. Tall, flat-sided scutes on the back of stegosaurs

Plesiosaurs. Paddle-flippered marine reptiles of the Mesozoic Era

Prosauropods. Early sauropodomorphs, capable of walking on both two legs or all four

Pterodactyls. Short-tailed pterosaurs

Pterosaurs. Winged reptiles, closely related to the dinosaurs

Saurischians. Lizard-hipped, longer-necked dinosaurs, including theropods and sauropodomorphs

Sauropodomorphs. Long-necked, small-headed herbivorous saurischians

Sauropods. Giant four-legged sauropodomorphs

Scutes. Armored bone in the skin

Serrations. Raised edges, as on the blade of a steak knife or the tooth of a theropod

Spikes. Cone-shaped pointed scutes

Stegosaurs. Plated dinosaurs, a type of thyreophoran

Thagomizer. The paired spines at the end of the tails of stegosaurs

Theropods. Two-legged, mostly carnivorous saurischians

Thyreophorans. Armored ornithischian dinosaurs, including stegosaurs and ankylosaurs

Titanosaurs. The most important group of sauropods of the later part of the Cretaceous Period

Triassic Period. The first Period of the Mesozoic Era, from 251 to 200 million years ago

Variations. Differences between members of a population

DINOSAURS BY EPOCH

DINOSAURS OF THE LATE TRIASSIC EPOCH
Coelophysis
Eoraptor
Herrerasaurus
Plateosaurus
Saturnalia

DINOSAURS OF THE EARLY JURASSIC EPOCH
Dilophosaurus
Heterodontosaurus
Scelidosaurus
Scutellosaurus

DINOSAURS OF THE MIDDLE JURASSIC EPOCH
Huayangosaurus
Mamenchisaurus
Shunosaurus

DINOSAURS OF THE LATE JURASSIC EPOCH
Allosaurus
Apatosaurus
Archaeopteryx
Brachiosaurus
Camarasaurus
Camptosaurus
Ceratosaurus
Diplodocus
Stegosaurus
Torvosaurus

DINOSAURS OF THE EARLY CRETACEOUS EPOCH
Altirhinus
Amargasaurus
Beipiaosaurus
Caudipteryx
Confuciusornis
Deinonychus
Gastonia
Hypsilophodon
Iguanodon
Jobaria
Muttaburrasaurus
Ouranosaurus
Pelecanimimus
Psittacosaurus
Sinosauropteryx

Suchomimus
Tenontosaurus

DINOSAURS OF THE LATE CRETACEOUS EPOCH

Anatotitan
Ankylosaurus
Archaeoceratops
Argentinosaurus
Edmontonia
Einiosaurus
Giganotosaurus
Homalocephale
Hesperornis
Hypacrosaurus
Majungatholus
Ornithomimus
Oviraptor
Pachycephalosaurus
Protoceratops
Protohadros
Rahonavis
Saltasaurus
Shuvuuia
Stegoceras
Triceratops
Troodon
Tyrannosaurus
Velociraptor
Zuniceratops

DINOSAURS BY LOCATION

AFRICA
Brachiosaurus (Tanzania, Zimbabwe)
Camarasaurus (Zimbabwe)*
Ceratosaurus (Tanzania)*
Heterodontosaurus (southern)
Jobaria (Niger)
Ouranosaurus (Niger)
Suchomimus (Niger)

ANTARCTICA
Cryolophosaurus

ARGENTINA
Amargasaurus
Argentinosaurus
Eoraptor
Giganotosaurus
Herrerasaurus
Patagopteryx
Saltasaurus

AUSTRALIA
Muttaburrasaurus

BELGIUM
Iguanodon

BRAZIL
Saturnalia

CANADA

Alberta
Ankylosaurus
Edmontonia
Hypacrosaurus
Ornithomimus
Stegoceras
Triceratops
Troodon
Tyrannosaurus

Saskatchewan
Triceratops
Tyrannosaurus

CHINA
Archaeoceratops

Beipiaosaurus
Caudipteryx
Confuciusornis
Dilophosaurus
Huyangosaurus
Mamenchisaurus
Monolophosaurus
Oviraptor
Psittacosaurus
*Scelidosaurus**
Shunosaurus
Sinornithosaurus
Sinosauropteryx
Tuojiangosaurus
Tyrannosaurus

ENGLAND
Camptosaurus
Hypsilophodon
Iguanodon
Scelidosaurus

FRANCE
Compsognathus
Gargantuavis
Plateosaurus

GERMANY
Archaeopteryx
Compsognathus
Iguanodon
Plateosaurus

HUNGARY
Magyarsaurus

INDIA
Titanosaurus

MADAGASCAR
Majungatholus
Rahonavis

MONGOLIA
Altirhinus
Harpymimus
Homalocephale
Iguanodon
Oviraptor
Proceratops
Psittacosaurus
Shuvuuia
Therizinosaurus
Tyrannosaurus
Velociraptor

PORTUGAL
Allosaurus
Hypsilophodon

* May have lived in this location

ROMANIA
Magyarsaurus

SPAIN
Hypsilophodon
Iguanodon
Pelecanimimus

SWITZERLAND
Plateosaurus

THAILAND
Psittacosaurus

UNITED STATES

Alaska, U.S.
Edmontonia

Arizona, U.S.
Coelophysis
Scelidosaurus
Scutellosaurus

Colorado, U.S.
Allosaurus
Apatosaurus
Brachiosaurus
Camarasaurus
Camptosaurus
Ceratosaurus
Diplodocus
Ornithomimus
Stegosaurus
Triceratops
Torvosaurus
Tyrannosaurus

Kansas, U.S.
Hesperornis
Tylosaurus

Maryland, U.S.
Deinonychus
Tenontosaurus

Montana, U.S.
Allosaurus
Anatotitan
Ankylosaurus
Camarasaurus
Deinonychus
Edmontonia
Einiosaurus
Hypacrosaurus
Microvenator
Ornithomimus
Pachycephalosaurus
Stegoceras
Stegosaurus
Tenontosaurus
Triceratops

Troodon
Tyrannosaurus

Nebraska, U.S.
Hesperornis

New Mexico, U.S.
Allosaurus
Camarasaurus
Coelophysis
Stegosaurus
Tyrannosaurus
Zuniceratops

Oklahoma, U.S.
Apatosaurus
Camptosaurus
Ceratosaurus*
Deinonychus
Stegosaurus
Tenontosaurus

South Dakota, U.S.
Anatotitan
Edmontonia
Hypsilophodon
Iguanodon
Pachycephalosaurus
Triceratops

Tyrannosaurus

Texas, U.S.
Coelophysis
Dilophosaurus
Protohadros
Tenontosaurus
Tyrannosaurus

Utah, U.S.
Allosaurus
Apatosaurus
Brachiosaurus
Camarasaurus
Camptosaurus
Ceratosaurus
Diplodocus
Eolambia
Gastonia
Iguanodon
Ornithomimus
Stegosaurus
Tenontosaurus
Torvosaurus

Wyoming, U.S.
Allosaurus
Anatotitan
Ankylosaurus

* *May have lived in this location*

Apatosaurus
Camarasaurus
Camptosaurus
Deinonychus
Diplodocus
Pachycephalosaurus

Stegosaurus
Tenontosaurus
Triceratops
Troodon
Tyrannosaurus

ABOUT THE AUTHOR

Dr. Thomas R. Holtz, Jr. is a dinosaur paleontologist at the University of Maryland, College Park, where he teaches courses in dinosaurs, general paleontology, and historical geology. He is also the Director of the College Park Scholars "Earth, Life & Time Program" (a two-year interdisciplinary program for honors students interested in natural history).

Dr. Holtz's main research interests are the evolution, adaptations, and classification of the carnivorous dinosaurs, especially *Tyrannosaurus rex* and the other tyrant dinosaurs. Additionally, he is studying the effects of plate tectonics on the history of dinosaur ecosystems. Dr. Holtz has written many technical papers and chapters, and is also co-author (with Dr. Michael Brett-Surman) of *James Gurney: The World of Dinosaurs*. He has consulted on, and appeared in, documentaries in the U.S., Canada, England, and Japan, including the award-winning BBC/Discovery Channel program "Walking with Dinosaurs."

Dr. Holtz lives in southern Prince Georges County, Maryland, with his wife, two cats, and whatever dinosaurs come to the feeders on a given day.

INDEX

Achelousaurus, 90, 91
Alamosaurus, 194
Allosaurus, 116, 119, 221, 230–231, 236–239, 240, 243, 247, 258, 260–261, 325
Altirhinus, 124–127, 130, 134, 144, 328
Amargasaurus, 176–179, 180
Anatotitan, 68, 136– 139, 312, 332
Ancestors, 18
Ankylosaurids, 48–55, 330
Ankylosaurs, 26, 35, 325, 331
Ankylosaurus, 52–55, 68, 331
Antelopes, 85, 102
Apatosaurus, 116, 172–175, 178, 180, 238, 313, 325
Archaeoceratops, 74–77, 78
Archaeopteryx, 284–285, 290–293, 302, 310–312, 325
Argentinosaurus, 188–171, 330

Armor plates, 195
Armored dinosaurs, 25–55
Asteroid, 336
Atlantic Ocean, 119, 324, 326
Australia, 112; and Antarctica, 115
Beaked dinosaurs, 96–144
Beast feet, 145, 197
Beipiaosaurus, 276–279, 304, 329
Bernissart, Belgium, 123
Bird, early, 298, 302; sea, 306
Brachiosaurus, 116, 184–187, 190, 325
Brontosaurs, 146
Brontosaurus, 172, 175

Camarasaurus, 116, 180–183, 186, 190, 238, 325
Camptosaurus, 116–119, 122, 325
Carcharodontosaurus, 260

Carnotaurus, 227
Caudipteryx, 268–271, 304, 329
Cenozoic Era, 313, 316
Centrosaurus, 90, 91
Ceratopsians, 56, 82, 325, 330–331, 333
Ceratosaurus, 116, 218–221, 222, 227, 228, 230, 231, 238, 325
China, 156, 160
Coelophysis, 210–213, 214, 216–217, 220, 231, 311, 319, 323
Coelurosaurs, 244–309, 325, 330, 332
Common ancestry, 21, 204
Compsognathus, 247, 248
Confuciusornis, 302–305, 311, 329
Corythosaurus, 23, 143
Crests, 114–115, 142–144
Cretaceous Period, 26, 315, 328–332, 333, 334, 337
  Early Cretaceous Epoch, 328–329
  Late Cretaceous Epoch, 330–332, 334, 337
Crocodiles, 17, 326; relatives of, 319, 320, 321
Cryolophosaurus, 239

Deer, 85, 102
Deinonychus, 111, 280–285, 290, 324, 325
Descendants, 18
Dicraeosaurus, 178, 179
Dilophosaurus, 214–217, 220, 323
Dimetrodon, 20
Dinosaurs
  ancestors, possible, 18
  armored, 25–55
  bird hipped, 21
  birds as descendants of, 198, 296–297, 298–305, 310–312, 338–339
  brain of, 266–267
  claws of, 197
  color, 81
  crests, 114–115, 142–144
  extinction, 331–335
  family tree, 24
  feathers, use of, 270–271
  finding out how dinosaurs change as they grow up, 91
  frill, use of, 81

Dinosaurs (*continued*)
  growing to full size, 183
  horns, use of, 85
  how they became fossils, 14
  lizard hipped, 22
  marginocephalians, 56–95
  name "Dinosauria," 20
  most primitive, 202
  ornithischian, 21
  ostrich, 250–257
  sails, purpose of, 179
  saurischian, 22
  sauropodomorphs, 145–196
  sounds made by, 143
  survival, 335–337
  tallest, 184
  theropods, 145
  thyreophorans, 25–55
  tyrants, 258–263
Diplodocus, 116, 168–171, 172, 178, 180, 190, 191, 217, 238, 325
Domed dinosaurs, *see* Marginocephalians
Double sail, 176, 179
Duckbills, 132, 330
  broad-snouted, 136–144
  hollow-crested, 139

Ducks, 311

Edmonton Formation, 48
Edmontonia, 48–51, 331
Edmontosaurus, 68
Egg thief, 272
Einiosaurus, 86–89, 331
Elephant, 146, 179, 182–183
Eolambia, 134
Eoraptor, 198, 202–205, 206–207, 212, 213, 311, 319, 323
Evolution, 18
Extinction, 333–337

Family trees
  dinosaur, 24
  marginocephalians, 57
  ornithopods, 98
  sauropodomorphs, 147
  theropods, 200– 201
  thyreophorans, 27
Feathers, 199, 246–249, 268–271, 304
Fin, 128
Fish eaters, 232
Flowers, 327

Fly, the ability to, 293, 304
Forked reptile, 178
Fossils, 10–16, 311, 325
 living, 167
Frill, 56, 76, 80–81
Fused reptiles, 48

Gargantuavis, 306
Gaston, Robert, 44
Gastonia, 44–47, 325
Giganotosaurus, 240–243, 260
Golden Age of the Dinosaurs, 324
Gondwana, 226–227, 329, 330, 332

Harpymimus, 256
Herrera, Don Vittorio, 206
Herrerasaurus, 198, 206–209, 212, 213, 313, 319, 323
Hesperornis, 306–309, 332
Heterodontosaurus, 99–103, 111, 324
Hollow form, 210
Hollow-tailed reptiles, 244
Homalocephale, 58–61, 332

Horned dinosaurs, 82, 86, 92
Horns, 85, 89, 92–94
Huayangosaurus, 36–39, 325
Hylaeosaurus, 20
Hypacrosaurus, 136, 140–143, 332
Hypsilophodon, 104–107, 111, 114, 123, 282–283, 328, 338
Hypsilophus tooth, 104–107

Ice Age, 316
Ichthyosaurs, 10, 12, 20, 320, 326, 329, 332
Iguana
 lizard, 104
 tooth, 120–123
Iguanodon, 20–21, 120–123, 124–125, 130, 199, 325, 338
 hip bone, 21

Jaw, nutcracker, 97
Jobar, 164-167
Jobaria, 164–167, 170
Jurassic Period, 26, 315, 322–327

Jurassic Period (*continued*)
　Early Jurassic Epoch, 323–324
　Middle Jurassic Epoch, 325
　Late Jurassic Epoch, 325–327

Lagosuchus, 18, 311, 319
Lambeosaurus, 143
Land connection between Asia and North America, 135, 330
Laurasia, 329
Lesothosaurus, 24
Lizard feet, 146, 158
Lizards, 320
Loons, 311
Lump reptiles, 48

Madagascar, 222
Magyarsaurus, 196
Majungatholus, 220, 222–225, 227, 242, 243, 296, 330, 332
Mamenchisaurus, 160–163, 166, 325
Mammals, 20, 316, 320, 329
Mammoths, 20

Marginocephalians, 56–95
　family tree, 57
Marsh, Othniel Charles Marsh, 174–175
Meat eaters, 197–309
Megalosaurus, 20–23, 199, 231, 338
　hip bone, 22
　thumb claw, 22, 228
Mesozoic Era, 313, 315
Meuse river lizards, 12
Microvenator, 271
Monolophosaurus, 239
Morrison Formation, 116, 169, 180, 220, 228, 236, 325
Mosasaurs, 12, 20, 329, 331
Muttaburrasaurus, 112–115, 118, 122, 126, 325

Necks, long, 145, 150–151, 162
New Mexico, 82
New Zealand, 167
Nodosaurids, 48
Nose horns, 89–91
Noses, big, 112, 125
Nostrils, 126, 138, 182, 187

Ornithischian dinosaurs, 22–24
Ornithomimus, 254–257, 332
Ornithopods, 96–144, 325
family tree, 98
Ostrich dinosaurs, 250–257, 334
Ostrom, John, 282–285
Ouranosaurus, 128–131, 325
Oviraptor, 270, 271, 272–275, 310, 334
Owen, Sir Richard, 12, 20–21

Pachycephalosaurus, 66–69, 331
Pachyrhinosaurus, 90, 91
Pachysephalosaurs, 56, 224–225, 330, 331
Paleontologists, 12
Paleozoic Era, 313, 314
Pangaea, 318, 324
Parasaurolophus, 143
Parrots, 311
Patagopteryx, 306
Pelecanimimus, 250–251
Pinky, 123, 126, 130, 212

Pisanosaurus, 319
Plant eaters, 25–55
Plants, 327
Plateosaurus, 152–155, 319
Plates, 36, 317
Plesiosaurs, 12, 20, 324, 326, 329, 332, 333
Prenocephale, 61
Prosauropods, 145, 148, 152–155, 156–159, 323
Protoceratops, 78–81, 82, 274–275, 286, 332
Protohadros, 132–135, 140
Protomammals, 20, 318, 320, 321
Psittacosaurus, 70–73, 74, 78, 325
Pterodactyls, 10, 20, 326, 329, 332
Pterosaurs, 315, 320, 324, 333

Rahonavis, 294–297
Raptor dinosaurs, 267, 280–285, 293, 296, 310, 325, 326, 334
Reptiles, 20, 319
Reptiles, flying, 10, 20

Rhinoceroses, 182
Ridge Heads, 56–95
Rocky Mountains, 335
Roman festival, 148
Romania, 196

Sabretooth cats, 20
Sac, 126–127, 138
　nose, 114–115, 187
Sails, purpose of, 179
Saltasaurus, 192–195, 332
Saturnalia, 148–151, 152, 313, 319
Saurischian dinosaurs, 22–24
Saurornitholestes, 289
Sauropods, 146, 323, 325
Scelidosaurus, 32–35, 217, 324
Scutellosaurus, 28–31, 217, 324
Scutes, 25–26
Sea
　bird, 306
　turtles, 332
Seismosaurus, 191
Shantungosaurus, 138
Shunosaurus, 156–159, 166, 325
Shuvuuia, 298–301, 332

Sickle claw, 267, 294, 296
Sinornithosaurus, 289, 304
Sinosauropteryx, 244–247, 250, 270, 304, 311, 328, 338
Skeletons, partial, 190–191
Spikes, 36, 88
Stegoceras, 62–65, 264, 329
Stegosaurs, 26, 35, 36, 323, 325, 331
Stegosaurus, 40–43, 116, 313, 325
Styracosaurus, 90, 91
Suchomimus, 232–235, 329
Supersaurus, 191

Tail, 170, 231
　see Thagomizer
Teeth
　of *Altirhinus*, 127
　of *Camarasaurus*, 182
　of *Heterodontosaurus*, 99–103
　of *Ornithomimus*, 256–257
　of *Pelecanimimus*, 252–253
　of theropods, 197
　of tyrant dinosaurs, 261–262

Tenontosaurus, 108–111, 114, 118, 122, 123, 284, 325
Thagomizer, 38
Therizinosaurus, 279
Theropods, 145, 197–309
Thick-skulled reptiles, 56
Thumb, 122
Thunder lizards, 146, 175
Thyreophorans, 25–55, 217
  family tree, 27
Titanic reptiles, 190
Titanosaur sauropods, 330, 332
Titanosaurus, 196
Toe claws, 197
Torosaurus, 68
Torvosaurus, 221, 228–231, 234, 238, 325
Toureg people, 164
Triassic period, 18, 315, 318–321
  early Triassic Epoch, 318
  middle Triassic Epoch, 318–319
  late Triassic Epoch, 319–321
Triceratops, 68, 92–95, 311, 313, 331
Troodon, 264–267, 332
Tuatara, 167
Tuojiangosaurus, 38
Turtles, 320, 332
Tylosaurus, 309
Tyrannosaurus, 23, 54, 68–69, 95, 142, 240, 242–243, 257, 258–263, 313, 332
Tyrant dinosaurs, 333

Ultrasauros, 184

Variations, 17
Velociraptor, 81, 286–289, 290, 294, 301, 332
Volcanoes, 322, 335

Waves, tidal, 336
Winged reptiles, 320
Wings, 198, 309
Wishbone, 198, 213

Yixian formation, 247, 268, 276, 305
Yucatan peninsula, 336

Zuniceratops, 82–85, 86–87

If you liked this book, you'll love all the titles in this series:

- Little Giant Book of After School Fun
- Little Giant Book of Amazing Mazes
- Little Giant Book of Card Tricks
- Little Giant Book of Dinosaurs
- Little Giant Book of Insults & Putdowns
- Little Giant Book of Jokes
- Little Giant Book of Kids' Games
- Little Giant Book of Knock-Knocks
- Little Giant Book of Optical Illusions
- Little Giant Book of Optical Tricks
- Little Giant Book of Riddles
- Little Giant Book of Tongue Twisters
- Little Giant Book of Travel Fun
- Little Giant Book of "True" Ghost Stories
- Little Giant Book of Visual Tricks
- Little Giant Book of Whodunits

Available at fine stores everywhere.